Sorcerers and Spirits

Gowri Rekha

PARTRIDGE
A Penguin Random House Company

To order additional copies of this book, contact
Partridge India
000 800 10062 62
orders.india@partridgepublishing.com

www.partridgepublishing.com/india

To my best friend, Bunn.

"Whither thou goest I will go,
And where thou lodgest I will lodge;
Thy people shall be my people,
And thy God my God;
Where thou diest will I die,
And there will I be buried.

Aught but death shall part thee and me."
~ Adapted from the Book of Ruth.

Contents

Contents

Preface

**Lenore, existing on the fifth plane, is a world where
both magicians and non-magicians are found.
This tale is from Andoreya, one of the eleven kingdoms of Lenore.**

Andalucia:

It wasn't always like this. There used to be safer times, when we didn't have to hide our magic, when we learned in schools how to control and harness our magic. That was a long time back, though.

But when the war started, seven years back, everything changed.

Magicians struggle to keep their powers secret; they don't want to be part of the genocide the war is causing. They don't want to die. Who does really?

Some really noble souls join the war, and fight against the enemy. I'm afraid I'm not really one of them.

Andoreya is my home, and I want to protect it. But I know fighting this war will not help, I will only die. I know I have to do something, but I don't know what. I need to figure out what I am, and only then can I do anything else.

Till then I will hide my magic from everyone.

Fabiana:

My mother died when I was just a baby. I don't really remember her, but I miss her a lot. My father's a General in the army, he's off fighting. The war has been going on for years now, seven years. Even before that it was bad. People like me, they didn't live long. They died mysteriously. I don't know why, but I have a feeling they were killed because of what they were. I don't know who did that to them, or if I'm just imagining things. But this feeling won't go away. I have to keep my abilities hidden until I know what's going on.

There's a war going on, I don't really know who the enemies are but I know it's not just the exiles. No, there's someone more powerful behind this. It's just this feeling, I know I'm right. But no one will believe me. I'm just a kid after all, just a teenage girl.

It isn't so bad yet, the war I mean. We haven't been severely affected, but it's only a matter of time I know.

It's something bigger than we can all imagine, it's something beyond people like us.

It's just this feeling. It won't go away.

"Really? Best friends?" I tilted my head and looked at the strange girl.

"*Always,*" said little Ann with a serious face.

"We'll be best friends for always."

1: Magicians by Dark

Andalucia

When I was ten, everything changed. Everything. Not just my life or my family's but our whole world changed. There was the war that caught all of us off-guard, perhaps not all of us, since we weren't defeated and are, to date, fighting, but the citizens never expected a war and I don't think anyone expected it to last this long.

But the tragedy hit us first.

When things go awry people turn to different sources of comfort; some to God, in our case the Spirits (the drink too), some to their lovers, some to art forms, some to friends and family. When I was troubled I turned to the Forests, wise and mercifully silent.

There was a reason why I couldn't run away to the Forests right now, and the reason was speaking to me. I blinked at her.

"I don't see why you can't dress like normal girls, Ann. It's really odd," said the reason. "Why must you insist on wearing his clothes? I mean… if you mean to remember him this way, you can keep them in your drawers, *must* you wear them?" I looked down at my boots so that she wouldn't see how bored I was. "And stop that incessant humming of yours! Singing is alright when someone asks you to, at a party. You must display your talents for your prospective in-laws to see, but you don't need to hum all the time, honestly child!"

I stopped. I hadn't even realised I had been humming. And she was clearly confusing me with someone else, I never sang at any party.

I sighed. She'd already taken me to three shamans, who all seemed absolutely nuts, and tried to *banish* the wild spirits in me. The first visit to the shaman was when I was eleven and had just picked up dressing 'oddly' as she said. It was terrifying. The shaman was this wrinkly old man, who had a really creepy smile, and sickening thoughts. The second seemed reasonably sane but completely clueless about magic. Take it from me. And the third? Ha! That was last year and I knew I wasn't mad, not really anyway. I rolled my eyeballs in their sockets and uttered gibberish in a deep voice, acting like the Spirits

3

had possessed me (any moron would know Spirits don't possess people, you'd die if they did!) and cursed him. The poor man had been terrified. Needless to say, my aunt was not amused. She didn't look too amused right now either, surveying me like I was a bad tomato. I really hate tomatoes. Her mouth was still moving, but the words didn't filter through to my brain. I looked about, trying to act like I didn't know who she was talking about (me, of course), or who she was either. The trees were calling to me; *solitude*. Being in a crowded marketplace, it was quite easy to ignore my aunt, though not the call of the forests, but her loud voice cut across like a sharp knife through the rabble of the crowd.

"And don't you look about acting as though you can't hear me, Miss."

I flushed as passers-by glanced at me. "No Ma'am," I murmured.

"Hmph, I'm going to have a word about your dressing to Reveria, once more."

I tuned out, as always, what she was saying. She loved to lecture me. It was like a hobby of hers. In general she loved doing that to everyone, but I was a particular favourite target because of my 'oddness.'

So what if I liked wearing men's clothes, in particular his clothes? As a child I had always loved playing dress-up, but unlike normal girls I never dressed up like a princess or a fairy. I dressed up as a pirate, a troll, a knight but mostly I dressed up to imitate *him*, my brother.

Wearing his clothes made me feel more… confident, more like him. And as a child, oh did I want to be like him! It was always Ryan this and Ryan that. "Look at Ryan how smart he is, how good looking, how well mannered." Which he was of course, but when it was just Ryan and me, we had a ball. We'd climb walls and trees, sneak around the Capital and play adventure games, pretending to be pirates or magicians or knights on quests.

But Ryan had a secret. Ryan suffered from a rare illness. I guess it could be said that he died of that illness, but there's more to it than that.

"Andalucia are you listening?"

"Huh?" I blinked, returning to the present. "Oh, oh yes. Yes, I am." I nodded vigorously for good measure.

She sighed with disapproval, then turned to the fruit seller. "How much is it for the oranges?"

I grimaced as she continued to haggle with the fruit seller, who of course stood no chance against her loud arguments about the unfair prices of fruits;

it was wartime, no one had much money, certainly not enough to be able to afford oranges at 6.75 silvers.

I observed my aunt, she was a stout lady with brownish-black hair and really thin lips, unlike her sister who was taller with fair hair – my mother. She was also a hopeless gossip and loved delivering speeches. I honestly had no idea how we ended up being related.

My eyes wandered to the temple of the Spirits. I had never been in there but I didn't need to. I had seen the statues through the eyes of others and even then I had been intimidated. The sculptor hadn't sculpted facial features, because no one knew how they looked. And yet it was easy to tell them apart. The tall, colossal man would be Thor the Warrior whom I favoured more than the others. Next to him, crouched with catlike grace would be the Shapeshifter. The twins stood on either side of the two, with an air of pride, the Sorcerer and the Dragon Spirit. I never could recall the names of the other three.

They were the first ever magicians in the whole of Lenore, though their history was muddled and we didn't know much about it, mostly because only scholars learned about such things and not students. We tended to look to them in times of danger, after all they were the first ever magicians, maybe they could help us.

Or maybe nothing could help us. The war had been raging for seven years, how much longer could it continue? All the other kingdoms of Lenore had already fallen, only Hunwery and Andoreya were left.

The village bell tolled. I snapped out of my reverie. Aunt Jenny was still lecturing me; she was harping on my improper attitude now. "Why did you snap at Mister Gunther yesterday at the party?"

That creep? Why is she defending him?

"I have to leave now Ma'am, I have lessons," I said, half turning away from her, ready to sprint up to the building.

She grabbed me by the arm. "Now look here Ann, I know you don't take whatever I say seriously."

I opened my mouth to protest, though she was right, but she waved me off. "No there's no use arguing with me, I can see it in your eyes that you don't agree with anything I say… but look dear, I'm saying this for your own good."

I frowned. Really? It wasn't as though she really cared about me. What she cared about was what people thought of that wild niece of hers, not *me*, as a person, with my own feelings.

"Do you know what the ladies here say about you?"

Confused, I asked: "Uh… how does that matter?"

She looked flabbergasted. "By the Spirits, Andalucia! It matters a lot! You are to marry one of their sons!"

No, not this again! How can she be serious about this?

She *can't* be.

"If they disapprove of you, do you think you'll ever have suitors? You'll die an old maid!"

"But–marriage?" I stammered. I took a deep breath. "I'm only sixteen!"

"Exactly! In one or two years you will have to get married into a good family."

Before rationality could stop me I snapped: "I'd rather kiss a swine than marry any one of these fools."

Maybe I'd said too much. Answering back isn't a very good quality in a 'lady', which is what I was 'supposed' to be, but clearly was not.

Aunt Jennifer's ears went red, a sign that she was angry. "Mind your tongue young lady!" she chastised me. "Get away now, go. Go for your lessons."

I bounded away with ignorable guilt, turning only to wave to my mother. She smiled at me. My sweet mother, innocent and fragile as a flower. I could see her wonder where Fab was. Even I didn't know where she'd gone but then I had come down for breakfast late. I hadn't seen her since our episode yesterday in the woods, when she accidentally set fire to my hair. My long hair, the one feature of mine that I actually liked, and she set fire to it. Accidentally of course, but even then, I could use this to guilt-trip her when I needed her cooperation. I chuckled to myself, then stopped. People would think I was mad if I kept doing this. But then again, who cares? Besides, they already thought I was a freak.

Rot in hell, society, I don't care!

Mostly, said the little voice in my head.

I brushed impatiently at my hair.

Where was this girl?

Though she was actually living with us now, as her father was away fighting in the war, I hadn't seen her in a while. I had been in the library and returned late, after Fab had gone to bed. I would've stayed longer but the library timings didn't allow me to. The librarian had very kindly escorted me all the way home; he was an old man and didn't think I should walk alone to my own house at ten in the night. Yes, because there are wolves waiting to jump on me. I rolled my eyes.

My mother had been fuming when I got home. Once she finished lecturing me, she had given me my dinner and then sent me to bed. Not that I had gone to bed, of course. I had sneaked out the kitchen window and gone to the forests. I sat chatting with Kiera till dawn. By the time I slipped back home, Fab had left for school. Luckily she hadn't mentioned to my mother that I hadn't been in my bed all night, she knew I had a habit of spending the night in the forests when I couldn't get sleep or when my mind was troubled like it was yesterday. Both the moons looked so pretty yesterday, and the combined moonlight lit up the darkness. It was better than the sun. I wished to see both the moons complete, but that only happened once in a lifetime. My mother has seen it; she said it was a sight to behold.

I sighed. I still hadn't managed to figure out what my magic was. And I had to. I was sixteen already, one more year for my Blossoming. Blossoming was a very special age for everyone. It was the age when, if you had any hint of magic in you, it would show itself or blossom, completely. You would reach your full potential. Right now Blossoming was also dangerous because of the war.

Because what's the most powerful weapon in war? Magic.

Every magician was tracked by the royal Hounds and taken from their families and their lives to fight in a war that had been raging for seven years. To have magic in these days, it can be said, is a curse. But my magic protected me and her. My magic was weird. Unheard of.

I was so bothered by not knowing what kind of magic I have that for the past two days I hadn't slept. And I knew now I needed to let it out. I needed to talk to her.

I could always search for her, but I was too tired and letting my barriers down in such a crowd wasn't something I wanted to do right now. I'd see her in class anyway. Let's see... first lesson – geography. I squared my shoulders and entered the school.

"Our land," the scholar read in his droning voice, "was a rich land, good for cultivation, for growing luscious fruits, but was a wild forest, filled with savages and beasts. Emmett and his wife Annabelle were believed to be the first presences in Andoreya. They were the first king and queen of Andoreya. They civilised the people, and brought them under their rule. After matters were settled in the capital, at that time Jonoria, now known as Oracle City, Emmett and his eldest son Edward went on a journey, to explore the rest of Andoreya. As they passed each place, they named it." He pointed at a map on the board. "Gondon, our city. To the southwest. Rivendell," he pointed at the village to the north of Gondon. "Rushwater, Raven Forest, the Northern deserts, Oracle City, Ice Caves, Nine Mountains, Mistwood, The Black Woods..." he paused. "These are the main geographic locations. Of course there are many villages, and towns. But they are not of much importance. You should know their names, that is all, unless you want to pursue Geography after this year and become a professor. The huge mountains there," he pointed next to the northern deserts, "past those are the wild lands. The Repctic Sea. Then to the northeast – Oracle City which opens to the sea, the Dark Sea." Some girls shuddered, the sea was supposed to be cursed.

Superstition if you ask me, though no one had ever sailed the sea and come back to tell the story. The ruined, wrecked ship and mangled bodies had washed ashore however. But only dimwits would try to sail our seas, the pull of the two moons was too strong.

"The architects of Lana built bridges that connected the kingdom of Lenore. While the journey between the eleven kingdoms is excruciatingly hard, it is still undertaken. With the entry of magic, however, it became easier. Dardenium has the one and only portal that can take you anywhere in Lenore..."

I fiddled with the tiny scrap of parchment in my hand before rolling it into a ball and adding it to the dozens on Shandre's mass of curly hair. It looked like it had snowed on her head. I grinned to myself. I glanced at Fab, she was busy doodling in her book. I yawned. I met Fab when I was ten. When I had moved into Gondon after we had left Oracle city because of the... misfortune that struck our family. Fab and I met in the forest. I had run away from home because my horrid relatives had come to offer their condolences and I had overheard them speaking amongst themselves that it was such a shame that he had died, and how there were rumours that something had been wrong with him. That he had dark magic within him. So, I, being his ever-faithful follower, leaped out from my hiding place and yelled at them saying they didn't know anything about him and they were all just big faggots. Of course, at that time I didn't know the meaning of the word. My father did though, and he shouted at me and asked me to apologise for calling my dear great-aunts such a thing. I did, reluctantly. Then hurt, angry and embarrassed I ran to the woods for refuge and there I crashed into Fab who had set her house on fire! Being scared and frightened she spilled her heart out there, admittedly to a unfamiliar girl, telling me how angry she was with her father for not coming home for vacations, to her mother for dying when she was really young (she had said the word 'mother' weirdly, like she didn't know how to pronounce it), to the boy next door who continuously teased her about her weight, and how she had finally set her house on fire with her mind.

Yeah. With her mind.

We ended up talking about my 'oddities' too and found out that we had told each other the secrets we had never told anyone else, which we had even been scared to accept ourselves. And obviously we became best friends after that. We should've known then, right then, that the wheels had been set into motion by a force much greater than we could ever imagine. We should've known right then that the whole encounter was weird, it was like we already knew each other, from before. But that wasn't possible, right?

In short – my best friend was a Sorcerer, more correctly Sorceress. I looked at her, sitting next to me. Today she was wearing an off-white flowery dress, her chestnut brown hair in a braid that just about touched her shoulder (she liked her hair short). I couldn't see her eyes but I knew they would be blue, so unlike my green. Fab looked groomed and well, lady-like. I looked, I had to admit, wild.

I yawned again. I had to sleep tonight at least. How many times had I yawned? Three? Four? I yawned yet again.

"Miss Gamori!" said the scholar in a sharp voice, making me drop the wad of paper I had in my hand. "What are you doing?"

Unthinkingly, promptly, I replied "Yawning."

The class broke into giggles.

Crap.

He turned red, and then in a hoarse voice said, "You can continue doing it outside."

Fab shot me a look that clearly said, do something. Something along the lines of apologise or fall at his feet, probably.

I nodded. "Um Professor... I didn't mean that."

"Out!" he yelled. I flinched. "Now!"

Fab wasn't grinning anymore, no one was.

Oh Thor, I thought as I tried to walk the walk of shame with some dignity, and leave the class.

Once I was safely away from the entrance to the class, in the deserted corridor, I groaned. Ugh. Stupid, stupid, stupid! Why couldn't I hold my tongue?

"Urgh!" I groaned again through gritted teeth. I would have to apologise to him, maybe even give him an apology letter. I did like him, Professor Burns. He was sweet, but his class was extremely boring. I never ever paid attention to his lectures, which isn't something I'm proud of… but my attention span wasn't very long, especially if I wasn't interested in the topic. Like Geography.

A group of boys walked past me in the corridor. Most of them were used to seeing me dressed so oddly but even then they stared at me with looks of incredulity and mild horror. I tried to concentrate on the opposite wall. Stupid gits.

"Why are you standing outside?" asked one of them in a low voice. I looked up to see my cousin Aero (his mother was Aunt Jennifer), his long blonde hair falling all over his face. He was slightly taller than me, which was saying something because I was the tallest girl in Gondon.

"Oh you know," I replied trying to sound casual. "Thought I could use some fresh air."

"Ohh…" he said looking confused, "Funny, they never let us out during class for anything."

I raised my eyebrows. "I can't believe you bought that. I was kicked out of class Aero!"

Evidently that only confused him more, because now he looked dubiously at me. I shook my head in exasperation. "Go, go for your next class," I said, almost sounding like Aunt Jennifer. "I'll explain later."

He shrugged and went. I suddenly remembered something and I called to his retreating back, "Aero, don't um mention this to Nick okay?"

He gave me the thumbs-up without turning back. At least he understood that.

Nick was my other cousin. Nick was, well… he shared Aunt Jenny's opinions of me and constantly reprimanded me. Though he was just a month older than me, he always acted like he was years older.

I ground the heel of my boot against the stone floor in anger. Who invented these rules anyway? Who set the decorum? Who gave them the right to decide what's wrong and right?

The town bell rang, and the class filed out. I joined Fab and was about to walk away with her to our next lesson, when Professor Burns called my name.

"Miss Gamori. A word with you please."

Fab and I exchanged looks before I followed him into the class. I stood quietly, my fingers digging into my palm behind my back as he looked through his drawers. He pulled out a heavy leather book and dropped it on the table; it made a loud thump. He gestured at me to pick it up; I did, and nearly fell down under the weight of it.

Okay, it wasn't *that* heavy. But being slightly theatrical is amusing. Well, inside my head at the very least. Was I supposed to run ten rounds with the book? Do push ups with it on my back? They made the boys do all that sort of stuff as punishment. But a girl? Albeit dressed like a boy.

Confused I asked, "Uh… what is this for, Sir?"

"Punishment," he replied. "You will read this whole book by Monday. Yes, Monday," he said, seeing the look on my face. "You have two days; write a brief summary of it. And hand it over on Monday."

I nodded, after all, what I had said was pretty rude. "I'm really sorry sir, I don't know, uh, why I said that. I didn't exactly – I mean I *didn't* mean it."

"It's quite alright Miss Gamori," he said stiffly. "I don't expect everyone to have an interest in the geography of the land they live in like I do. Tell me Miss Gamori do you know the names of the other kingdoms of our world?"

I gulped. "Um there's Hunwery. And err…. Gana? Lama?"

"There are eleven: Leda, Delphie, Pixos, Hunwery, Lana, Kyrium, Myreia, Grewarv, Dardenium, Usward, and Andoreya."

Well, I did remember Lana. Sort of.

"You know Geography is immensely interesting. I know all about the other kingdoms, though of course I have not been, and cannot go there."

The kingdoms of Lenore were separated by vast seas; in fact, Lenore consisted of more sea than land. And the seas were treacherous, sailing them was suicide. The only way of communication came from Dardenium. They had a portal (our bridges were never used anymore, what with all the trolls and plunderers) which could take them to any of the other kingdoms and all the kingdoms had some route (that didn't involve the seas) to Dardenium. But since Dardenium fell, all those routes were barricaded. Their magicians were really skilled, though fewer in number than Andoreians. We got the famous Solfovenillas from there, the sweetest fruit imaginable. Our Leapers had tried, but leaping can only be done to a place the Leaper has visited once before, besides which the balance of our world had been tipped. The exiles had the upper hand, the scales of magic were unstable. With Dardenium's fall, Lenore had no hope.

For most of us, though, nothing existed beyond Andoreya. And I couldn't even imagine what we would do if Andoreya fell. We had the best army but we weren't immortal.

"Are they at war too, Professor?" I asked.

"At war?" He looked shocked. "Dear child! What do they teach you at school these days?" Then he frowned, realising he was one of our teachers. "Ahem, I mean of course they are. Though most of them have been defeated. Dardenium was the first to fall and that's why the other kingdoms fell so easily. Because now the enemy has access to the portal." He sighed. "Of course if you paid attention during geography and history class you might know this. I want the essay by Monday morning. Good day."

I waited until he left the class before sinking into his chair with a huff of frustration.

In trouble? said a soft velvety voice in my mind.

I pouted; *I'm always in trouble Kiera.*

The speaker came into view. With velvety black fur, and her tail swaying majestically, she jumped onto the desk. My cat, Kiera. Well, not exactly *my* cat. She would come and go whenever she wanted. I stroked her back and she purred.

Spoilt brat, I said.

She purred again.

I sighed. *I have dance lessons now,* I said mournfully.

She mewed almost like a laugh.

Better go then before you get into more trouble.

I reluctantly got up; trying to sound heroic I said *yes, dance awaits me. My graceful elegance will be missed if I do not hurry. Therefore I must not tarry.*

Cut the drama, she interrupted.

I put my hand over my heart and tried to look offended; she coolly turned her back to me and stalked out of the room.

You're heartless you know.

I know, was her reply.

I trudged after her, till I reached the hall where our class was to take place. It was an airy hall – with portraits of famous noblemen and women and pretty cream tiles – buzzing with chatter. Everyone was there already, all the girls and boys. It was the only class we had with the boys and everyone tried to make the most of it.

Ballroom dancing was a class I did not much like, dancing was my personal hell. I lacked the grace, the talent and the interest to learn dancing. And Fab, being my partner, had to suffer as well.

"Watch it!" Fab hissed when I stepped on her foot for probably the zillionth time.

"Sorry," I mumbled as I circled in our spot.

"I'll probably have to amputate my foot by the time our dance lessons are done," she said pulling me back into the duo.

"I can do it for you," I offered.

She cocked her eyebrow. "You *are* doing it." But the corners of her mouth twitched.

You have to be lucky to get a tolerant partner like Fab. Kal wasn't that lucky though. If by chance she stepped on Shandre's foot or embarrassed her in any way – good morning apocalypse.

I saw Nick dancing with a fat boy called Fedrico. Nick's expression was that of someone in agony. I grinned, our eyes met and he raised a brow. I looked away quickly and tried to look contrite. Nick's eyes took in my dress, which was a loose grey tunic and cotton trousers, he looked disapproving. It was amusing really, the way he'd lecture me despite knowing that I wouldn't listen to what he said.

When the lessons in hell ended, Fab had blue-red toes and Shandre, a red face like a bull's ready to explode at the next chance. I steered clear of Shandre, I had got enough punishment for the day. Besides she was already angry with me, as one of the girls had been so kind as to point out to her that she had a lot of paper bits in her hair when everyone else had laughed at her. Shandre's eyes had immediately sought mine and she glowered at me as I tried to look blameless. I really shouldn't have done that. I had meant to tell her before we went for the next class because I knew she would be furious to be seen like that in front of the boys. I shouldn't have done it but I knew I would do it again. Damn me. Damn Society. Damn...

At least Kal was way better than me; I wondered what Shandre would have done if I had been her partner.

I chuckled at that thought.

Fab glared at me, and I immediately rearranged my face to look sober.

Unfortunately, ballroom classes were compulsory. So I had to suffer through this, no point in complaining. Not that I *didn't* complain.

Once a year, the mayor would host a ball for all those above fifteen years of age. It was a public event, to meet prospective brides and grooms. Also, to interact with people. It was a good opportunity for girls who liked to show off their dancing skills and etiquette.

When I thought about last year's disaster, I shuddered. Ma had insisted I go, so had Fab. So grumbling, I went. Ma had given me her first ball gown, a light pink silk gown. It was a really pretty one, but I hated the colour. I had made a big fuss to put it on, and Ma had done my hair. She did some complicated knot that made my hair look shorter than it was but better, I think. She wanted me to look like a girl for one night at least, and she took ample advantage of the situation.

Fab had worn a dark blue gown that brought out the colour in her eyes. My mother had done her hair too. She had pulled Fab's hair up and pinned it, so it made Fab look older than she was. She looked beautiful.

Kal had worn a simple green gown, but Shandre had overdone it, wearing a sort of shimmering golden gown. It had a little too deep V-neckline; most of the elders hadn't approved of it although I'm sure the boys did.

I had been asked to dance thrice. Twice by Nick, whom I was sure Aunt Rose had forced to ask me, as courtesy, though it was more of torture for me. The third was by a boy whom I didn't know personally... he was two years older than me. I had seen my ma's satisfied smile when he asked me. But too bad for her and the boy, I managed to trip him, accidentally of course, onto the table where some of the elders were sitting and right into the punch bowl. The poor boy, whenever he saw me he would turn around and walk in the opposite direction. Couldn't blame him of course, I'd embarrassed him a lot that day. He shouldn't have asked me in the first place. Funnily he was Professor Burn's son, and after that day I liked him much more than I should. Damn his niceness.

I should stop swearing.

This year too there would be a ball. This year too my ma and everyone else would force me to go. And this year too I would make a fool of myself. Though I hoped, after witnessing last year's events, no one would ask me and I could manage to get out before I broke someone's leg.

But... this year I may not be there for the ball, right? I just might be in Rivendell. If I wanted. I mean, I should go, I shouldn't hide my magic anymore. It was wrong. But as much as I wanted to get away from everything and go somewhere... Rivendell wasn't the best option. Going to Rivendell meant I would have to finally give in. I would have to stop hiding and come out with my magic.

The magic in Lenore was scarce, it wasn't always, but it was now. And those children who had even a trace of power in them were selected by the Royal Sorcerer Ilatagite. In the olden days, everyone had some sort of magic or other. Green thumbs – any plant they touched thrived; Weatherseers – they could predict the weather for any time or day, even a year from now; those with Yoresight – they could see a person's past; Leapers – they could travel from one place to another in just a leap; Healers; Mind readers, Mages and so on. I couldn't list the different types of magic that were once a part of Andoreya even if I spent a whole year trying. Because once you thought you had it all, you'd find someone else existed with a new unheard-of power; it just wasn't possible. These were just the small powers, though they didn't exist anymore and their existence was extremely valuable now. But there was magic which was much, much stronger and more powerful, but also kind of extinct. Like sorcery, Sorcerers were rare—two in a generation or something but most Sorcerers died when they were young, I don't know how but not many lived long. Ilatagite was old, and the last Sorcerer alive.

Wrong.

He was the last Sorcerer who was known. There was another Sorcerer who wasn't known by anyone but me. That Sorcerer was my best friend.

I glowed with pride as I looked back at her walking next to Kal. She caught my eye and raised an eyebrow. I grinned then looked away.

There was other magic too, which I knew was unidentified, because however much I searched through books and legends for it, I never found it.

Magic that no one knew about, that wasn't in the big fat record book in the library, *my* kind of magic.

My small bout of happiness deflated and I sighed in gloominess. Not knowing what kind of magic you possessed was weird; not knowing why you had not one but multiple powers was even weirder. Let's see – can talk to animals, can read minds, has conversations with Spirits. The first two were known magic, but no one possessed both of them together. It wasn't heard of.

And talking to some mysterious light? That was simply absurd, and creepy. This is why I hadn't told anyone about it till now, other than Fab of course. Well, that's not exactly true. I didn't... I didn't want to talk about my magic, it made me uncomfortable. My powers were simply unheard of. Besides, our family did not need the attention my magic would bring. *I* did not need that attention. Anyone with magic would be taken directly to the castle and would have to fight in the war. There was no distinction between males and females when it came to this. Everyone with magic would fight. As it was, most of the able men of Gondon were already fighting. It was only because my father had a heart condition that he was exempted. And thank heavens for that. Boys above the age of sixteen were taken and men below the age of sixty five. It was a wonder that there were any men around anymore. A shame that Nick is still around, I thought dolefully.

But honestly, the war was a scary thing. Since Gondon was so far away from the wastelands, the warfront, we weren't affected much. But if you were unlucky enough to be able to read people's minds, and sometimes when you were really emotional you just ended up getting images of someone else's life, you would have a good idea of the horrors the soldiers and magicians had to face. Which is why I knew a lot of things others didn't, but that didn't mean I understood. Like what kind of dark magicians did the other side have? They seemed immortal and so strong... and evil. And how long could this go on? I knew we couldn't withstand much more. The enemy seemed to be growing stronger.

We needed magicians. We needed a Sorcerer. I glanced guiltily at Fab, I hadn't told her the whole truth about what I had seen when one soldier, an old man, had returned last year because he couldn't fight anymore. His ill-health and age made him weak. He had also lost a leg. I shuddered. All the images of war I had got from his mind. My father had insisted we go see him. Mister Winkle, he was really old and haggard. And as soon as I saw him, and looked into his dark blue eyes I was lost in a chaotic stream of memories. The despair, pain, hunger, exhaustion....

It took me a while to recover from that.

I hadn't told Fab everything, I didn't want to scare her. As much as I hated keeping secrets from Fab it was for her own good. At least that's what I told myself, that I was *protecting* her.

"Hey! Wait up!" Fab called, and I turned with a yawn. She said 'bye' to the others and headed towards me. I had been walking alone, lost in my thoughts. I usually walked with Fab, Kal and Shandre; I guess you could say they were my friends too.

"Why did you run?" Fab asked, once she reached me and we started walking together.

"Who ran?" I asked, confused.

She gave me an exasperated look. "Sorry. Let me rephrase. Why didn't you walk with us?"

"Oh, that," I said. "I was thinking."

"Well, that's new," she said with a grin.

"Very funny," I rolled my eyes. "As I was saying, I was thinking about our magic."

Her expression became serious. Whenever we talked about this, she would instantly become worried and tense. "Relax will you? No one's attacking you," I chuckled.

"It's just... I still can't digest the fact that... I'm...."

"Probably the last Sorcerer to exist, besides Ilatagite? Also the first female one in almost a century? Old news." I yawned again. I must be really sleepy, not surprising though, I hadn't slept a wink last night. How can you if you keep dreaming about your dead brother talking to you and saying he's planning to kill you?

Can the dead walk?

"Still... it's scary," she said frowning. "I can't believe that I'm the first female Sorcerer, there's never been one and maybe I can't do it."

"So? There can be one in this generation then!" I said, interrupting her. "Just because it's never happened before doesn't mean it won't ever happen! What about the first female healer? Or the first female royal advisor, first female swordsperson, the first female teacher? And all those others?" I asked crossly. "If they all had sat wailing like you, would they have reached where they are today?" Seeing the expression of amusement on her face I added, "Okay, so they're not alive *today*, but they still made it, and now there are stories and books about them! Just imagine, Fabiana Lilywhite Mecatrus—the first female Sorcerer, books about you, stories, and songs. You might even have a statue built of you or something!" I said. She looked at me, sceptically. I continued. I was having too much fun to stop. "Maybe a prince will ask for your hand in marriage, just imagine that, and you could rule together prince and Sorceress, or maybe like the princess and frog tale, you could disenchant some prince? Of course you'd have to give your first kiss to a frog." Then, as an afterthought I added, "Okay that'll be gross ... or, or maybe..."

"Ann!" she cried indignantly. I had extreme moods; right now I was hyper, bouncing with madness. It would die soon, and I'd become dead serious, maybe miserable too. But while it lasted, I might as well enjoy it.

"Yes?" I asked trying to look innocent. "But Fab if you're going to kiss a frog, let me know first," I said. "I'll talk to it first and make sure it's a good frog." I beamed at her.

She looked at me with an expression of disbelief and amusement.

"Ann," she said, shaking her head and turning serious, "it's not funny. You know ... my father's last letter suggested ... he wants me to get married. And he's already asked Aunt Lina to look for alliances for me."

And just like that, I deflated; my bubble of erratic joy had just been popped, very suddenly and unpleasantly.

"*Marriage?*" I repeated, probably sounding like I'd never heard of such a thing before. "But you're only sixteen!"

"I'll be seventeen in a few months. And Lina got married when she was seventeen. Even your mother was married at sixteen."

"Yes, but," I frowned, "that's different. We ... you ... marriage is too ... big Fab! I mean, do you really want to chain yourself to someone you hardly know for the rest of your *life?*"

"That's what's expected of us Ann! And don't make it sound like prison. It's not *that* bad." I snorted. "It's either that or admitting to being a Magician and fighting." She paused then added, "Soon, your parents will be looking for alliances for you too."

I snorted again, though a small, really small voice in my head agreed with Fab. In fact, I knew they were already looking. A fact I tried to overlook. I would not get married if it was the last thing in the world. I'd rather kiss a swine. Well, unless maybe the man looked like Thor or something, in which case he definitely wouldn't marry *me*.

"I can't believe this," I said, grimacing. "You are the first female Sorcerer ever, and you're going to get married and have children? Fab, you have *so* much potential. I mean, not saying that you shouldn't marry!" I knew Fab wasn't against marriage like I was; I wasn't going to put any of my mad ideas in her head, but to just get married at this age and well ... throw away her life like that? The girl hadn't even seen anything outside the confines of our little town.

"I'm not saying don't marry Fab," I said, trying to calm down. "But you haven't really explored your magic. We don't know much about our magic. There's so much more to learn. If you get married..." I gestured wildly, unable to find words to express how wrong it sounded.

Fab frowned. "Ann, no one but you and I know about my *so-called* potential."

We had discovered only last summer that she was perhaps the first female Sorcerer in years, though we didn't know how long, and we didn't know whether she was the last Sorcerer alive. But it did look like she was. Recently the kingdom had been desperately searching for young ones who might have the unique powers to be Sorcerers. They had come to Gondon many times on their search, but they had never found Fab out.

Because I could shield her magic from others, as I could shield mine as well. That was another power too, not much of a power... but a good defence.

"And even then," Fab said sadly, "I can't tell anyone, not even the man I marry."

"I know." I sighed.

If she was the last Sorcerer she did have her responsibility to Andoreya. We needed as much magic as we could use because of the war, and Ilatagite was well ... ancient. No one knew his age, but he'd been around for almost forever. We needed a young Sorcerer. And here was Fab, meeting all the requirements except that of being a male. I bet a female Sorcerer would be equally good, probably even better at magic. But it didn't matter because no one knew about her magic, because we chose to keep it that way. Fab was afraid of how people, especially her family, would react if they found out that she was a Sorcerer. We were scared, and by the time we reconsidered our decision it was too late, because if she was found out so would I be. I was too involved in this to not get involved. And my magic wasn't explainable, and it was creepy. You can't just tell your parents over tea, "You know I talked to one of the Spirits who decided our fate yesterday? Yeah we had a nice chat about how the world was going to end soon." (Well, I think that's what they meant when they said 'Abyss shall open and consume everything you know.')

No. Not possible. My parents were great, caring and understanding. But this they would not understand. And even if they did, what would happen next? I'd probably be forced by the world to go to the Capital to be studied and classified. And once that was done, I would never come back home. All possible magic was needed during the war, even the most insignificant. That's why most people were hiding their powers, not easy if they couldn't shield them like I could. So most got caught, and taken away.

And they never came back home.

Yeah we were selfish, but we didn't want to get taken away against our will. Not for something that we didn't even want to be part of.

The war had started when I was nine, right after we were struck.

What was the reason for the war?

The exiles had decided to rebel. See, like good magic there was bad magic too. There were people who possessed real strong, dark magic which would inevitably cause harm.

I don't believe in good and dark magic. I believe there is only one kind of magic: magic. The way a person wields their magic is what categorises them into good and evil. But obviously I was alone in this thought. Well, in a minority at least. Come to think of it, mindreading could be considered as dark. By Thor, no! I wasn't a dark magician! I didn't use it for evil! Well, except for a few times ...

I shook my head. Anyway, when a person was identified with dark magic they had the option of giving it up or being exiled to the wild Wastelands. Most gave it up, but some didn't. I don't know how a person could give up their magic but it was apparently possible, and those people who didn't agree to do that were duly exiled. Over the years their numbers grew, and seven years back, all hell broke loose. The queen was killed along with the minister, and the little prince was kidnapped from the castle.

Dracone Helle was no ordinary castle. It was a huge, three-hundred-acre castle, with dozens of mazes and passageways that you could lose your way in and never get out of. The head of the exiles is a dreaded figure. No one's really seen him and no one knows his real name. He was called the Night Prowler because he was the only person who had managed to sneak into the castle and get out all by himself, the same night he killed the queen. He was the mastermind behind all the battle plans and atrocities. But he had never come to Gondon, maybe because Gondon was off the main chart. I dearly hoped he would never come here.

But he might, said a small voice in my head, he might come for you.

I frowned, don't be silly Ann, you were little. You could easily have been confused.

Ryan was bleeding.

His breathing came out in gasps, suddenly it stopped altogether.

I was running, running for my life. Someone was chasing me. I looked back, I heard a laugh.

Ryan was swaying weakly, walking … towards me.

I blinked, where was I? Cocking my head I noticed we had reached home, walking in silence, deep in our own thoughts. What had I been thinking about? Oh yeah the castle … I blinked again, my head felt light.

Fab gave me a look of concern and I shrugged. I had to remember to talk to my mother about these sudden bouts of light-headedness. I sighed.

Ma welcomed us home with her cheerful smile and our mood lifted when we discovered dessert was apple pie. My father joined us halfway through the meal and we chattered away like any happy family, laughing at the silly jokes of my younger brother Arni. I looked at Arni; he was born after Ryan's death. He was eleven years younger to me. He had an uncanny resemblance to Ryan, but he had a much more sensitive disposition than either Ryan or I had. Sometimes I thought he was the reason my parents were still together. The accident had shattered our family. It was only after Arni's birth that things got better, but even then …

After dinner, Fab and I helped Ma clear the table and wash the dishes, then we retreated into my room for the night.

We changed into our nightgowns and I sank into my bed. Fab sat by the desk, writing a letter to her father. I was half asleep when I realised she was sitting on her bed and looking at me.

Sleepily I lifted my head, "You okay?"

She shook her head. Even without the dim light of the lantern I knew she was crying. I quickly got off my bed and knelt by hers.

"Hey, it's okay. Relax." As I said this I was unconsciously sending tendrils of calm to her mind, it surrounded her like an aura. In my mind it looked like ropes of green light were surrounding her, but to anyone else it wouldn't even be visible. Right now I had let my barrier down to help her, and so I knew that downstairs my parents were having an argument in their bedroom while Arni, whose room adjoined theirs, sat on his bed, listening fearfully, I could feel the tension in the air. I also knew that our neighbours, a young couple, were going to have a baby soon by the joyful feeling that came from the lady of the house. My cousin Aero was stealing bread from the pantry, I could sense his fear that he might get caught by his mother. I could feel almost the whole of Gondon's citizens' emotions right now.

I knew what each one of them was doing, I felt dizzy.

I tried to draw back, it wasn't easy. My mind was too distracted by the various thoughts and emotions that filled me – rage, sorrow, passion, love, hunger, lust – I clenched my fists into balls. Concentrate, Ann. I pulled back with a lurch and fell on the ground. Now Fab was the one kneeling next to me.

"You dolt, why did you do that?"

I was breathing hard, gasping for air like I had just nearly drowned. This was the drawback of my powers. I could use them but this was the toll it would take on me. Not worth it. But most of the time I did this unconsciously, when I tried to console anyone this would usually happen and then ... well.

"I didn't do it on purpose," I groaned, as my head throbbed. I tried to shake off the feelings that didn't belong to me. Ugh. It was crazy to know what went on in someone else's head. I never knew Nick had such feelings for... I shuddered. Yuck.

"Heavens above! You have got to stop doing this, Ann! You didn't need to do that. We could've just talked, it would've been enough!"

I sat up, slowly. "Okay, talk. Why were you crying?"

She raised an eyebrow. "I'm not about to tell you that after what happened to you now. What am I, heartless?"

"Yes," I answered. "C'mon Fab, just tell me, I hate when you keep secrets." I felt a twinge of guilt. My mind screamed 'hypocrite' at me but I ignored it.

Fab sighed and I got up slowly, but the room tilted and I quickly sat down on her bed. I crossed my legs and we waited for my head to stop throbbing and the room to stop spinning.

"Okay. Shoot," I said, nodding at her.

"Ilatagite will be here soon," she said. "I heard some of the scholars discussing his arrival. He's coming himself this time."

"Alright, so?"

"Well," she pulled her knees close to her chest and hugged them, "Ann, you can shield me from Hounds, which is really amazing, but do you think you can do it from a full-fledged, royal Sorcerer?"

"Ah." I frowned. "Yeah, um probably not."

"Exactly." She sighed, falling back on the bed so I couldn't see her face anymore. "Which means I'm doomed and so are you. He's going to tell everyone what I am. Can you imagine how my father will react? How your parents will? How everyone here will? Spirits above! They'll all be so mad that we didn't tell them! Why didn't we? I knew we should have! Ilatagite's going to be furious! Ann!" She sat bolt upright and stared at me, horrified. "We could go to gaol! We hid from them! And I'm a Sorcerer! I shouldn't have! We shouldn't have! Ann! I don't want to go to gaol –"

I interrupted her babble with my laughter. "Fab!" I said amidst bouts of amusement, "You'd think we haven't had this conversation before. By Thor! Calm down."

She looked mutinous. And I struggled not to laugh. "Fab, remember when the Hounds first came?" I asked, grinning.

"Yeah, just after your eleventh birthday."

I nodded. "And? Remember what happened the day before they came?"

"You had a dream." She fidgeted. "A Spirit visited you and told you to keep our magic a secret."

"Exactly. And who knows better than the Spirits?" I asked. "Nobody, that's who. I like to think it was Thor."

She rolled her eyes. "You said the voice was more feminine."

"Well yeah," I conceded. "Still, a girl can dream."

She shook her head, smiling. "Thing is Ann … how do you know we can trust Ilatagite?"

"Ah." I frowned. "Well, he is the royal Sorcerer. And …"

There was a knock on my door, Arni's little head peeped in. I got up from Fab's bed knowing where this would be going.

"What is it Arni?" I asked looking at him.

He had dark hair like mine and light blue eyes like … Ryan had. He would look exactly like Ryan when he grew up. I'm not sure if that's a good thing or a bad thing.

"Anna," he said, "can I sleep with you and Fabi tonight?"

Fab looked at me and shrugged, I sighed.

"Sure you can, come on." I said lifting the covers for him. He quickly scrambled into my bed and I dropped the blanket on him. I sat next to him and Fab and I exchanged a look. She got up and folded her letter, and then she blew out the candle and the lantern went dark and the room was submerged in darkness.

I got into the bed beside my little brother. I could feel the tension in him; he didn't understand why our parents were fighting though. How could he? He didn't even know about Ryan.

I listened in.

"We couldn't have done anything Suphinius!" Reveria cried. "It wasn't our fault."

"We *should've* done something."

"It's in the past Suphinius and let it be. Thinking about it won't bring him back. It won't. We have Ann and Arni. Let's give them what we can't give him."

It was painful to hear them argue over something we couldn't do anything about. Something we couldn't change. My mother was right, it was in the past and we should let it be. But could we? Could I? He was such a big part of my life ... even in death. I tried not to listen, to yank my barriers up again but I couldn't. It was painful but I had to listen. I felt sick. With a wrench I pulled back.

I held Arni close and influenced his mind, making him drowsy.

For a long time I stared at the ceiling, mulling over Ilatagite's arrival, one hand unconsciously stroking Arni's hair. In a way it would be an escape for me. I just wanted to run ... but I knew I couldn't. This was the ideal opportunity, but was it worth it?

I heard Fab turn over in her bed with a sigh. I bit my lip. I didn't know what would happen once Ilatagite found out about our magic. He would take me to Rivendell, he had to. But was that what *I* wanted?

Besides there was the question of my magic ... my magic! Mine wasn't even explainable.

I remembered the night of the 'incident', that was how everyone referred to it, and I had got used to treating it that way. Like something that happened to someone else. Not to our family. Not to me.

Thing is, the more you lied to yourself, the more you started to believe in it.

I heard a door slam downstairs, and knew without using my magic that my father had left the house and my mother was sobbing. I knew Fab had heard it too. I rolled over, my back to Arni and her, and shut my eyes tight, as tears streamed down my face.

A thousand miles away, a lone man raised his head, his blue eyes glinting at the sky, before he picked his way through the carnage of dead soldiers.

2: The Royal Sorcerer

Ilatagite paced the room restlessly. He had arrived at Oracle city, the capital, during the early hours of the morning.

He had come to the hall straightaway and waited for the king to arrive. At around midnight he had got a message from the king's messenger, telling him to immediately hurry to the castle. After settling some matters at the Academy, he had transported himself and his nine students to the castle. He hardly used magic to travel unless it was absolutely necessary, but since the king wanted to see him immediately he had done so. But of course you couldn't appear inside the castle, it was protected with strong spells cast by the Sorcerers before him. So he had arrived at the capital in the morning and they had made their way to the castle. He glanced at his students, three were girls. They were all magicians. He had done his best with them. But even his best wasn't enough anymore. They needed more. They needed a new Sorcerer, a younger one.

Ilatagite sighed. He was getting too old. He was worried about what the king wanted to say. Ilatagite had started the Academy just five years back because the magicians who were recruited had no control over or knowledge about their powers. Long back, much before the war started there was another Academy, in Dardenium, a much bigger one with magicians from every part of the world pouring in. They pooled their knowledge, studied, experimented and discovered. Ilatagite himself was an academic there. The Academy was burnt down the same day the war started. How the exiles managed to do it was a mystery. Many magicians died. Some, like him, escaped. But most had died, including most of his friends and colleagues.

Right now they had a scanty twenty-seven magicians with them including his current students, it used to be forty six in the beginning when the war had just started and they had sent the Hounds to bring out anyone with magic to help the war. Many had died.

One of the guards came in and called Ilatagite, who gave his students a stern look before leaving them alone at the entrance hall. He entered the throne room, where the king sat on the throne, looking weary.

Ilatagite bowed, "Your Majesty," he said, "you look ill."

"I am ill," said the king. "I have been for a long time."

Seven years back, the king's health had started deteriorating, since that horrible day when the queen had been killed and the prince kidnapped by the murderer. There had been utter chaos that day. Ilatagite had been summoned from the Academy just like this, and he had hurried here to find a grieving king without a wife or heir. Edwin had been the only child, the heir to the throne. He had been a brilliant boy.

The murderer, whoever he was, had come in the dead of night, killed the minister and the queen as well. The prince's screams had woken up the whole castle, the guards tried to pursue the murderer but he had already vanished with his prize. The king had been devastated and the prince and his scent had vanished, without a trace.

That same day, another boy had vanished too; his family held his funeral. His younger sister had seen him die. The girl wouldn't talk. She had said only one thing and after that, nothing. No amount of coaxing had helped. Ilatagite had even tried to read the girl's mind but it was so enveloped in grief, in darkness, he couldn't make out anything. She had said, "They killed him." Of course Ilatagite had run an enquiry but they hadn't been able to find out who had killed the boy and the body had vanished. The minister's sons did admit later on that they had beaten him up but left him alive. Some quarrel over their sister and the boy seeing each other. But the body was never found. The family moved out of Oracle city a few days later.

"We cannot, will not, last long, Ilatagite," said the king. "My soldiers are tired, it's been years. They are loyal to me, but that does not make them invincible. There are soldiers dying every day beyond our borders. General Mecatrus reported twenty-nine men dead today. He also asked me for two days' leave and I denied it, we can't even afford to give them leave. They miss their families, they are not happy. And the more we lose, the more they gain. They turn our men into their docile servants who drink blood and fight with lust. I think it's time we started considering evacuation. Our kingdom is the only one yet to evacuate. Why did we wait so long?"

Ilatagite had no answer. "Is there enough place in Drell?"

"It's a fortress that has magic to protect the inhabitants from being attacked or harmed. Till we can do something about this, I think it is necessary to evacuate. Many of the other kingdoms evacuated their people and I do not want more innocents dying."

"Very well, your Majesty," Ilatagite said.

"Only the royal family knows about it. My great, great grandfather built Drell. He was a seer; he must have known we would need it. I wish we didn't," he sighed. "Did you bring your magicians, Ilatagite?" he asked, and Ilatagite nodded again. "They are outside, my King."

"They can join my ranks," said the king, "I hope these are not as big cowards as last year's."

"We must not be so harsh, Sire; everyone is scared to join the war. They hide from the Hounds. Soon I will go again, for new students, *myself*. And hopefully this year we will have a bigger number and better students."

"What about an apprentice for you, Ilatagite?"

Ilatagite sighed. "I haven't found anyone with even a hint of Sorcery in them."

"If Dardenium hadn't fallen you could have made it there and searched all of Lenore. The fall of Dardenium is the fall of Lenore."

Ilatagite bowed his head gravely.

"It is no wonder we are losing. The portal can take the enemy anywhere. Is there no way to close the portal?"

"I cannot alter the nature of our world, Sire." Ilatagite said. "No Sorcerer can. If Andoreya falls too … they will have Lenore."

"I cannot even contact the kings of the other kingdoms. Who knows their condition? We are such wretched folks Ilatagite," the king sighed, "and we are not getting younger. We need a new Sorcerer. How long does it take to train one?"

"I had five years of training," Ilatagite said. "But I am afraid if we find an apprentice, everything must be taught in a matter of months."

"Yes, we don't have time."

They both looked at each other and saw the same thing, tired men who wanted to give in to Death.

As Ilatagite left, the king said very quietly, "We cannot hold this for long, the walls of protection are already breaking and the soldiers are dying in masses. The other side is very strong Ilatagite, and they have powerful dark magic at their disposal."

Ilatagite didn't say anything; he walked out with a heavy heart.

3: Lessons and Anntics

Fabiana

I woke up early in the morning and took a bath and got dressed. We didn't have school today. Ann was still sleeping, one arm around Arni and her mouth slightly ajar.

I pulled on my stockings, my underskirt, and my dress. Then I finished the letter to my father. I told him I didn't know if I was ready for marriage but I would do as he wished. Ann would be furious. I sealed the letter. I told myself I must remember to give it to Ann's father before he left for work. I looked at the clock in our room, it was barely past six.

I picked up a novel and flipped through it, my mind elsewhere.

The only time I asked my father about my mother was when I was six. An older boy had said my mother was dead.

"Papa," I asked, leaning on his knee, my hands folded on them. "What is a m – mudder?"

"Speak up, my love," he said, folding the newspaper, "Papa can't hear you if you mumble."

"A mudder. What's a mudder?"

He frowned. "A mudder?"

"Like a father," I said, trying to make him understand, "but not like one. Like me but a father."

He smiled, his eyes crinkling and shining. "A mother, you mean sweetheart. Well," he pulled me up and seated me on his lap, "a mother is like a father but she's a woman, a girl like you."

Of course he had to then explain the difference between males and females which I didn't really understand.

"A father and mother get married and have children like you."

"What's married?"

He laughed.

"Well, it's what my little sweetheart will do when she gets older. You'll marry a boy and have children."

I wrinkled my nose. "Why do people marry?"

"So we're not alone."

"But I'm not alone. You're there," I said frowning.

"I won't always be there."

"Why? Where are you going?" my eyes widened.

"Not now love. Later. When I become old."

"So we won't be together always?"

His face clouded and I patted his cheek softly, the stubble pricking my palm. "I won't leave you ever Papa."

"That's what your mother told me too baby," he said smiling sadly, "but she went."

"Where did she go?"

"To Heaven."

"What's that?"

He laughed. "You're full of questions today love!"

I smiled. I missed my father greatly. He hadn't been allowed to come home even for two days, the king had denied it; I didn't know when I would see him again.

"When did you get up?" Ann asked me, sitting up.

"A while back," I said.

"Wait, I have to show you something."

She got up, went to the bathroom and came back, her face dripping with water. She went to the bedside table and pulled out the heavy book Professor Burns had given her.

"I found something in here," she said, wiping her face on her sleeve.

"When did you read this?" I asked, going over to her.

"Last night."

"I thought you were asleep!"

"I only slept in the morning, around four." And I noticed the dark circles around her eyes.

"Ann..."

"It's not my fault!" she protested immediately, "I couldn't sleep." I saw her shiver.

I clicked my tongue like a mother hen. She rolled her eyes. "Look."

I took the book from her and she pointed out the paragraph she wanted me to read.

"It was the 27ʰ year under King George the Fourth's rule when the first signs of magic began to materialise. But it was dark magic and with it, it brought great evil. Theft and murder became daily happenings. The king took severe measures in order to decrease the malevolence. Those who were caught were put on trial. Executions were carried out if the person was found guilty. Strange stories began to circulate about mysterious beings that hypnotised people to do their will. Many of the accused said that they had no memory of doing such evil acts. Around this time the forests became the most dangerous places in Andoreya, believed to be the abodes of evil beings and spirits. Beings who possessed dark magic such as lycanthropes, night walkers, jinn, fair folk, gnomes, goblins were said to live in the forests; coming out after nightfall to wreak havoc.

When a single massacre of the town Quintel transpired, leaving more than four hundred people dead, the king finally called on the Royal Council and decided that Andoreya was no longer safe and it was better if they left. (Note: this was before the portal existed; there were no means of travel or communication between the other kingdoms.) There were rumours that there was a place far from Andoreya where they could ask for sanctuary. There were also rumours that the magic came from here.

It was decided, and within a week every single inhabitant of Andoreya including the wild tribes, the northern snow clans, and every single village and town, abandoned their homes to follow the king.

Seventy and six days later, the Andoreians gradually losing faith in their king, they reached the shores of the Silver Sea (now known as the Dark Sea) where an armada of boats awaited them. Most were reluctant to sail the sea with so few victuals, not knowing what lay beyond, hence the king ordered a battalion of the royal army to sail forth and see if there was any land ahead.

Two days gone, a single soldier returned bearing the news they most wanted. There was an island with fruits so sweet, water so wonderful and magic so evident.

The people rejoiced and set forth. The island was just as the soldier described, an ideal haven. And Lo! There stood the rest of the soldiers all dressed in the finest clothes, and beside them stood the most beautiful lady they'd ever seen. Rumours said that she was a goddess. The Andoreians settled in the magical city, while the king discussed the problems they were facing and asked for help.

The lady then called her brothers and offered their service to the king.

"*Thank you dear lady, but if my soldiers cannot defeat these creatures I cannot hope that some voodoo magic can,*" *said the king. For the only magic he had ever witnessed was those of witches, Lycans, vampires; dark magic. Hence he did not trust magic.*

The lady smiled, "*We are the First Four, the original magicians. We possess the strongest and rarest magic. Together we are invincible.*"

She gestured towards the first man, who stepped forward. "*This is Thor the Warrior. He has unimaginable strength. Thor, if you would demonstrate.*"

The almost giant-sized Thor lifted one of the huge boulders and threw it across the garden, past the city, over the cliff and into the sea. The splash was enormous, and when the boulder hit the seabed, the island shook violently like an earthquake.

The second man came forward. "*This is Lennox, the Shape Shifter. He can shift into any animal and become the exact clone of any human. Lennox if you please.*"

The lanky man quickly shape-shifted into a wolf, an eagle, a bull, and finally into a replica of Thor. The king stared at the doppelgänger.

The third man came forth. "*This is Lucifer, the Sorcerer. He can control all the elements. He can fly through the air, and cast spells of power.*"

The Sorcerer made each of the elements appear in his hand from thin air and directed each of them against the rocks behind the king. Then he flew through the air and retrieved an apple from one of the trees and presented it to the king. And as the king held it, the Sorcerer made it bigger and bigger till it finally burst and released sparks into the air. Lastly he cast a spell that created a giant crack on the ground, revealing the kingdom of the dead. And before the king could register what he had done, the crack sealed itself.

"*I am the Dragon Spirit, Cora. I can ... well let me show you.*"

"*Hello George*", *said a musical voice in the king's mind,* "*I am Cora and this is my dragon Zephyr*".

The king turned and Lo! Before him stood a huge purple dragon, its glittering scales gleaming in the sunlight.

"*My army will aid you and your kingdom.*"

And as he watched, a dozen dragons of different colours appeared in the sky, flying above them in circles.

"*This is what we offer you, King George of Andoreya, do you choose to accept our offer?*" *Cora asked.*

The king did. The four left Athanus that day itself with only the dragons as an army.

For six nights and seven days they did not return. Then on the seventh night, the night of the Midsummer Solstice they returned, victorious.

After days of celebration, the Andoreians returned to their homeland. Some chose to stay, but the four magicians decided that they would leave Athanus with the Andoreians. All but the Dragon Spirit could leave, for she was the Guardian of the city and could not leave the island ever. The eldest two did not want to leave her alone, and so they stayed back. But the Sorcerer left. It is the descendants of the Sorcerer Lucifer that roam the lands of Andoreya now..."

"Um Ann, we've learned all this before."

She looked stunned. "When?"

"In History. Pay attention," I said. "And the book is called Myths and Legends, there has never been a Sorcerer who could control all the elements."

"Yeah, well, you're missing the point!" she said dismissively. "See, if these other three are ... well exist, then we just need them! And Ilatagite! And we'd win the war!"

"Since when have we been discussing war strategies?" I asked her dubiously.

"I need to take a bath," she said, taking her toiletries from the cupboard and going in. I followed her. I sat on the basin counter as she pulled the curtain around the bath. I heard the water run and a splash as she started to bathe.

"So?" I prodded.

"Well, I was just thinking that if the war ended we wouldn't have to hide anymore."

"That's all fine and dandy," I said as steam filled the bathroom. "Slight problem, they don't exist."

"How do you know?" she asked.

"I pay attention in class," I said, smirking. "They died. Long, long back. And they didn't have children or anything. But the Sorcerer must have. He did I mean."

"Wow. So technically Lucifer is your ancestor?"

I shifted uneasily, "I guess."

"Well, I still think it could work. I mean maybe they did have children and maybe those people are just hiding. Or maybe, hey, maybe they're in that place. That haven place."

"Ann, you *need* sleep."

"I'm just thinking of possibilities. It could be. You never know."

I shook my head. There was just no way it could be true.

I sighed. By heaven's grace I hadn't been surrounded by people when my power first manifested. I had been alone. And later I only told Ann. Ann had seen the dark side of possessing magic and even then, Ann was strangely old in the ways of the world. Perhaps it was being a witness to her beloved brother's death that made her the way she was, cautious and hard. Over the years we learnt how wise that one decision was. Over the years I practised my magic, alone or with Ann, hidden under the mystical shadows of the forests or behind four walls. It's tough to control your magic when you have no one to show you how. It's tougher to test your limits; you don't know what you can do and how it will turn out. A fact I'm ashamed of is that even though I am a Sorcerer I can't cast a single spell.

I turned my mind to the present. Ann is easily carried away, mostly in her own world. She's observant and not blind to the harsh realities of life; she sees everything but she closes her eyes to problems most of the time. Sometimes I feel like she's gliding through life, with only a part of her conscience actually involved in the present. And sometimes I feel like she's bashing herself, head-first.

I, on the other hand, am constantly trying to be practical, pushing myself to do better with the shameful feeling that I won't be able to do so, insecure and brooding and unable to comprehend the magnitude of my powers.

I heard the water drain as she pulled the plug. A few moments later she came out, bathed and dressed in a red tunic with cream trousers, her hair wrapped in the towel. I could smell the soap.

"So genius, tell me where does our magic come from?" she asked, as she towelled her hair.

"Well," I frowned, trying to remember, "from the Spirit world. And our genes. Andoreya was full of normal people. No magicians until, like you read, the dark magicians came, and later the good ones. I've never heard of this haven place. I think it's a myth. But the point is magic isn't native to Andoreya. So maybe this haven does exist."

She sighed. "You burst my bubble all the time, Fabiana Mecatrus."

I grinned, "Your head's way up in the clouds, someone has to pull you to the ground."

She grunted.

When we entered the room, someone was knocking. Ann opened the door.

Her mother looked at us in surprise. "Oh! You're already awake. Good, well breakfast is ready. You can come and have it once you're ready."

We nodded.

"Is Arni..." she saw Arni sleeping on Ann's bed soundly. "Oh, when did he come here?"

"Last night," Ann replied staring hard at the wall. "I think he had some *nightmare.*"

I frowned at Ann and she bit her lip guiltily.

"Yes, well," Ann's mother looked tired and preoccupied, "come down once you're ready. And Fab," she said, giving me a tired smile, "your father's sent us word – he should be back in a month."

"Thank you Mrs. Gamori," I said, as my heart did a somersault with joy.

"It's no trouble at all," she said smiling, before leaving the room.

Ann stared at the empty space where her mother had been standing till just a second before. I guessed what she was thinking. She turned her back to me and rummaged under the cupboard for her boots. Then she went back into the bathroom.

"Fabi?" Arni said, sleepily sitting up. "Where's Anna?"

"She's getting dressed," I said, smiling at him. "It's almost time for breakfast."

"Oh," he said, opening his little mouth into a yawn.

I stretched and had to stifle a yawn. It was a Saturday, we didn't have classes today. I wondered what Ann had in mind for us today. Most Saturdays we went to the forests and I practised my magic and she jumped from tree to tree chatting with the forest animals, literally.

Ann came out of the bathroom. I looked at her eyes to see if she had been crying, but I couldn't make out. She looked at Arni and smiled, tiredly. She walked towards him, jumped on her bed and began to tickle him relentlessly. Arni squealed for her to stop. They wrestled each other, laughing loudly.

I laughed at the two of them. It's moments like these that make me wish I had my own family, a *proper* family.

I ached for my parents. But I knew it was me, the demon in me that had done it. I fell to the floor and began to weep.

Finally Ann stopped and lay down on her bed, gasping for breath.

"Now scram," Ann told him playfully. "We have to get dressed."

I sealed the envelope with wax, I'd have to remember to give it to Mister Gamori as he left for work; he usually sent the letters through some travellers. I picked up the stack of letters to put in the drawer, the last letter was about the marriage. "See..." I said, handing her the letter. She hesitated. "Oh go on, these lines." I pointed out the lines.

She read aloud: "*Daughter, I've asked your Aunt Lina to start looking for good alliances for you. I realise you will soon be seventeen. It should not be that I am neglecting my duties as a father. We will look for eligible matches and then we shall see.*"

"See."

"There's nothing to see," she said coolly, handing me my letter. "He said he's looking. You're still safe. Thank Thor. Jeez. Marriage. But hey... if ever you can't find a good alliance Fab... there's always Justin."

I groaned.

"Fabiana, please, will you accept these red roses that match that lovely blush on your face as a token of my love?" she imitated him, falling on her knees and looking at me with adoration.

"He was not on his knees," I said, though he had been.

"Oh he was," she said smirking "'Dearest Fabiana, I can't imagine living without you … you have such a beautiful smile.' Well Fab you certainly never smile this beautiful smile for me."

I made a growling noise.

She smirked.

Justin was the shopkeeper of the lace shop, their family business, and a really sweet fellow. I had only talked to him a few times and then one fine day he had met me while I was coming back from Shandre's house to Ann's, and proposed. It was horrible. I had no idea where it came from.

"I bet he's skulking around waiting for you. I'm telling you one thing though … I am not going to save you from him anymore. I hate that look on his face when I take you away. Like his heart's been burned."

"Ann!" I cried indignantly.

"Anyway, do you feel like going to the library?" Ann asked me, lacing up her boots.

"Why?" I asked back.

"To do more research on the Spirits."

"Are you asking me?" I asked her, grinning.

"It doesn't matter," she rolled her eyes. "You're coming anyway."

"I could turn you into a warthog for all you know."

"I think I'd make a nice one," she said, before leaving the room.

I smiled to myself as I got ready for what I thought would be a very long day. Spending my Saturday in a library wasn't such an inviting thought, but we do what we have to.

Ann and I sat on the floor of the library between the dusty shelves filled with thousands of books. The library was the only one in Gondon and was simply huge. Not many people came here though. It was mostly just historical books. There were geographical ones, philosophies, many on magic too. We were in the Magic section of the library. The old librarian was checking on us every half hour, I guess he was flummoxed as to why two young girls would want to spend their Saturday in the dusty library. After two hours of reading and not finding anything, I was beginning to side with the librarian too.

"Miss Mecatrus," said a voice, and I glanced up from my book. "How nice to see you."

I stood up quickly and brushed the dust from my dress. "Good Morning Mister Burns," I said smiling. "I didn't know you liked to read."

"I don't" said Gerry. "I was here to get a Geography book for my father. He wanted a book and he's not feeling too well. I came up here to get it for him."

"Oh, is Professor Burns unwell? He seemed fine yesterday," I said.

"Just a common cold, that's all."

"Fab," Ann said coming from behind some shelves with a pile of books. "I found..." she turned red on seeing Gerry who was red too. I guess they were both recalling the ball last year.

"Oh— um— Mister Burns, um— what are you doing here?" she stammered.

"I'm looking for a book for my father, Miss Gamori," he answered with a bow of his head.

"Yes, of course," she said, looking embarrassed. "Um, I just – we were looking for a few books too. Just to pass time, you know..."

"Of course," he said, bowing slightly. "I won't disturb you then. I'll see you around, Miss Mecatrus, Miss Gamori." He bowed again and left.

I couldn't help but grin. "By the Spirits, Ann," I said, "it was a year back and an accident. Why are you still fretting about it?"

"I'm not," she lied, turning her back to me.

I raised a brow, and she sighed. "If I didn't know better, I'd say you liked Gerry."

"Rubbish," she said dismissively. "Here," she said, handing me a book. "We'll take this book. It has some information. But other than this, I can't find anything." She looked frustrated. "I don't understand. If the Spirits are so important why don't we have any books about them?"

I shrugged; I didn't know the answer to that one either.

One month later

"Where do you think she's hiding?" I heard Kal ask Shandre.

"Heaven only knows! She always has some tricks up her sleeve."

"Too right I always do!" a voice said from somewhere. Ann. I could hear her from my hiding spot, which wasn't much. I was just hiding behind the doors to the staff room, behind the curtains. I was near the window so I could hear everything that was going on outside. Almost everyone had been caught and so they were now looking for the both of us. One of the girls in our year, Melissa, passed by my hiding place but didn't find me.

"Try the playground," said Kal. I saw her looking about as she said this.

"I can't see them anywhere. It's like they've become invisible," Shandre said.

"Hmm. What an interesting theory, invisible," Ann said.

"But that's not possible, you can't be invisible!" Shandre yelled.

"Nothing is impossible Shaaandre," said Ann in a sing-song tone.

I knew Shandre and Kal from when they were eleven, and Ann from the age of ten.

I feel like I've known Ann practically all my life, but we're very different from each other. She has waist length, jet black hair and green eyes that always seem to be sparkling with mischief. No one I knew had green eyes like Ann. They weren't the normal green, they were... different. They often reminded one of animal eyes, like a cat's but more feral. And she was tall – taller than me.

I, on the other hand, had short hair, well not very short but shorter than hers and it was a chocolaty brown colour. I was also shorter than her, but I was slimmer. And my eyes were blue, sea-blue my father always said...

But it wasn't just looks, we had entirely different characters, yet we were similar. When it came to character, I was more social than Ann, I could get along with people easily enough and I never got into fights. Ann always got into fights. She always argued, even for the smallest things. She was always in trouble. Contrarily, she spent most of her time alone, staring at the clouds or stars, or reading.

But Ann and I always did things that our friends, mainly Kal and Shandre, didn't approve of at all. Like going into the forest and coming back at dusk, we practised our magic there. But we couldn't help it; we weren't the type to tell others our problems, we preferred to try to sort them out by ourselves, between ourselves.

And I'm pretty sure Ann wasn't born to be a lady. The very thought of Ann sitting coyly and well-behaved was silly. Alright, we weren't bad people or anything. Just different. I guess I was a lot more different than anyone else, but I didn't have a choice. Being the first female Sorcerer in centuries was a bit … frightening. And that's one of the reasons we kept it a secret.

"Are you going to find us today or not?" Ann said bringing me back to the present. We were in school, it was our last day before the vacations and our lessons were over. But we had to stay back, because apparently there was some important announcement. So the girls had decided to play hide and seek. Everyone had been caught except us.

"Found Fabiana!" cried Melissa. Apparently she had decided to scour the area again.

Okay, everyone had been found but Ann.

"C'mon," said Melissa. "Help us find your friend."

I nodded, registering the 'your friend', but nevertheless followed her out. As soon as I went out into the courtyard I knew exactly where she was and I looked for her, until I caught her eye and she winked. I nodded, understanding her plan.

"Didn't you find her yet, Shandre?" I asked, walking towards Shandre and Kal. My skirt rustled in the wind, some of the boys were sitting on the fence and pretending that they were not looking our way.

"No!" Shandre said, stomping her foot, and sneaking a glance at the boys. "She must be cheating! I can't find her anywhere!"

A smile crept over my face. "Have you looked … up?"

Shandre looked confused as she slowly lifted her head to look at the tree she was standing under. As though from nowhere, Ann jumped down from the tree with a loud "Aarhh" and landed right in front of Shandre, on all fours! She looked like a wild cat.

Shandre screamed loudly and grabbed me. Ann began to laugh and not lady-like laughter, oh no, she was bent double and laughing, slapping her knees and clutching her stomach. I joined her, my eyes streaming with tears. Even the boys were laughing their heads off.

"Ooh— priceless expression, Shandre!" Ann said, in between bouts of laughter. But Shandre was red with embarrassment and fury. I think Ann sensed this because she choked on her laughter and sobered. "Oh c'mon it was a joke."

"I didn't find it very funny, Ann."

Now Ann looked guilty. "Well it was meant to be a joke, I …" the other girls had crowded around us now, uh-oh.

"Gosh, I'm sorry," she said awkwardly. "It was just a joke."

One of the boys whistled, which got Shandre rattled and she burst into tears before stalking off, with a few girls behind her. Ann looked guilty and murderous; furiously she turned to the boys.

"Who the hell whistled?" she asked, bristling.

Some of them looked at each other and back at her. Ann, no, we'll get into trouble!

"I asked, who whistled?"

"Ann, leave it," I muttered to her trying to pull her away. She shrugged my hand off.

One of the girls 'tsk-ed', I frowned at her, it was Vandra. She studied with us but we didn't talk to her much, because for some reason Ann didn't like her.

Ann turned on her.

"You have a problem?" she asked.

"No," she said, looking at the girls who were standing behind her and watching.

Ann's eyes were cold, her expression hard.

The other girls started murmuring amongst themselves, showing that they were behind Vandra, so she said a bit more boldly, "There is something very wrong with you Andalucia. Ladies just don't go around climbing trees and jumping like … like apes. You need help."

Ann snorted, "I hardly think any of us are *ladies*."

"At least we dress like we're supposed to," snapped Vandra.

The boys had gathered around us too; it was like a circle in which Ann and I were facing Vandra who had a band of girls behind her, and on the other side were boys whom I hardly even knew. There was no adult around, no one to chaperone us. This was bad.

"Ann, leave it. Let's go," I urged.

"Yeah kitty, leave it," jeered one of the boys.

Oh no. Why? Why couldn't they keep their mouths shut?

"What did you call me?" Ann asked vehemently.

The boy was two years senior to us. I vaguely recalled his name being Trevor or something.

He smirked, and the two goons next to him mirrored his action.

"Here now, girls don't go about climbing trees, dressing like men and picking fights, do they, boys?"

Most of the boys agreed they didn't. I tried to look for a familiar, helpful face in the sea of boys but couldn't find one. Of course I wouldn't! The boys I knew were gentlemen, well, in public at least! But these boys were trouble makers.

They practically goaded Ann who I knew was already upset about Shandre. "I do. And I'll fight with whoever I think is being cocky like you are now."

My heart skipped a beat at her language. She could be in serious trouble for saying such a thing!

"Ann!" I said in shock.

"And aren't you being just that now?" Vandra asked nastily. "Such vulgar language, really. You think you're pretty superior to us don't you? With your dressing like a man," she took in Ann's clothing, which was a tunic and trousers unlike our dresses and skirts, "and climbing trees, and picking fights? It's not. It's really unacceptable."

"Unacceptable according to who exactly?" Ann's voice was hard, flinty. She was on the path of self-destruction. "I don't give a damn about what you or anyone here thinks about me. I will dress as I please and if the Spirits are going to eternally damn me for my aberration, then so be it. I don't give a rat's fart."

I counted the times she had said damn, only twice right? Oh Ann. Why can't you shut up?

"Ann. Enough. We're going," I said, dragging her.

"I'm calm, Fab," she said, shrugging my hand off. And she was. The calm before the storm.

"What makes you think you're better than us," Vandra asked through gritted teeth, "when everyone, including you, knows that you're not?"

Things had really gone too far now. I was praying that a teacher would come.

"That's really too much," I told the girl, Vandra. "She did say sorry."

"You shouldn't get into all this, Fabiana," she told me.

"No it's not –"

"Yeah, Fab. Stay out of this," Ann murmured to me.

I glared at her indignantly, but I was alarmed by her expression. She looked ready to cry.

"Ann, let's go," I said pulling her shirt sleeve. I succeeded in dragging her out of the circle, when one of the stupid boys, the one who had spoken before, said to Vandra, "I think you touched a nerve."

Ann spun around. "Maybe I can't hit her but you're stupid and vulgar, Trevor, and I will not hesitate to beat you up."

Have you seen the size of him, Ann? Have you? Look again.

The murmur grew louder; the girls were looking at Ann like she had just slapped them. The boys looked surprised. Ann had really crossed the line, saying such things aloud were going against society's norms. She's called him by his first name. She's *threatened* to slap *him*. She's used profane language.

Oh, we're doomed. I give up.

The boy stepped forward with a sneer. "Slap me?" he laughed, some of the boys joining him. "I'm surprised, you really are a rebel aren't you? I wonder how much of a rebel you truly are..." he said his eyes taking her in. I shuddered.

I glanced at Ann, who was shivering though it wasn't really cold. I knew she was frightened. I was beyond frightened.

"You're disgusting," she spat. "Now unless you want me to make your dirty secrets public, you'll keep your opinions about me to yourself."

A murmur went through the crowd. Trevor didn't look so smug anymore. In fact he looked uneasy.

Ann began to walk under my coercion when he said under his breath, but loud enough for Ann to hear, "Doubt she's a girl even."

I saw Ann's jaw clench.

The next lines he said came out loud and clear. "Unless she can prove it."

She moved too quickly, I couldn't stop her.

BAM!

Right in his face.

My hands were on my mouth as I stared in horror at the blood streaming from his nose. He staggered and one of his friends caught him from falling.

Everyone backed away from Ann and me.

"And I'm vulgar?" she spat. "Your brother's ten times worse."

Vandra looked horrified as she knelt down beside Trevor.

Brother? Oh no. Oh noooo. This was bad. The cold stares we got were nothing compared to the curses that were flying from Vandra's mouth. Her language was much filthier than what Ann had used, much filthier.

One of the boys, I think Trevor's friend, started to make his way towards Ann with a nasty expression. He was twice Trevor's size and thrice Ann's.

Ann was trembling, but she didn't back down.

"What's going on there?" called a voice. I saw Professor Wijoh coming towards us.

I dragged Ann away from there. It was better for us to disappear before he caught us. Ann pushed my hand away, and ran. I chased after her, she ran till she reached the forest.

She flopped down on the grass and hid her face in her hands. I sat by her and patted her back weakly. I didn't realise she was crying until I heard her sniff.

I couldn't believe this had happened. Ann always had a bit of a temper, but she never lost it like this. She did get into arguments but she always checked herself. This time however...

She sniffed loudly, "I'm a horrible person."

"Of course you aren't!" I said immediately. "He deserved the punch after what he said! Though... maybe we could've avoided the whole situation altogether."

"I didn't think Shandre would take it so badly," she said looking up at me through puffy red eyes. Her kohl was smudged. Ann was the only one I knew who wore kohl. She said it helped reduce her headache. I wondered if it was her headache that caused her to fly into a rage like that.

"Neither did I," I sighed. "But you know her, she's so self-conscious around boys.

"I didn't realise they were even sitting there until later! That stupid bloody Trevor! Ugh! I hate him!"

"Nice punch though," I said.

"Got him right in the nose, huh!" she said with sadistic joy.

"But Vandra… and Shandre," I said, and immediately she looked weary.

"I shouldn't have said anything. Stupid, stupid, stupid!" she cursed.

"Yeah, but... past is past."

"Yeah past… is in the past," she said her eyes unfocused.

There was silence for a minute or two before she said: "You know that's what they all think, right? That I'm vulgar and weird? And you know you're going to be branded too, since you're my friend? You probably shouldn't be."

I got angry. "Ann please, give me some credit. I won't leave my best friend just because she punched a gutless jerk," I continued, "in his face, when he deserved it too. Though I think you could've gone without the whole fight, if that stupid Vandra hadn't interfered but... c'mon, seriously?"

She looked downcast before she mumbled "Sorry, it's just that... ugh! I'm so tired of people who think I'm odd because I climb trees and dress different! I mean how's it disturbing them in any way? I'm the one walking around like this! Not them!"

"I know, I know," I said soothingly.

She sighed. "I'm in deep shit, aren't I?"

"Don't say shit Ann," I said reflexively and she snorted.

But she was in deep shit. I couldn't lie about that, the teachers would find out. Trevor's parents would want to know how he managed to get a bloody nose and so Ann's parents would find out and... I sighed.

"We'll do something," I said, getting up and helping her up.

"Maybe I can live in the forests for a few days till everything cools down. You could bring me some food and stuff."

"No can do," I said, pushing her gently.

"But—but I'll be killed!" she said, protesting. "They'll butcher me alive."

"Who will?"

"Society! And Aunt Jenny and Shandre's mother are pretty close friends, so them. And then Trevor's parents. Trevor's parents… oh Spirits! I can't Fab! They... our... our families have history!"

"What kind of history?" I asked. I couldn't recall her ever mentioning Vandra's parents.

But she went on: "Just typical, of all the people to punch in the nose I had to punch someone from that family. Oh dear heavens, I am so dead. So, so dead. Agh!"

"Well... you should've thought about that before. I tried pulling and dragging you away from the fight but did you listen? No."

She sobered. "I know. Guess I have to face the music now."

I nodded. Then remembering something, I asked, "What was that thing you knew about Trevor that got him so uneasy?"

"Oh that?" she said, a watery smile spreading across her face. "He's disgusting, but he hasn't done anything as such. I was just bluffing. He fell for it."

4: Nightmare Come True

Andalucia

I was pretty sure I was expelled. I sat on one of the chairs in our hall as a crowd of people sat opposite and passed judgment on me. My parents were there, the Mayor (who was also the Principal), our history teacher, Vandra's parents with Trevor whose nose was bandaged, Aunt Jenny, Shandre's mother with Shandre.

Seeing Vandra's parents only made my parents more uneasy. My father was sitting straight, his face impassive. But I could sense the emotions running behind his mask. Grief, anger, despair, loss...

Fab was sitting with them and we were having a telepathic conversation.

Oh god, I wish this was over.

Consequence Ann, you should have listened to me.

Yeah, I know. Stop making me feel worse.

I felt her silent amusement. I felt no amusement, only tension and guilt for having put my parents in such a position. Our families didn't exactly have a good history, we did have history though. I didn't let Fab see these thoughts of mine; I really didn't want to have to explain all this.

Kiera leaped onto my lap and curled up there and went to sleep. I stroked her fur, happy for the warmth she gave.

Our Herb-lore teacher, Professor Wijoh cleared his throat. "We're here today to clear the matter about the commotion that happened on the last day of school which led to physical assault."

Definitely judgment day.

"As I have understood," he continued "Miss Gamori scared Miss Swen so that she broke into tears."

I interrupted here: "Actually one of the boys whistled and so..." I stopped because of the look my father gave me.

"Let him finish, Andalucia," he told me sternly.

I nodded, red in the face, and mumbled, "Sorry."

"As I was saying, Miss Swen left in tears. Then one of the girls, Miss Rose, I take it?" without waiting for an answer he went on, "she defended Miss Swen." I yearned to interrupt but Fab was telling me to keep quiet till he finished his recital.

I looked at Fab. *They've got it all wrong! Now it sounds like I'm the one at fault!*

You can explain once he's done, she said calmly.

"And then Miss Gamori used some vulgar language and when Mister Rose here supported his sister she punched him in the face." He looked quite grave. "This is what I gathered from the students who were present that day. And also, this is not the first time Miss Gamori has gotten into trouble. She's been involved in a lot of tussles; she's thrown the key to the dance room into the pond..."

"That was an accident!" I protested. "It slipped from my hands!"

"Just when you got near the pond?"

I bit my lip and stared pointedly at the ground. It had been an accident... of sorts. I don't know what had possessed me, I was in one of my extreme moods, extreme joy, and it just... *fell* into the pond.

He continued with his list of the trouble I'd been in and caused. He referred to things which had happened years back, like the time I filled frog spawn in one of the senior boys' shoes. Okay that was only a month back but he had called Shandre fat, ironically. I was just getting back at him for being rude, that's all.

Finally, after what seemed like aeons, he stopped. Everyone looked at the Mayor. He was a portly man with a sad, stern face. His two sons had died in the war just two weeks back.

"As per previous discussion, we have come to a decision that Miss Gamori must be expelled."

I expected that and yet I shivered. I had one more year of schooling left!

"And as punishment she will not be allowed at any social events."

Well, that's not too bad.

"Or public spaces, until she proves she can behave better."

What? How dare they!

"Andalucia, do you want to defend yourself?" asked someone. I blinked at Trevor's mother. Why was she asking me to defend myself? Of all the people! Oh Thor!

I nodded hastily so that I wouldn't lose the chance. "Firstly I didn't mean to embarrass or hurt Miss Swen," I said looking at her. "And I'm truly sorry I did." I meant that, though I felt she was really stupid for crying because I scared her, it wasn't like I had knifed her or anything. "Secondly Sir, you've got the story wrong or at least it's a biased version. Miss Rose," I avoided looking at her parents, "said something rude to me and I defended myself. I don't think that's a bad thing. I admit I did say a word or a few words I shouldn't have and I shouldn't have lost my temper either. I apologise for both." I took a deep breath. I hated apologising, especially to people like Vandra and Trevor.

"But for punching Mister Rose's nose I refuse to apologise."

And now thou shalt be damned Andalucia, forevermore. May Hell claim thee.

Everyone looked shocked, my father opened his mouth, but I continued. "He said something which was really vulgar and which I'm sure he would never say in the presence of elders. But he did to me that day, you don't have to take my word for it, but he did." I looked at his parents. "Something I'm sure would get him expelled too."

Fab's voice rang in my mind *Nice, but maybe a bit overdone?*

I'm expelled anyway. What does it matter? My hands were sweaty, and I felt like I had just died about fifteen times in the past few minutes. Expelled. Wow. I didn't think they'd actually expel me. What would I do now? This is a sign Ann! Run away now! It's time!

"Is this true, Miss Mecatrus?" Professor Wijoh asked her.

Fab nodded. "Everyone was at fault here," she said quickly, but I knew her attempt to save me was futile. "Mister Rose did say inappropriate things as well. Very inappropriate. And it's not all Ann's fault."

"Trevor will be suspended," the Mayor said cutting her off, "but you are still expelled Andalucia. You cannot be excused."

Fab slumped into her chair just as I did.

"Anything more?" my father asked finally in his gravest tone. He looked at Professor Wijoh and everyone else in the room expectantly.

"She needn't be expelled," Trevor's mother said. "Really. A bit too much."

"It's done," the Mayor said, getting up to leave. We all stood up as a sign of respect. My knees were trembling. Expelled? Expelled!

Fab! I'm expelled! What am I going to do? What will I do now? By the Spirits! Why did I ever punch him? Stupid Shandre! This is all her fault! No, it's mine. That's why I'm expelled.

Fab looked at me, worried, panicking, *Ann, relax. We'll find a way. Don't worry.*

"Well, if that's it, then…" said Professor Wijoh, breaking the charged silence, "I guess we can all leave."

Trevor opened his mouth to say something but then he caught my eye and stopped. Guess I had freaked him out. Ha! But so what? I was the one expelled! *What am I going to do?*

As they left our hall, I apologised profusely to Shandre and her mother. Her mother was quite sweet about it, telling me that such things happened, it didn't matter. Whereas Shandre said she wasn't angry with me, but she kept a stony face when she addressed me.

Trevor just walked out of the hall avoiding looking at me entirely; I braced myself for his parents' cold stare but was shocked when his mother took my hand and apologised sincerely, with tears in her eyes.

Oh Thor.

She seems nice, Fab commented.

Nice was an understatement.

The whole meeting was very upsetting for both families, since our pasts were intertwined together.

I bit my lower lip as she continued. "I know he can be really rude sometimes, I'm really sorry if he said anything that upset you." She was a short woman with dark red hair like Vandra's.

"Oh no Ma'am, please don't apologise. I'm really sorry that all this had to happen."

His father stood by. "But not that you punched him?" he asked.

I glanced at my parents who were standing close to him before saying, "No sir. Though I'm sorry I lost my temper. I could have avoided the whole situation, it's my fault."

But he didn't look angry. Only… could it be, impressed?!

"You've got a brave girl Suphinius," he told my father, and with a nod towards his wife he left.

His wife hugged me, to my utter disbelief, and whispered, "I am truly sorry for everything Andalucia. I know…" she paused. "I'm sorry, it should never have happened."

I didn't say anything, what could I say to that? Memories rose up and burned my mind.

"Mister Gamori," she addressed my father, "we will talk to the mayor. She won't be expelled."

"Oh no, Ma'am. What's done is done," my father said. "At any rate there are other prospects for her."

Huh? I looked at my father but he was still smiling politely at Trevor's mother.

When they all left, my father took me aside.

"Father, what do you mean by other prospects?"

His jaw was clenched and I knew he was angry.

"Father, I'm sorry... I told you..."

"You could have avoided the whole thing. Look what you've done."

I felt like he had slapped me. It didn't matter that I was expelled. What mattered was my father's reaction.

"Father—"

"How could you do this to us, Andalucia?" he asked angrily. "You know the association we had with them and how awry it has gone. Why must you rehash it? Are you determined to go the same way as your brother?" My father's jaw clenched, I could see sorrow and anger in equal measure. I had no words. He never mentioned Ryan in front of me, ever.

"How could you put us in such a situation?" he asked, exhaling loudly. He looked so old suddenly. I felt tears well up in my eyes. "I'm so disappointed in you."

"Father I—"

"Your brother gave us enough pain. We are still suffering because of him. I will not let you do the same to this family. If you can't go to school and behave like every other girl your age then I will find you a boy—" my eyes widened in horror. "You're getting married. And that is all."

He walked out of the hall and I sank into my chair. I heard my mother try to come in but my father stopped her.

"I've had enough of her antics," he said.

My heart sank. Marriage!

I felt suffocated, like I was drowning. I opened the window, and the Devil damn me, jumped out of it and ran to my forests.

I ran and ran and ran, my tears streaming wildly.

Oh my God, if there is a God, please, please don't let this happen! I can't get married! I won't! Spirits, please, please, if you exist, I will do anything but get married! Please, please! Thor! Please, listen to my prayers. I tried hard to remember the other Spirits' names but couldn't. Thor, please, please Thor, I promise you I will never ever behave badly if you stop this from happening. Please, please, if Spirits exist, please help me!

It was only morning so I was safe. If it was night I would be in trouble for coming to the forests. But what was the point? I was doomed anyway.

I cried until I could cry no more. I willed someone, some Spirit, some god to talk to me and tell me they'd save me.

When I had calmed down I tried to think rationally. Marriage isn't so bad. Who was I kidding? I couldn't get married. There would be even more restrictions! And to have children? I couldn't imagine myself as a mother. I couldn't even imagine what I would have to go through to conceive. I felt like gagging. No. I wasn't ready! In fact, I may never be ready!

My head throbbed and I realised someone was pressurising my barriers to break through. Someone familiar.

Fab? I sniffed.

By heavens, Ann! Come home now!

No. I'm running away.

What?

If I come, I have to get married. I won't.

Ann, please, be reasonable.

I will not marry Fab. I won't.

Ann, your mother is worried and looking for you. Come home, we'll sort it out. I swear. And if we can't, I'll run away with you.

You will?

Yes. Now come.

Swear?

I swear Ann.

My father wasn't home when I got there, which was fortunate. I looked like I'd rolled around in a pigsty. I trudged up to my room.

"Annie!" my mother cried, hugging me.

"Ma, I'm all dirty," I groaned.

She let go of me, her eyes wet. "I just went to the forest to think," I said guiltily. My mother was always worried about me and I felt a twinge of guilt, I didn't do much to ease her mind.

I looked at Fab who grimaced.

"I won't get married Ma," I said stiffly entering my room. I removed my boots and massaged my legs with my fingers. God, they hurt.

Please Thor, please help me.

"Ann, we're only looking."

I gulped, "But I can't."

"Ann, my darling, it has to happen someday."

"It's too soon!" I cried angrily, "I'm not ready!"

She frowned. "Of course, you can't behave wildly when you're married. And when he takes you in bed..."

I felt queasy. "Ma! I don't want to hear all that!"

Fab looked uneasy at the thought of being *taken* in bed. My stomach churned and bile rose in my throat.

"It's... I'm too young. I'm not ready to die!" I was actually sobbing hysterically.

"You're not going to die, Andalucia," she said sternly, "and every woman goes through this fear."

"Fear?" I spluttered "I'm not scared! I'm... I'm..."

Scared, admit it, just admit it. Of what? What am I so scared of? You know it, my conscience said haughtily, you know you'll be caged and reformed. You know whoever you marry can never accept you the way you are, wild and reckless. Nor will his family. Then what? He'll treat you with disgust, try to change you and finally give up. You'll be rejected.

"Even Fab's father is looking. So are all your friends' parents." She got up. "Lunch will be ready soon."

I'm going to starve myself to death.

"Fab." I sobbed, looking at her.

She came and hugged me.

"Ann, you make it sound like a death sentence."

"I won't get married Fab! I won't," I cried. "You promised you'd run away with me."

"You'd do that to your parents?"

"Yes. No." I cried more.

"They're only looking, Ann."

That was true. Maybe they wouldn't find anyone. In fact, no one would probably be interested.

"But I'm expelled. What am I going to do?"

"We need a miracle," Fab said, sighing, "to get you out of this mess."
Now where could we get a miracle?

I found my miracle during lunch.
"Ilatagite's coming the day after tomorrow," my father said.
Fab and I froze.
My parents continued to eat.
"He's looking for magicians. And he's going everywhere by himself. The kingdom must be in a desperate condition for him to come himself in search of magicians."
Fab was staring at me anxiously. He's looking for... and that's when the miracle landed in my lap, wrapped up like a gift.
"I have magic," I blurted.
Fab looked like she'd faint. My parents both stopped eating and looked at me, shocked. Everyone was shocked, I was too. What was I doing!
"That's what happened that day with Trevor!" I fabricated quickly, "I was ill and something was happening to me."
"Alice told me her son had a fever before his magic came," my mother muttered to my father.
"Is that why you lost your temper?" my father asked doubtfully.
I nodded vigorously. Fab's mouth was hanging wide open. I kicked her under the table and she quickly recovered.
"I didn't realise until now. I was so hot and bothered. And then it came."
It's a good thing that my parents weren't magicians, if they were they would've known that magic doesn't just come overnight like a zit or something.
"It?"
"My magic. I can— I can talk to animals."
Fab choked on her food. I had let it out. My secret. Well, a *part* of it.
"Andalucia, you do realise what this means?" my father asked.
That I won't have to get married!
"You will have to fight in the war."
And that.
"You may never come back home again," my mother said, almost crying.
Ah.
I chose the lesser of two evils. Death over marriage! Suddenly I didn't feel too happy. It didn't seem like a very good idea at all. I should've shut up. But so what? He was coming. He would find out. What was I *doing*?

"Suphinius, can we hide her?" my mother asked.

"What?" I said. "Hide me?"

"You can't go!" she cried. "You'll never come back."

"That's not true! Some people do…"

"We can't hide her Reveria," he said quietly, looking really upset. "Ilatagite himself is coming."

"Ma, what are you saying? How can you hide me?"

"I won't let you go! I can't let you go! You…" And then all hell broke loose. My mother collapsed from her chair to the floor, just like that. We jumped up in shock. My father lifted her and gently laid her on the sofa. He told us to leave the room. We cleared the dining table and went up. I wanted to stay but my father had shaken his head.

"She doesn't want to lose another child," he muttered under his breath.

"Oh Fab, what have I done?" I fell onto my bed, my face in the pillow.

"She'll be fine Ann, don't worry."

"This is ridiculous!" I cried. "It's death anyway! Torture and death." And rejection. Who would accept me really?

Fab grimaced. "It'll be okay…" she mumbled weakly.

But things only got worse.

Next day Fab's father came. And as glad as I was for her, I couldn't help but wish she could stay with me right then when everything seemed to be going wrong because of me. My mother had recovered and went about doing her chores like nothing had happened, except for when she would glance at me with shining, fear-filled eyes like she expected some vulture to grab me and carry me away from her.

"Papa!" Fab had cried, running to him and hugging him as he entered the room with my father.

He laughed. General Mecatrus was a jolly man, with a huge brown moustache and laughing blue eyes like Fab's, only a little lighter. You'd think that being in the army, he would be grave and serious, but he was exactly the opposite.

"Was it a difficult journey home, Sir?" asked my mother, offering him a cup of tea which he gratefully accepted.

"Oh no," laughed Fab's father, "it wasn't as bad as usual Ma'am."

"Manzeria was just telling me," said my father looking at me, "that a few of the other soldiers have come back too. Like—"

"Nellie!" I cried. "Oh gosh, he's here?"

"If you mean Lieutenant Nelson," said Fab's father smiling at me. "I believe he is. But before you run off, tell me how much trouble did you and Fabiana get into this time?"

I gulped. My mother smiled, "Fab didn't get into any trouble, she was a gem."

"That's more than what we can say for some people here," my father said, looking at me.

I flushed.

"How is the situation, General Mecatrus?" my mother asked him.

His smile faded, and lines creased his forehead. I sensed his mood, grim and downhearted.

"It's really bad Ma'am," he replied. "I don't know how long we can keep this up. The other side..." he shuddered, "they're... unstoppable. The Royal Sorcerer is a great help. I think it's only because of him we're still fighting. But... he's old and he's not there all the time. The Magicians are quite helpful too. But we need a miracle to win."

The atmosphere was grim. I felt suffocated. I didn't even want to look at my mother. What if she fainted again?

"Andalucia says she has magic," my father let drop.

Fab's father looked at me, alarmed, and I was afraid he would say: "Hide her."

"I see," was all he said.

"There's no choice but to send her, eh?"

He nodded. "I'll look out for her."

"Would you send Fabiana if she were in this situation?" my mother asked softly.

"Ma!" I hissed, shocked.

"Would you?" she repeated.

"I cannot deny Ilatagite," he sighed, staring at the ground.

Fab and I looked at each other grimly.

"But..." he said, "there is always hope." He smiled. "As long as we have magicians and Ilatagite, we should be good. I think we can defeat them, the chances aren't too bad."

I didn't know if he was saying this to ease the tension, but it did work. He kept his empty cup on the table. "I guess we should get home then."

"Of course," said my father bowing his head slightly.

"Take care," my mother said quietly.

Fab gave me a nervous look before she left too, with her father. She was worried, I knew. But I couldn't feel worried just then. I pushed away the worry for later. Right now, there was a chance of happiness.

Once they were gone I jumped up and down, "Can I go? Can I go?"

"Where?" Ma asked even though she knew where.

"To see Nellie!" I cried eagerly. "Please, please! Say yes, say yes!"

"He just got back home," said my father. "Let him rest."

"Aw Ma!" I said, disappointed. "Let me go, please! I'll just pop in, say hello, and come right back."

Ma looked at me sternly. "Annie," she said in the tone that suggested I was going to get a lecture, "you know it isn't good to go alone, that too into a house full of young men."

"Young men?" I guffawed. "If you mean Nick," I snorted, "ha! I'm more man than him!"

"Yes," said my father, "and that frightens me," while my mother reprimanded me, saying "That's no way to talk about your cousin, Ann."

"Ma," I said, "come on, let me go. I promise I'll behave!"

"No," she said firmly. I felt my shoulders sag.

The bell rang and my mother went to see who it was.

I scowled at my father's amused expression.

"Well," said my mother removing her apron, "someone up there must really like you Annie."

"Huh?"

"Rose just invited us all for dinner to her house, everyone will be there."

I shot out of my chair, unable to believe my luck. "Are you serious?"

"Yes Ann," my ma said smiling. "If you help me with the chores in the house. Now, that is."

"I'll do anything," I promised.

"And..." my mother smiled widely, "wear a proper dress."

"*No!*" I cried, my eyes wide.

"You did say anything," my father pointed out very unhelpfully from the dining table.

"Wear a dress," Ma said, "or don't come."

I had to go. I so badly wanted to see Nellie. And everyone else would be there, how could I miss such an opportunity?

I pouted. "Alright, I'll wear a dress."

Nelson was my cousin; he was twenty-six years old and my favourite. He reminded me a lot of my own brother; they were around the same age and had similar personalities.

Nellie was the one who had helped me, along with my own brother, to climb trees and ride. He was also Nick's brother, unfortunately. Nick was the total opposite of Nellie. Nick was stern, no fun and a goody-goody. He was of the opinion (like everyone else in the world) that girls should be well-behaved, properly-dressed, speak a little and only politely in a soft voice – in short, everything I was not. He always tried to boss me around. He was never considerate of how blatantly he pointed out my mistakes in front of others.

Zorine opened the door. Zorine was seventeen, just a year older than me, and very pretty. She looked like she sprang out of a painting or one of those novels with beautiful heroines in it. Her hair was a soft brown, and her eyes were a grey-green. She was thin, tall and graceful. She was my second cousin and lived with Aunt Jenna, after her father had died in the war and her mother had run away with her secret lover. It was Gondon gossip for months.

"How nice to see you," she said smiling. "I hope you're all doing well."

"Zoor," I said rolling my eyes, "it's just us, what's with the formality?"
My mother shot me a reproachful look, as Arni ran past Zorine into the house.

"Well," said a voice from behind, "some people believe in being polite. How are you doing, Sir?" he asked, shaking my father's hand.

I groaned. Nick was such a moron and from what I had gathered whenever my barriers were down, he had a huge crush on Zorine that extended a bit too much in his imagination. I shook off the image I had got from his mind, feeling like some dirty spy. But the disgust remained in my mind. After all, she was his cousin, his brother's fiancée.

"Can we come in?" I asked Nick grudgingly, "Or is it polite to keep your guests standing outside?"

"Oh my," Zorine said, opening the door wide. "I'm so sorry, please come in."

Nick's house was smaller than ours, but spacious, all the same.
"The others are in the tea room," Nick said, "but the elders are in the lounge."

"You go with them then," my mother said. "We'll see you at dinner."

I nodded and smiled at them before following Nick and Zorine through the narrow passage. There was a painting on the wall, of our great grandfather Thesus.

"I heard you got expelled." I grunted.

"I expected it much before." I didn't say anything, so he continued. The moron!

"Everyone's here," he said finally.

"Everyone?" I asked feeling a bit uneasy. I had expected a few cousins, but not everyone. He couldn't mean everyone though. I mean… all of them?

"Yeah," he said in a low tone, smirking. "Other than Zorine you're the only girl, glad you dressed properly this time."

"Are you allowed to actually say that?" I asked sweetly. "You know, comment on a girl's clothes?"

"You're no girl," he shot back.

I gritted my teeth but didn't say anything.

Nick opened the door. The room was a spacious, airy one, though right now it looked very crowded, which it was. He had spoken the truth – everyone was there. There was Aero and his brother Andrew who were playing cards with Zayn, Zorine's brother. Both Andrew and Zayn were soldiers too. Then there were my second cousins Liam, William, and Ralph; all between the ages of twenty and twenty five. Liam was a soldier; the other two were brothers and helped their father in his shipping business. Or they used to, but now they were also fighting in the war. No able-bodied man was spared. They had to fight, like it or not. Nick and Aero would be taken too this year, they had reached the appropriate age. Liam's younger brother who was Arni's age was there too,

Nathan. He and Arni were running around the room pretending to be soldiers and wielding imaginary swords.

But where was Nellie? I craned my neck, my eyes searching, but I didn't find him.

"BOO!" said a voice from behind. I jumped.

"Nellie!" I cried, outraged.

He laughed. "Should've seen the look on your face!"

"Just like the look on that girl's face when she did the same thing, that is before she made the girl cry and punched a boy in anger," said Nick, looking smug.

"You punched a boy?" Nelson asked taking my hand and shaking it in congratulations. "I'm proud of you!"

I grinned, though abashed. He squeezed my shoulder affectionately.

"She has a list of things you'd be proud of," Nick said, walking over to the table where Aero and Andrew were playing. "Filling Paul's boots with mud..."

"The Paul we used to play with?" Aero asked, looking at Nick. Nick nodded.

"He said he wanted to cut my hair and turn it into a mop!" I cried indignantly.

Nick raised an eyebrow. "What about the time you threw the keys of the dance –"

"They slipped from my hands!"

"Right when you reached the pond?"

"Why does everyone ask that?" I cried indignantly. Everyone gave me the look, the look that said you-know-why. Well now.

"What about the time you tripped Detrias into horse shit?" The image of Detrias with his face covered in horse shit popped into my mind and I laughed.

"He deserved it," I said amidst giggles. "He was bullying the kids!"

"And that's up to you to decide eh?" Nick asked as he shuffled the cards. "Who should be punished or not?"
I rolled my eyes. What a moron.

"Maybe it is," I said a bit aggressively.

"Okay, okay," said Nelson loudly, realising that I was getting angry. "Let's calm down, I'm sure the list goes on... but let's do something less anger initiating."

"Let's all play cards," Zorine suggested.

I pouted as I sat next to her. Nellie sat on her right with one arm around her shoulder—they were engaged. And somehow, whenever they exchanged small gestures of affection, it was okay. The world didn't scream at them and throw a fit about 'society' and the damn 'norms'. Maybe because it was Nellie and Zoor— the two most unlikely people to ever do anything *wrong*.

Opposite me was Liam, he was nice. So was Ralph. It was William I didn't like; he had this stupid notion that I was his affianced or something, which was why he kept looking at me and smiling loftily. He wasn't bad looking, it was just... I wasn't planning on getting married to him or anyone.

"Andalucia, are you playing?" Andrew asked bringing me back to the present.

"No," I said grumpily, "I don't like cards."

"Girls don't know how to play cards, that's why!" jeered Liam. I rolled my eyes at him. But I felt warm. It was nice to be somewhere amidst family, outside the confines of society... mostly. At least we didn't do the Miss and Mister formality among ourselves.

"I'll play," said Zorine, smiling.

Nellie squeezed Zorine's shoulder affectionately and was looking at her like she was the only person in the room, like she was the only one he could see. I shuddered. Love was creepy enough without it being so intense.

"So how's it, being in the army?" I asked loudly.

"Boring," said Nellie.

"Boring?" Andrew asked with raised brows. "We don't have a single moment to ourselves to even go to the loo in privacy."

I chuckled and Nick shot me a disapproving look, so I chuckled louder. Well, hello, it was funny.

"But the war isn't going well," Liam said grimly. "We've lost scores of men to the wastelands. They have witches and all number of dark magicians on their side. The fight isn't fair; we hardly have enough magicians to counter theirs."

I felt uneasy.

"They just spread dark fire across our army. We can't get the fire out by normal means. It's only because of Ilatagite that we're surviving."

"And the Hounds have been identifying the enemy magicians so that we could kill them; till now we've killed about eleven. But there are hundreds. Some of them are just... they just don't die!"

"How can they not die?" Zorine asked.

Liam shrugged. "Search me," he said, as Arni jumped on the settee beside him, yelling "DIE!" at Nathan who had been hiding under the table, unseen by us.

"Well put Arni. Well put," Liam said, shaking his head.

"Arni," I said sternly, "get down now." He stuck his tongue out before bouncing off the settee and chasing Nathan through the door.

"Um so," I said trying to keep calm, "are they out looking for more magicians?"

"The Hounds are searching," said Andrew, "and General Mecatrus is here to recruit, but the kingdom is also asking for magicians to step forward. Personally, I wouldn't advise anyone to."

"Why not?" asked Nick.

"You'll be stuck in the war until you die, mate," he said. "There's no way they'll let you go once they get you. It's lucky we all got to come home even. And that's only because Ilatagite's at the warfront for these two days. It's only those who haven't been home for more than a year who were allowed. The others are still fighting."

I didn't feel good suddenly. Had I chosen right? Death over marriage? Smart move Ann, real smart.

"Which reminds me," Liam said looking at Nick and Aero, "aren't you and Aero signing up? You've reached the age. Passed it, actually."

"Well according to what you have all been saying," I said quietly, "they needn't sign up. They'll be taken anyway."

"Yeah," Liam said, "but when you sign up at least you can fool yourself and others that you're going because you want to and not because you're forced to."

"Let's talk about something else. This is too depressing," Nellie said. "Aero what's been going on around here? Any new gossip?"

They chattered about senseless things and the mood lightened, except in my eyes. I saw the boys fighting desperately and wondered how it would be if one of them died. I would even grieve for William. Or maybe not.

I tried to distract my mind. But I didn't succeed.

"So, tell me," Nellie mumbled to me, "any *beaus*, Ann?"

"Ha!" I murmured back, "I'm not mad and it seems no boy here is either."

He laughed. "But you know they're looking for alliances for you. I heard my mother talking to Aunt Jenny about it today."

"I got expelled."

"I heard."

"Father thinks marriage is my only other option."

He grinned. "Well. I'll tell you this. Your options right now are William," I mimed gagging, "or... Gerry Burns."

"Gerry?" I felt my heart jump. "But I tripped him and humiliated him! He'd never agree!"

Nellie raised both brows, his eyes twinkling, "If he did? You like him eh?"

"Of course not!" I said indignantly. But a small voice in my head was guilty. My daydreams consisted of me travelling around Andoreya with Fab and learning more about my magic. But sometimes, when I was really exhausted and lonely and feeling *crazy*, I'd think about someone who would understand me and my magic and my oddness completely and well... love me. Gerry was really nice. And he always spoke nicely to me. But that was more politeness than anything. Maybe I should've chosen marriage. Horrified at myself I brought myself back to the conversation... like Gerry would agree to marry me!

Something brushed my leg. I frowned. A cat? Keira? No. It was someone. I looked across and William smirked.

I wondered how much trouble I could get into if I punched him on the face, but then decided it wouldn't be worth it. I had already gotten into enough trouble.

"Are you alright?" Nellie asked me.

"Do you think I can punch William?" I asked him in a whisper.

"Is he annoying you?" Nellie looked serious. He glared at William who immediately broke into conversation with Andrew who was sitting beside him.

"No, no," I said quickly. I didn't want to cause any more trouble, though I was grateful that Nellie was concerned.

"Gerry is a decent boy though."

"I'm not getting married," I said, scrunching my nose. "I'm going to Rivendell to train under Ilatagite."

"*What?*" he shouted.

Everyone looked at the two of us, stunned. "Aunt Reveria," he said vehemently, turning to look at my mother, to my utter shock, "you can't be sending her to Rivendell!" My mother paled.

"Nelson, what –?"

"Uncle, no, she won't come back!"

"Nellie, shut up!" I whispered horrified.

"Annie," he said choosing the name Ryan used to use for me, "you have no idea what we're up against."

"What is this about?"
"Rivendell?"
"Does she have Magic, Reveria? Why didn't you tell us?"
"You can't send the child!"
"She can hardly keep herself out of trouble here!"
"She'll be dead in a minute."
"What a tragedy!"
"Why didn't you say anything?"

"You have to hide her!" Nellie said sharply, louder than the others. My mother was covering her forehead with her hand, looking thoroughly beaten.

"It's Ilatagite, son, we can't hide her," my father said grimly.

"Send her away then! Somewhere else! Don't you get it? She won't come back!"

I shivered. "Nellie, please, drop it."
He looked at me squarely, a look so like the ones Ryan used to give me, that I trembled. "Annie, you will die. You won't survive. It's suicide!"
"Nellie!" I hissed.
"Nelson, behave yourself," his mother said.
"Mother, she's a child."
"I'm sixteen!" I protested. If I could get married at sixteen I sure as hell could fight in the war.
"And you'll die."
"Rose, I think we should go now," my mother said, getting up.
"Rev, no, sit down," my aunt said, throwing a dirty look at Nellie. "We're just worried for her."
"I understand," my mother said, "and we're having a hard time already. You must understand we... we... don't want to lose her as well..." My mother's face crumpled and most of the family looked around uneasily, ashamedly. Even Nellie looked guilt-ridden. Everyone was silent. My father murmured an

apology and excused himself. My mother picked up Arni who had fallen asleep on the couch next to Nathan, and walked out with him.

"I'm sorry Aunt Ro," I murmured. She nodded understandingly. I glanced at the rest of my family, shrugged apologetically and walked out, but not before glancing at Nellie whose face was set in stone, though his eyes told me another story.

Everything seemed to be spiralling downwards.

5: Arrival of Reality

Fabiana

My father and I sat up most of the night, talking. He told me the small incidents that he had witnessed and we talked about Aunt Lina and her baby and I told him about the stories of school and Ann.

In the back of my mind, a small voice was urging me to tell him I was a Sorcerer and that I too would have to go to Rivendell but I just couldn't bring myself to do it. Especially after he told me how he really felt about Ann's magic.

"It's dreadful," he said. "You realise the gravity, love?"

"She might survive," I said, trembling.

He shook his head and my heart sank. "Things are going really badly. I came back to send you away."

"Send me away? Where?"

"There's a fortress. I'll be leaving day after and both of us can go together. I'll take you to Ilatagite and he'll send you there to safety."

Oh, the irony! I thought of telling him then, but his next sentence killed that thought. "I would be devastated if it was you. I can't imagine losing you too." I gulped. "Don't worry love, I'll keep an eye on her," he assured me.

If only he knew how entangled our lives were. I smiled weakly.

My father and I were having breakfast when someone knocked on our door. My father went to see who it was, and returned a few minutes later. "I'm so sorry dear," he said, grabbing his cloak, "but I have to go to the war office right now, they need me."

"But—?"

"I'll be back by noon, I hope. You should go over to Ann's house, please." He planted a kiss on my forehead before leaving. His unfinished meal sat there. I sighed. My appetite lost, I cleared the plates.

I felt angry. I never got time with him. It was always like this. I knew I couldn't blame him. But I knew who to blame. I shook off the unwelcome thought and went to my room to change.

A memory from long back gripped me. I was thirteen. I had come from school. My father was going back to fight and I was going to live with Aunt Lina. I came home and shouted for him but he didn't respond.

I went up slowly, and I could hear sobs. From the staircase I saw the door of my mother's room slightly ajar, my father kneeling on the ground, clutching something and crying.

There's something about a man crying that is very raw, and when that man is your father, it hits you harder.

That night I went to my mother's room. I never went in there much and if I did, I never touched anything, fearful of tampering with anything. That night I let my hands caress the polished mirror, the tables, the hairbrushes... I sprayed some of her perfume, a little, fearfully. I sat at her writing table. I let my fingers glide over the parchment that was once hers.

When I was back in bed, I inhaled the smell of her perfume on me and cried for the loss.

I blinked in the mirror. "Get a grip, Fab." I told myself, as I brushed my hair and braided it.

I pulled on my boots and left for Ann's. She was sitting on the fence munching an apple when I reached her house.

I leaned on the gate and looked up at her. "My father's gone—"

"To the war office, I know," she said.

"How do—?"

She shrugged, "I was trying to sense Ilatagite coming. Unfortunately that meant I would have to lower my barriers so, I sensed uh... what happened in your house."

"That's eavesdropping!" I accused.

"No it wasn't!" she said.

"Of course it is!" I wasn't angry. Well, a bit, but not much. I was glad she hadn't heard last night's conversation.

"Okay maybe it was, but I couldn't help it really!"

I looked sceptical.

"Fine," she groaned "sorry. Happy?"

I grinned, "Yes."

"When is he coming? Do you know?" she asked.

I shrugged. "No idea."

We looked at the trees. After a while I said: "This is it Ann. We're going."

"I guess." She sighed.

"What happened?"

"My family." She huffed and told me what had happened yesterday at her Aunt's place.

"Whoa, it became such a big issue?" But then, it would, of course.

"Yeah." She looked grim. "I feel terrible now. But you know, Ilatagite would find out anyway... and Fab, maybe I could shield us, but how long will we hide? How long can we? Both of us will Blossom soon and then what? How can we hide it then?"

When people Blossom, their magic is much stronger than before, the potential is complete and even normal people can sense the magic in them.

"And don't you want to know how to cast spells? How to control your magic? See the extent of what you can do?"

"So basically you're saying we can't hide but we shouldn't even want to anymore."

"Yeah."

"But what about our parents?"

Her face fell. "Can't help it."

"We never had a chance," I mumbled.

"By Thor, we sound morose."

I gave her a sideways glance. "You call on him too much."

"Maybe he'll listen," she said grinning. "That'll be amazing! He's really handsome."

"Ann, he's a Spirit."

"Yeah, so?"

I shook my head, chuckling.

It was afternoon when Ilatagite arrived in Gondon. I was still at Ann's place. Her mother was a bundle of nerves. She even yelled at Arni for running around too much. Ann shot her mother a disapproving look before going after him to stop his tears.

I was helping Ann stack the washed dishes when her mother came behind us and scared us. "He's come." I jumped. I felt all the blood drain from my body. Her mother looked like her blood had been drained too.

"Ma," Ann said softly, "will you calm down?"

"Of course." She smoothed her dress and tidied her hair. She busied herself, arranging tea and biscuits, her hands trembling. "Your father, Fabiana, is the one who's escorting him."

I nodded.

Her mother looked at us like she would burst into tears. Ann took her mother's hand. "Ma, I won't die. I swear. Just calm down."

She sniffed, kissed Ann, and then took the tray and left the kitchen.

Ann shook her head at me in exasperation. "Gosh."

"I'm terrified," I admitted.

"So am I," she said.

We held hands, and I saw her lips move in prayer, no doubt to Thor.

When we were called we went, still holding hands.

I saw Ann's parents sitting on the sofa and opposite them my father was sitting, tense, beside a handsome sixty-something man. His robes were a deep plum colour that matched his eyes, and he radiated vibrations so strong it seemed that we could see the air crackling.

Who else could it be? I felt bile rise in my throat. I felt a tingling sensation all over me as Ann's nails dug into my palm. I saw his eyes widen and narrow. He knew. He knew what I was.

Through my peripheral view I saw Ann shake her head slightly. Was she shaking her head at him? What was she saying?

"Can I see the girls alone?"

"Both?" my father said, alarmed, and I felt a bolt of pain for him.

"Yes, both," he said.

Our parents got up slowly and left the room, after assuring us everything would be alright. Judging by their terrified looks, they needed more assurance than us.

The doors were closed and we were left alone with one very angry Sorcerer.

He raised his hand and a flash of purple light burst from his fingers, and washed over the room, and then vanished.

"It's a spell to ensure we won't be overheard," he said, looking at our expressions. He didn't ask us to sit down so we didn't. We just stood there, our hands behind our backs, as he glared at us.

"You are a Sorceress," he said finally.

I nodded, not trusting myself to speak.

"Since when have you known?"

"Since I was ten," I stammered.

His eyes flashed angrily.

"Have the Hounds not been here?"

"They didn't find me."

"How is that possible?"

"I shielded her," Ann said. His eyes bore into Ann's and then he jerked back, surprise evident. He turned to me and frowned.

"Your mind is protected too," he said.

"Yes," I murmured.

He was frowning hard, his eyebrows scrunched together.

"What are you?" he asked Ann.

"I don't know, a Tongue I guess." She was lying, but why?

"Why did you not speak up?"

He looked so scary. I moved closer to Ann.

"We didn't want to die," she whispered.

"Everyone dies eventually," he said, his violet-grey eyes narrowed.

"We didn't want to die in the war," she amended.

"How do you know about her powers when no one else does?"

"I was there when they manifested."

He leaned back in his chair. "And you have only trusted each other?"

We nodded.

"Do you know what you have done?" he asked. "Do you know the magnitude of what you have done? Do you know how many people have died because of lack of magicians? Of a Sorcerer?"

I shrank beside Ann. I wanted to tell him the Spirits told us not to say anything, but Ann didn't seem to want to tell him, so I kept quiet.

"And your parents?"

"They didn't want their children to die," Ann said quietly.

"I just had this feeling that I shouldn't tell anyone because… of some danger," I blurted. It's wasn't a lie. It was true.

His eyes widened momentarily.

"Can you cast spells?"

"I can only summon and manipulate fire."

"That's not enough," he said. He looked angry, troubled and relieved as well. "It's not enough at all."

I glanced at Ann but she was staring resolutely at Ilatagite.

"There's something out there killing Sorcerers specifically. That's why you're the only one left," Ann said suddenly. I stared at her. "The only reason Fab is alive is because of the shield."

"And how do you know this?"

"Logic," she said weakly. "There are no other Sorcerers, known ones anyways. And Sorcerers are rare too, so obviously that means the ones who are alive are in danger from something. Because the others are dead, and not from natural causes, as Sorcerers live a longer life than other magicians do. So two died in the fire at the Academy, and one apprentice of yours died a year before the war. Suicide?"

"How do you know all this?" he asked sharply.

"Public records," she said. "I read about it."

"You're lying." The tone made me shiver. It was so powerful. Ann held her ground.

"You can check," she said shrugging. I knew this tone of hers. It was what she used when she told Trevor she knew something nasty about him. It was the tone she used when she was lying outright. How the hell did she know then?

"You're saying no one should know about your friend except for us?"

"Yes." Ann nodded.

He studied her before giving a slight nod, more to himself than us. "She shall be our secret weapon."

Weapon? I could taste the bile now. It took all my willpower not to hurl.

"Naturally, you will both come with me to Rivendell," he said, almost daring us to oppose him. Like we would! "I will tell your parents."

With a nod, he dismissed us. I don't know who looked worse, our parents or us. I was glad I wouldn't be in the same room when Ilatagite told my father that I too would be going to Rivendell.

"I will expect you both, with your belongings, near the town bell at six in the morning," Ilatagite said, as he left.

"Ann, come to the kitchen. Fabiana, go to your father."

I glanced at Ann who grimaced, and then went back into the hall.

My father looked ashen, like he had aged suddenly. He didn't say anything, he just opened his arms and I walked into them and he held me like he would never let me go.

I woke up at three to pack my belongings. I had hardly slept. I had dreamt and dreamt of battles and dead soldiers, Ann amongst them, with her eyes open and glassy, my father crying over her dead body as Ann became me.

I didn't know what to expect of our future. I didn't even want to imagine what lay ahead of us. From marriage to wars. What a turnaround.

I picked out my violet dress, my favourite one with its white sash and pulled it over my underdress. I laced my boots, braided my hair and then I surveyed my room.

My room was a small one, and lightly furnished. I never used it much, so it didn't even feel like my room. I was almost always in Ann's house. There was a bed, a desk, a drawer, a bookshelf and a bathroom. The light came from the lantern which my father must have lit earlier. I wondered where I would be sleeping tonight? The thought made me a bit uneasy.

After so many years, seven to be exact, someone besides Ann knew about my secret and a part of hers too. I wondered why she didn't tell the whole truth. Probably she didn't want to become a slave of the kingdom, but who would want that? But then again every single magician, regardless of how small or big their power was, would be dragged to the castle.

I, on the other hand, had less choice; I needed to learn more about my magic. I needed a teacher.

When he took me to the castle, to the king I would definitely be stuck there. But Ann may not have to be… because according to the information her parents and Ilatagite had, she could communicate with animals and had a certain degree of telepathic abilities. It wasn't nearly as helpful in a war, but then again, she would have to stay in the castle. However, I was the Sorceress. I would not be with her or the others. I would be with Ilatagite.

Sadness filled me when I thought that I may have to be in the castle alone. I remember the months before I met Ann, how lonely I had been. For the first three years of my life, my father had stayed home to look after me along with my nanny. When I was six, my nanny had died. And my father had been promoted to General. I used to stay a lot with Aunt Lina then. She was sweet and looked after me until she had to move away when I was thirteen. By then I had met Ann. I thought back to the day I met Ann, how odd and exciting she had seemed.

"But Papa said he would come!" a little girl was saying. "He said he would!"

"I know dear," said Lina, "but the king didn't approve his leave request. I'm sorry dear." She kissed the little girl on the head.

The little girl brushed away her tears and ran out of the house. She was staying with her cousins because her father was fighting in the war. She ran to her house, and sat on the doorstep crying.

Why did her papa have to fight in the war? Why couldn't he come home?

She saw a little boy walk past her, holding hands with his mother.

Why didn't she have a mother? She sobbed, why was she always alone?

It isn't fair! I want to see my papa. She sniffed, tears running down her face.

Why, why didn't the king allow him to come home?

She clenched her fists, angrily. Why didn't they want her papa to be home with her?

Anger welled up in her, and suddenly her hands were on fire! She screamed, waving her hands up and down. The fire burst into bigger flames and her house started to burn.

She ran out, shrieking.

Her hands were still on fire, she tried blowing on them and slapping them on the grass but it didn't work, though at least now the fire didn't burn. It was blue in colour.

She stopped, and looked at it in awe.

She was in the forest, no one was around. She looked at the fire, what was it? Why wasn't it burning her?

From nowhere a girl jumped down from the tree she was sitting under, a thin girl who looked about her age but towered over her. She was wearing a white frock which was now very dirty. Her hair was very dark but it was her eyes that caught her attention. She had green eyes, green like the forests. She looked like she had been crying, but she looked at the girl with blue fire curiously, and her face lit up. "Firai," she murmured, beaming at the other girl.

"You're a Sorcerer," said the tall girl. "You must be."

The little girl gasped. "No I'm not!"

"You are," said the girl, nodding her head. "That's why you have fire on your hands, blue. It looks nice."

"How do you know?" she asked, cocking her head.

"I just do, I'm Ann by the way," said the girl, then she frowned. "My broth—brother told me about Sorcerers. He's dead." Her face went wrong, as though she was trying not to cry.

"I'm sorry. My mother's dead too."

Ann's eyes widened. "That's sad."

The girl nodded. "She died when I was a baby."

"My brother died last week," Ann sighed.

The girls didn't talk for a while; they just stood staring at each other.

"I can talk to animals," said Ann suddenly. "When my brother died, something happened... and I could understand animals. I can read minds too..." she said, fidgeting with her dress and looking fearful.

"Can you read mine?" asked the girl.

She nodded. "You miss your papa, and you feel lonely." She smiled suddenly. "But don't worry. We can be friends if you want. Best friends," she said, nodding.

The girl cocked her head, and then smiled. She had never had a best friend, that too one who could climb trees. "Really? Best friends?"

"*Always,*" said little Ann with a serious face. "We'll be best friends for always."

My reverie was broken by clunking sounds. I frowned. Where was that coming from? I looked about. *Clunk.* I turned my head, looking everywhere for the sound, when I saw something hit my window: *clunk.* Someone was throwing pebbles! Ann?

I quickly went to the window and to my horror I saw Justin. My heart rammed against my ribs in panic. I gulped and opened the window.

"Mister Denner," I hissed, "what are you doing?"

"I've joined the army Miss Mecatrus," he said, not bothering to keep his voice down, "and I just heard you're going away too. To train as a magician. I always knew there was something magical about you."

"My father will hear you," I said, almost pleading.

He looked around and then back at me and grinned. "I shall come up then."

WHAT?

Darn the vine near my window! I watched in horror as Justin climbed the vine. I hoped no one would see him.

"Fabiana," he said, breathless, hanging on to my windowsill, one foot on the vine, the other on the ledge, "I wanted to say goodbye and good luck."

"So you climbed up my house?" I asked, horrified.

A vision of another man leaning through a window took hold of me. *I wanted to see you before I left, will you wait for me?* I blinked.

Justin smiled at me with adoration.

"I had to say goodbye." He looked hopeful and I think he expected... I'm not kissing you mister!

"You have to go!" I said, trying to separate the image of the man and Justin. The man looked so familiar.

His face fell, predictably. "I will wait for you, Fabiana."

I'll wait for you.

"Miss Mecatrus!" I chastised.

"Fabiana, such a beautiful name." He was almost singing it.

"Please go," I begged.

"Here, take this, as a token of my love and fidelity."

Fidelity? Spirits above! He was giving me a ring! A golden ring!

"I can't take that!"

"You have to," he said, and then with one hand he grabbed my hand and forced the ring on my finger before I could even blink.

"What have you done?" I asked, confounded, wrenching my hand away and yanking the ring off. "Take it back!"

"It is yours to keep, as is my heart." And then he beamed at me and climbed down my vine, blowing a kiss at me and vanishing.

Come back soon.

I dropped the ring into the flower vase, still shocked and flushed from the encounter. Stupid Justin, what was he thinking? He hardly even knew me, let alone love me! He didn't know anything about me and what he knew was superficial. But even then he was a sweet, innocent boy. I glanced guiltily at the flower vase. He'd given me a gold ring, how could I just throw it away? I should return it. But how? It wasn't like I could ring his doorbell and hand it to his mother. Guilt overwhelmed me and I fished the ring out of the vase. Arh! What do I do with this?

I'll be waiting.

6: Leaving the Known

Fabiana

I had a harried morning. Saying farewell was a huge task. My father and I had to visit the house of each of our acquaintances, as per the norm, and tell them of my terrible fate. I think I bore the looks of pity and sympathy quite well but my father was losing his calm by lunchtime.

During lunch he was filled with anxiety and would not stop advising me on how best to stay alive. From what he said I gathered Ilatagite hadn't told him what kind of magic I had and I guess he didn't want to know. I was a magician, I would have to fight, that was all he cared to know and it took such a toll on him. I was glad he didn't know I was a Sorceress; he might just die of a heart attack. I shuddered.

In the evening however, he had to go to supervise the enrolment of soldiers at the war office (a recent addition to our town). So I went over to Ann's.

Of all the times I have been to Ann's I had never got such a feeling of desolation ever. Everyone was quiet, even Arni. Ann and I exchanged looks but said nothing of the funeral-like silence in her house. I helped her pack, she was terrible at it.

I picked up a dress and stared. "You bought a dress?"

She yanked it from me, and scowled. "My mother bought some. I couldn't say no. You saw her."

I did indeed. Mrs Gamori floated around the house doing her duties with such a sombre expression I felt my heart ache for her. She was one of the sweetest people I knew, and the best cook ever, and I hated seeing her like this.

"Oh, that reminds me," Ann said, closing her rucksack, "Ma wanted to see us together. Come on."

I followed her out of our room.

"Are you worried?" I asked her, as we slid down the banister.

Don't worry; we'll get through this together. An echo of words said long back. I shook off the feeling. Ann turned her eyes on me; her eyes sort of slanted down, and her irises had rings. She really had wild eyes.

"Do you even have to ask?" she said.

"Me too," I sighed.

Ann's mother was busy preparing a goodbye feast. My father and I were having dinner here too because she'd insisted.

"Ma, she's here," Ann said jumping onto the counter and picking up a bun and biting into it.

"Ah, sweetie," she said dusting her hands, "I wanted to give you both something. Wait, I'll get it."

"What do you think it is?" I asked Ann.

"Search me," she shrugged.

"Ilatagite seemed surprised we could protect our minds."

"I think all magicians have some amount of telepathic ability," she said, finishing her bun and drinking some water. "You want a bun?"

I shook my head. "Isn't that... scary? They can read anyone's mind. You know that's forbidden? Well, not forbidden, but well... forbidden."

Ann wriggled.

"You can't help yours Ann. Well, sometimes you can."

"It's overwhelming," she said. "I can't do it when I'm angry and stuff."

"Ann!" her mother called. "Both of you come!"

I raised my brow at her and she shrugged.

Her mother was in her study. It looked a lot like my mother's. I was suddenly overcome by the image of my father kneeling on the floor, crying. I shook it away.

"Close the door, Fabiana," she told me.

Ann turned to look at me with this *what's going on* expression.

Her mother was leaning on the desk. She was a pretty lady with fair hair, full lower lip and a straight nose which Ann also had. She looked like she was carrying a huge burden. Her eyes were full of pain.

"Manzeria suggested we go to this sanctuary," she said.

"What sanctuary?" Ann asked.

"It's some fortress," I told her, "protected by magic."

"Just till the war ends," her mother murmured.

Like that'll ever happen.

"But that's great! You'll be safe!"

"The evacuation hasn't started. And even if it does, I don't think we should go."

"Why not?" Ann shouted.

"Because if we do, how will you contact us? How will we know anything about you? Once we go there we'll be cut off from here. What about you?"

"Ma, please, be reasonable—"

She interrupted Ann, "I've spoken to your father, Fab, and he agreed too. We thought it would be a good idea to give you both this."

"Ma... what—"

"Huh?"

She took a pouch from the table. "There's money in this. For both of you. We pooled some of our savings to give this to you."

Ann was taken aback, so was I. "What—?"

Ann's mother stopped her with a hand. She looked around the room fearfully, as though she was afraid someone would overhear her.

"If you get a chance," she said in little more than whisper, "run away from the Academy. Don't let them take you to the castle. You won't come back then. You'll have to fight till you die."

"Ma! What are you saying!"

"It's Ilatagite, Mrs Gamori."

She looked pained, her eyes filled up. "I know. We know. And we can't stop him from taking you. But the enemy... there are things you both don't know." Ann looked sceptical. "We may not win this war. At all. We're fighting on the losing side. Just escape and hide until..." Until what? But I don't think she knew either. "Until... things seem safer for all of us. And if... you get a chance to run away or if anything happens... we want you to have something." She held out the pouch to me. I glanced at Ann who shrugged and I took it. I pulled the strings loose and saw more than a dozen gold and silver coins.

"Mrs Gamori, we can't take this!" I cried staring with horror at the large amount of money she had handed us. "I mean... I can't..."

"It's your father's contribution too. And you're our own just as Arni and Ann are," she said.

I felt tears prick my eyes.

Ann took the pouch from me. "Ma! Are you crazy? Where did you even get all this money from?"

"We pooled—"

"You sold Grandma's necklace, didn't you?"

Her mother pressed her lips together stubbornly.

"This is too much! I don't believe you!" Ann cried. "You're all over-thinking it! You're making it sound..." she faltered.

"We're under-thinking it, if anything," I said softly to her.

"You will take it girls, and that is all," her mother said. "These too. It's only copper but I think it looks nice, doesn't it?"

She handed us two identical copper bands. There were swirly patterns on the band, making it look magical.

"I feel like I'm going to die now," Ann grumbled.

We are, whispered the wind.

"And Fab, make sure she doesn't get into more fights with boys. There are worse boys than Trevor," she said meaningfully. I nodded.

There was a silence as we waited for her next piece of advice. Instead she took our hands, my left and Ann's right. "Promise me you'll try to escape. Please."

"Ma..."

"Please, Annie, I can't lose one more child."

"We will," I assured her, though I knew it was a lie. How could we? Ilatagite was a royal Sorcerer! We were just youngsters.

"Take care of each other," she said hugging us. I could hear her heartbeat. She was holding us so close, I thought we'd suffocate. Ann and I were nose to nose.

Don't say anything, I told her with my eyes.

This is terrible, she said.

"We promise," we said together.

With all the farewells, grim atmosphere and everyone's behaviour, I honestly just wanted to get away. Ann only cried when she had to say goodbye to Arni. He was completely unaware of what was going on but even he seemed sad. It was too much.

Our fathers took us to the execution site, I mean, the town square where Ilatagite had asked us to come.

I don't know why but I just assumed that Ann and I were the only magicians in Gondon. I was proved wrong when we arrived at the appointed place.

Our town wasn't big and sprawling like the Capital, it was tiny with neat rows of houses and shops leading to the roundabout junction where the great town bell tower was. The sun wasn't even out, and the sky was cloudy. I liked the atmosphere. It soothed my trembling nerves.

My father held my rucksack in one hand, marching along to my right with an expression fit for a funeral.

As we reached the square, I saw more people and that's when it struck me, there were others! Ann and I weren't the only ones!

Of course you're not, I chided myself, what makes you think you two are so special?

Well.

"Fab!" Kal cried when she saw me, "I'm so glad to see you! I was afraid there'd be no one I know!"

"You have magic?" I asked dubiously. My heart lifted. Kal was coming along!

I give you my magic, for now and forever. Be brave.

She looked guilty. "I can heal, but only a little. My mother didn't let me tell anyone because…" I nodded understandingly. Because no one wants to die.

"Are those the Weber twins?" I asked looking at the two blonde-haired boys. They were handsome, shorter than me, and too young to be asked to fight or train, just thirteen or so.

"Yes," Kal nodded.

"Oh! Those poor boys," I said sadly. So young to be taken away from their family.

"And there's Vandra," Kal sighed.

"What? Vandra's a magician?"

Kal cocked her head, "She blossomed two months back, didn't you hear? She's got Heartsight."

"Is that a useful power?" I asked, sounding, I have to admit, slightly smug.

"Well, in war it must be. I mean if you know the weakness of your enemy… because it shows the loved ones as well as what touches you, I think, yes."

"She can see our weaknesses?" I asked, horrified.

"Supposedly," Kal said, lowering her voice. "I don't think she's that advanced, though."

I felt relieved. And then I felt like laughing. I'd almost forgotten that my mind was shielded! What a relief.

"Your parents seem really upset," I told her. Her mother and father were standing and talking to my father. They looked like they hadn't slept the whole night.

"Yours too," she said and I realised my father looked the same. I looked around and saw that the faces of all the parents looked alike, ashen and broken-hearted. The mother of the Weber twins was sobbing uncontrollably into her sister's shoulder. Her husband had died in the war; all she had left were her sons and they too were being taken away.

I felt a pang of sorrow for the parents; how thoroughly heart-wrenching it must be to lose your children to the war, in the name of saving your world. I blamed the Night Prowler, he was the one who started it all!

No, Fabiana, this started much before. It started with the exiling of dark magicians. It started even before that.

I clenched my fists. I'd told Ann about the voice I would hear in my head sometimes. And she'd said it must be the Spirits.

But I'd studied this and Spirits never contacted mortals. It was against the rules! But who else could it be? Which meant a Spirit was contacting us, Ann and me, I think the same Spirit, and if it was true, how was the Spirit doing it? And why?

"It's time." I looked at Ilatagite in his dark blue robes that clashed with his auburn hair. "Is everyone ready to leave?"

There were murmurs.

"Place your belongings here," he said. Once we all did, he waved his hand over the pile and lo! Everything vanished. Vandra didn't look too pleased.

One of Ann's cousins was coming along too. I saw her talk to his mother who was a sweet lady, better than Ann's Aunt Jenny.

And then Ilatagite addressed our parents. All he said was "Andoreya needs magicians. I will do my utmost to make sure they are up to the task."

I don't think it reassured any of them.

And then it was time. Ilatagite called us and made us form a circle. We held hands, like he told us to, and in front of our parents' eyes we vanished.

We moved slowly, like slugs, through a blur of colours. I felt nauseous, I didn't know what magic this was but it didn't feel good. It also made me uneasy because I knew I couldn't do magic like this.

As our feet touched the ground, a bell tolled ominously somewhere. It was eleven in the night. We were in Rivendell. I couldn't make out much about the place, because the lanterns cast a dim light.

Someone gasped and I looked up to see the building. It was like a mansion, where ghosts lived.

The tall, iron gate was locked.

I was standing next to Ilatagite so I heard what he said, *"Eiyshe torqe."*

What language was that?

The gates creaked open. We all entered the grounds with trepidation. Ann was beside me.

"Creepy?" she asked me.

"Very," was my reply.

"Oh look! Dogs," she said, and scrunched her nose. The black dogs were huge, and resembled horses more than dogs. "Maybe I'll befriend them later, they can eat anyone who annoys me."

"Do they eat people?" I asked fearfully.

"No, but they could. Don't you think?"

"I don't like them."

"Fifi and Fergus," she said chuckling dryly, "their names."

"They look nothing like a Fifi or a Fergus should."

"Agreed."

As we entered the mansion there was a collective gasp. It was a grand room with a huge chandelier hanging from the ceiling. There was a huge flight of stairs that separated left and right. I looked up and saw numerous doors on both sides, and a tapering ceiling from which the chandelier hung.

Even the Mayor's house isn't so grand and that's where we had our ball last year.

On the ground floor too, where we stood, there were many doors. This place was full of doors! And from one of these rooms a lady appeared, and hurried towards us. She was wearing a grey dress and her hair was tied back in a bun and covered by a cloth piece like those worn by the peasants who worked on the fields. She was also wearing a brown apron. Her eyes were a dull brown colour, but they seemed kind.

"This is Larissa," said Ilatagite, "the housekeeper." House? My house was half of this! But I knew it was nothing compared to the original Academy, the one that caught fire killing seventy-five magicians, years ago. It would have been wonderful to have studied there in the time before the war. "You are now part of this household and therefore I expect you to treat it as your own and not destroy it. The rules that applied at your old home will apply here too. I do not want anyone sneaking into the wrong side or doing anything that they should not be doing. You will be here for the next six months. In the past, the training period was longer but due to our current situation we have had to change that. I expect you all to work hard and wield your magic with ease but presence of mind. You will meet the rest of the magicians tomorrow."

He continued, "Larissa will show you to your rooms, and tomorrow I will see you all at seven o' clock sharp for breakfast, then we shall see. You must all be there on time." He glanced at Ann and then me, "Goodnight," he said, and turned his back on us and left.

The lady looked at each of us. "Well, come along then. I bet you are all tired. I have your beds ready. Come on," she said, gesturing at us as she climbed the stairs.

We all exchanged looks before following her up.

"Boys to the left. Your doors will have your names on them; your luggage is already in your rooms and everything that you'll need."

She looked at us as the boys trooped up their side of stairs. "Well, girls to the right. Come on then."

We followed her up the right side of the staircase.

There were a number of doors. Why so many? There were only four of us right? However I was wrong, the first door had a name on it. 'Irena' was carved on the door in calligraphy.

"The professor," said the lady, "changes the names every year according to the students. We respect your space and your room is truly your own. Every morning I will clean it, and I should warn you that thieving is not tolerated here." Then she smiled. The second door had a name too, 'Kristine.' So did the third and fourth, 'Josephine' and 'Lyra.'

"These are the other girls who will be studying with you; they're eager to meet you," she said.

"I doubt it," Ann muttered darkly.

The fifth door had one of our names on it. 'Kalindra' it said.

Larissa the *palace-keeper* unlocked Kal's door and showed Kal her room, while we got a sneak peek. It was a lighter shade of beige. Larissa smiled and said "I suggest you keep your window slightly open, there's a good breeze outside."

Kal hesitated before entering her room and vanishing behind the door.

Ilatagite's spells baffled me. I hadn't known we could do all this!

"Fabiana?"

I raised my hand. "Yes, that's me."

She unlocked the door and handed me the key. I opened it.

I entered my room. There was a rosy glow from a lantern which hung by my bed. There was also a writing desk, a drawer and a door which I supposed led to the bathroom. My trunk was next to the drawer. There was a framed picture of mountains with snow-capped peaks and a sun shining softly. It looked real, too real.

Ann whistled.

"We'll leave you to it," she said. Ann winked at me and left, closing the door behind her.

I removed my boots and sank onto the bed, *my* bed. This is where I would be living for the next six months. Then I would go to the castle and then…

I was just dozing off when someone knocked. I groaned and got up, expecting Ann and instead finding Larissa.

"Um," I looked at her quizzically.

"The Sorcerer wants to see you," she said quietly.

Now?

"Okay." I closed the door behind me and followed her out barefoot.

She took me down the stairs and to one of the doors on the right, just below Kal's room I think, and knocked.

"Come in," I heard him say. Larissa gestured at me to go in. Alone? I blanched.

Larissa pushed me and I took a deep breath, before turning the knob and entering. His study was bigger than our rooms, furniture was sparse but I felt like I was in a king's room. There was a desk, and a chair in front of it, a grandfather clock, and a shelf. The carpet was red.

"Ah, Fabiana," he said. He looked up from something he was writing, and, joining his hands together as though in prayer, pressed them to his lips. "I realise it is late."

I didn't say anything. I wasn't sure what to say.

"But we don't have much time. A Sorcerer's training lasts seven to eight years but we have just six months which is not enough. That is why we cannot lose a moment. Tell me, how much magic can you do? Truthfully."

"I was being honest the last time as well. I can summon and manipulate fire."

"Is that all?"

"Um yeah, that's all."

His eyes widened and I shrank into myself. He looked at me over his fingertips, still horrified. "There is a lot for you to learn then."

"My training started when I was eleven," he said, "but I have a feeling that... we may not have so much time. Well, we'll just have to manage," he said with a sigh. "The only Sorcerer that had full power was the very first one. No one else has had so much power after him, but well, he is no longer alive."

"What powers did he have?" I asked curiously.

Ilatagite frowned. "He could control all the four elements." My jaw dropped. "Yes, all four. Amazing isn't it?"

All I could do was nod.

"And he could cast the most powerful spells."

Spells. I couldn't cast even one.

"The first step to understanding your full potential, is knowing what you can and what you can't do," he said. "Sorcery is different from other magic. It is more powerful, without a doubt. After the first Sorcerer, Lucifer, no one has had the ability to control all four elements. My master, may he rest in peace, could control three." He paused. "But the ability to control three elements was already in him, he just had to unlock it. Now, not all Sorcerers can do that. Every Sorcerer has had the affinity for one element at least. You are young. Have you Blossomed yet?"

I shook my head.

"It is impossible to tell if you can control the other elements or not. But you can try. Not now though. Now we shall concentrate on spells and since we don't have sufficient time to train, we will begin training now."

"Now?" I asked, surprised.

"Yes, now," he said standing up, and with a sweep of his hands, the furniture shifted to one corner of the room. I stood up, feeling both excited and nervous and tired as hell. Wasn't this too sudden? What if I couldn't do it?

"The first thing about casting spells is concentration," he said. "If you don't concentrate, it can go disastrously wrong."

"Right..." I said slowly.

"So from today onwards, every night you will clear your mind and meditate."

I nodded, solemnly.

"Second, there is a secret to casting spells." He paused. "If you don't have confidence in yourself, it will never happen."

Ah. I licked my lips. Confidence? I had confidence... right?

You must believe child.

"I want you to summon fire for me, now."

That's easy. I lifted my right arm, and whispered and cupped a small bonfire in the palm of my hand.

He cocked his head, "You say something when you bring fire?"

"Yes," I murmured. I didn't need to, but it was easier to focus when I had a word.

"What do you say?"

"*Firai*," I whispered, and the flame in my hand roared.

His eyes widened again. "*Firai?* Where did you hear that word?"

I hesitated "Um... Ann. That's what she said when she first saw me produce fire."

"Andalucia, said the word *firai* to you?" he asked.

I nodded again. "But... when I asked her, she told me that she had said fire."

He frowned. "How... and does she use other words like this?"

When I didn't say anything, he pressed, "It might be important, Fabiana."

"Well... sometimes in her sleep... she says weird words," then I added quickly, "but it's just gibberish I think, I mean she's sleep talking."

"Probably..." he deliberated.

"Now, spells..." he said, but I had a feeling that his mind was still elsewhere. "There are certain movements you have to learn, it's only so as to get the channelling of magic right."

"How does moving our body help?" I asked.

"At the first stage it does," he said. "For instance," he waved his hand and let the furniture return to its original position, "if I tried that when I first started training I wouldn't have been able to do it. Now I want you to try and put it against the wall."

"Me?" I said, shocked. "Like, right now?"

"*Like*, yes."

I blushed. "I don't think… I mean I think…"

"See, there itself you've stopped the possibility. Confidence. Otherwise it won't happen."

"But…" I stopped, seeing his expression. "Okay… um… I'll try."

"Try putting your hands in front of you, imagine actually lifting them, and assume that position."

I put my hands in front of me, and stood in a stance as though I was about to run, a half-crouch. I felt stupid. But Ilatagite nodded encouragingly.

"Now concentrate on a word like shift, and imagine with conviction the furniture moving."

I nodded. Taking a deep breath I concentrated on imagining the furniture moving, as I said, "Move."

Nothing happened.

"Again," said Ilatagite. "This time with more confidence."

I tried around ten times before I actually managed to move something. And it was only the chair that moved, but I felt exhilaration flood me even though I felt completely, utterly, exhausted. I had managed to do it! Well, a part of it! At least I had done something.

But Ilatagite wasn't happy.

"This is a very small thing, Fabiana. There are much bigger and more demanding spells that you will most certainly have to do in the future."

That took away the satisfied feeling I had had.

"You can go now," he said. "Tomorrow, same time, same place. Make sure no one sees you."

I nodded, leaving.

I felt stupid, what if I couldn't do it? I mean I couldn't even move a few pieces of wood around, how could I do much more demanding spells? And by the last thing he had said, about the fact I would have to cast spells of power in the future, I knew I was fated to become a magician of the kingdom.

7: In the Shadows, Evil Lurks

He watched from the shadows as she vanished into thin air. Was she the one? Could she be? He groaned; things were getting too complicated. If she was the one, how would he kill her?

It would be easy for Him to do it, but could *he*?

He would have to tell Him... of course.

He let his eyes sweep over the town he had been accustomed to sneaking around to spy on her, before he vanished, leaving a raven's feather behind him.

"Is it her?" He asked. In the dim light, he couldn't see Him properly, but it didn't matter, he didn't want to either.

"I cannot be sure," he said. "There are no evident signs."

"But the other one?"

"Yes, she is the one you are looking for," he said.

"We need her."

"I can bring her to you now."

"The one you don't want to kill will follow."

That was true. And he didn't want that.

"I will kill whoever has to be killed, Master," he said defiantly.

"Will you?"

"Without hesitation."

His master leaned forward and the dim light revealed a wrinkled face with deep furrows, yellowing eyeballs with eyes the colour of coal, thick veins jutting out and scraggly stubble. His teeth were like yellowing bricks, and saliva coated his lips; whenever he spoke he would send spittle flying.

"One wrong move and I will take the life I gave you," his master said. It didn't matter that the man looked weak and ugly, something that should be dead. He couldn't be underestimated, *shouldn't* be. "One wrong move and I will kill her."

"You can kill her anyway," he said coolly. "My ties are broken. I only went there to keep an eye out for you. I have done everything you asked. And yet you don't tell me what their role is in your plan."

"I need them as I need your body," He said, "and when the time comes, you will give it to me willingly!"

"Yes Master," he said, and on dismissal, left.

The old man leaned back in the chair, disgusted with His weak mortal body. He twisted the ring on His hand; the power from the souls entered His body and made Him stronger as they made Him weaker. He could not enter Andoreya without severe repercussions to Himself even if He possessed the boy. Soon, He told himself, soon you will be free. All good things come to those who wait. He smiled.

Once He won this war, He would have the upper hand.

8: Cats are Crazy, People Crazier

Andalucia

I thrashed around for a good few minutes until I finally opened my eyes and found myself in a strange room. I swivelled my head, trying to understand. Where was I? What was going on?

Someone had just tried to break through my barriers! When I was asleep! By Thor, what the hell was going on?

I scrambled off my bed, turning around, trying to understand.

You're in the Academy, yes, you came here yesterday Ann.

Yes, I did.

This is your room here.

I looked around the little room bathed in the dim light of the sun. Yes, it is.

Someone tried to break into your mind. Someone you don't know, that's for sure. But who? And why?

I stared blankly at the clock in my room, one hand on my hip, trying to figure it out, before it hit me that I was late.

Crap! I had to bathe! I threw open my rucksack and fished out my toiletries. I think I had the fastest bath ever. Feeling proud, I quickly dressed.

Someone knocked on my door and I opened it. Fab stood there, accompanied by a girl with curly red hair who looked like an elf.

"Ann, this is um, Lyra," Fab told me, shrugging. "Lyra, this is Ann."

Why have you brought her here?

She caught me. And stop barging into my head.

But I love your head! It's so mercifully empty.

She rolled her eyes.

"Hello. I'm sorry you must be feeling awkward..." You have no idea! "But I saw Fabiana leave her room and I just had to say hello! And since she was coming along..."

Right then we were interrupted.

I fell back onto the floor with an "oof" as Keira tackled me. I didn't even know where she came from!

By Thor, Keira! Stop it!

But she continued to scratch my face and neck and whatever else she could.

Keira! Get a hold of yourself!

You left! You left! she meowed loudly.

What on...

I searched and searched!

Keira...

"What is that?"

"It's her cat, don't worry. Ann, you want help?"

Keira hissed, *how dare you leave me behind!*

What is wrong with you? You come and go as you like...

Do you know what could've happened to me?

Good heavens! I'm sorry...

You don't get it, you mortals.

What are you going on about?

"Ann?"

Get off! Fab mercifully picked her off me and I blinked blood out of my eyes. She was still waving her claws at me and struggling against Fab. *Keira enough! You don't stick around long enough! It's your fault!*

My fault? My fault? You have no idea, you have...

And then she scratched Fab who she normally likes much more than me. Fab dropped her with a gasp. She jumped out the window and vanished.

"What was that crazy cat doing?" Lyra cried looking at us. "Do you want me to call Larissa? Or..."

"No, no," Fab said, "it's okay. Keira was just in a bad mood."

Bad mood? She was hellish!

"What the hell is the matter with her?" I demanded. "Oh Fab, are you okay?"

"Just a scratch." she said, wrapping her fingers around her bleeding arm. "You look like you fell into a thorn bush."

"Perfect, just perfect," I groaned, touching my face gingerly. I hissed. It hurt so much.

"I can ask Larissa..."

"No," both Fab and I said together.

"We don't want her to know about Keira," Fab said.

"We'd get into trouble."

"Are you two sisters?" Lyra asked.

We stared at her dubiously before we broke into laughter.

"Come on," Fab said giving me a hand, "we'll wash this, we're already late. Do you want to carry on, Lyra?"

"Um yeah," she said and I got that she was feeling unwanted so I smiled at her. "Gosh, Lyra, I'm terribly sorry. My cat's just crazy. And in case you're wondering, I'm not crazy. I'm a Tongue."

Lyra looked surprised. "It's okay. A Tongue? That's nice." She smiled a little. "Um, if you don't mind me asking, why are you dressed like that?"

I looked down at myself and sighed. I did mind but I couldn't tell her that. "That's just the way I dress."

She didn't say anything more. "I guess I'll see you two downstairs."

We both nodded.

I quickly washed my face, moaning when I saw my reflection in the mirror. Oh Thor, I look demented! What is wrong with that cat?

"Why did she do that?" Fab asked, as she dribbled water on her hand.

"Something about leaving her behind," I muttered. "She comes and goes as she likes and she has the nerve to say I abandoned her!"

"Poor thing," Fab said softly, "to be abandoned."

"I didn't abandon her!"

Fab grinned. "I know. By the way, I've started casting spells. Well kind of."

"What?" I shouted.

She laughed. "Yeah, Ilatagite summoned me to his study yesterday and we've started training."

"Already?" I asked, shocked.

"Yeah, and Ann, it's really hard."

Now it was my turn to laugh. "Please Fab, I know you. You think you can't do it, no wonder it's hard."

She scowled at me. "We're late, let's just go."

We were so late that we had to skip our breakfast which was really bad, because I was starving. When we entered the dining hall everyone was already done and Larissa was clearing up. Timing sure was important here. Everyone was standing in a line facing a wall. What? "What's going on?" I asked one of the Weber twins, Cassius I think.

He shrugged. "No idea."

Marcus, the other twin, looked at us and smiled shyly. "Did you hear about the small victory we had?"

We both shook our heads. "I believe your father won it, Miss Mecatrus," he said as Fab blushed with pride, "at Werrintop."

"That's good news," Fab said, nodding.

They looked so young, too young to be here. It just seemed wrong.

Can the dead walk?

Ilatagite entered, in dark red robes. He didn't even look at us, just walked straight through the wall.

"Are we supposed to just walk through it?"

"How does that work?"

"What kind of magic is it?"

"Wow, Sorcerers must have an easy life."

One by one, hesitatingly, we walked through the wall. It was like the wall didn't really exist, like an illusion of a wall. Wow, Fab can do this! She just needs a little faith in herself. I looked at her and she looked uneasy. I waggled my eyebrows at her and she narrowed her eyes.

"Form a circle," Ilatagite said. He was standing at the end of the room; it was a long, bare room with a glass roof. Nothing was in it except for the carpet. There were no doors or windows but the glass room was good enough.

There were fifteen of us; of those I knew, only six. Only fifteen people were there in the whole of Andoreya who had some form of magic. That was really few. Two decades ago there used to be a hundred every year. They used to roam free and wield their magic according to their will. There used to be a school in the Wild West that taught Magicians how to harness their powers. Everyone used to go there before the place was burnt down. Ilatagite had started his own school for Magicians later; it was really small compared to the Academy. I had read about the Academy. It sounded amazing. I wished it was still there, I wished that I was born decades ago when there was no war and Magicians didn't have to be worried about hiding their powers or anything.

But wishing wouldn't get us anything, however much we wanted it to be true.

"This is where we will practise all your different magic. I will teach you where your power comes from, how to control it, how to make it do things you never dreamed of," he said, moving slowly across the bare room. "I want each of you to introduce yourself, first name only. I want you to be on a first name basis. Also state your power. You will respect each other's power and space. I will not tolerate any indecent behaviour."

Ilatagite passed us and I caught him whisper something to Fab who immediately turned pale.

What? What happened?

Ann! You're in my head again.

I picked up bits of her thought, *So what are you going to tell them? You have to lie about your magic right?*

Yeah. I don't know what I'll say.

"Why don't you start?" he asked pointing at a short, thin boy with gold rimmed spectacles. The boy reminded me of a canary bird with his blonde hair and demure looks.

"I'm Elvin, and I'm a healer." Kal looked excited; apparently she was a healer too.

"I'm Marcus Webber and I'm an Animai." There was a collective look of amazement on everyone's face. Animai could change their form into an animal.

I wondered what he could change into, as the next boy, Dawn Ava introduced himself. He had Yore-sight. He could see into people's pasts. I frowned, I didn't really want anyone seeing my past… but my mind was shielded so I guess he couldn't read mine.

Aero said he was a Leaper. Then Cassius said he was also an Animai. And then there was a handsome but rather arrogant boy, James, who said he was a telepath. Two thoughts entered my mind then – Oh wow, a telepath and Oh no, a telepath – along with suspicion. Someone I didn't know had tried to break into my mind, could it be…? No that made no sense!

"I'm Quinn Woolfe." I looked at the dark boy who had a coffee complexion, with his wild black hair and weird, deep accent. He hesitated before saying softly "I'm a Lycan."

"A Lycan!"

"What is he doing here?"

"Is he even allowed?"

"Aren't Lycans… exiled?"

Most people moved away from Quinn like he carried a transmittable disease or something. I was fascinated, to be honest. A Lycan amongst us!

One of the exiles! The exiles lived on the wastelands where, frankly, I had no idea how they managed. Whatever I have heard of the wastelands wasn't good, it's like a drought land where nothing ever blooms. Looking at him, I knew immediately he had lived a hard life. I didn't need to even lower my barriers to know. He was quiet because he expected this reaction; he was used to it.

"Enough," Ilatagite said and we shut up to look at him instead. "Quinn is here under my jurisdiction. He is half a Lycan and is a student like any of you. No one shall say a word against him." He didn't even need to say 'Or...'

"But professor..." a girl with straight red hair muttered. I looked at her, she looked like a Spirit with her creamy complexion, high forehead, prominent cheekbones and full red lips that matched her hair. She looked willowy, like an elf.

He was only half a Lycan, that was alright then, wasn't it?

"He will be treated just as you all will. That is all. Continue introducing yourselves."

I couldn't help but feel how much like a tyrannical dictator he was.

"I'm Irena Wilde," the redhead muttered smugly. "I have the power of telekinesis."

I don't like you, telikinet yourself away from me.

"I'm Lyra Wilde," the girl who had come with Fab said. Oh! Sisters! I didn't think Lyra was too happy about it. I looked at the two of them. Apart from their red hair and similar complexion they looked miles apart. "I'm a seer," she completed.

I don't know which was worse, the reaction to Quinn or to Lyra.

The buzz didn't last long though, Ilatagite made sure of it. By Thor, he's scary!

"Kalindra, I'm a healer."

"Hi, I'm Josephine," said the petite girl with brown ringlets of hair and wide blue eyes. "I'm an Empath but I'm still dormant."

Wow, an Empath. I had powers of an Empath too, I guess. Some of the magic would lie dormant in us till the age of seventeen.

"Vandra Rose," Vandra said almost as smugly as Irena. "I have Heartsight, or so I'm told." She looked grudgingly at Ilatagite.

I barely stifled my snort. Heartsight. What use was that?

Someone elbowed me and I realised it was my turn.

"I'm Ann, and er, I'm a Tongue."

A Tongue is someone who can talk to animals. I decided it was the safest of my powers that I could reveal.

"Kristin," said the golden head, who was taller than me, dang. "I'm a Scribe."

Scribes have a mental ability which had more to do with pens than swords, but hey a pen is mightier than a sword, right?

And it was finally Fab's turn. She looked uneasy and pale. She was even sweating.

Ann, what do I do?

I guess she felt me in her head *this* time.

Um, I frowned, *you have to tell them something.*

But what? I can't very well tell them I'm a Sorceress.

"Fabiana?" Ilatagite prodded.

"I'm Fabiana Mecatrus...." I felt her panic which made me panic and without knowing what I was doing I did it. I didn't mean to but I just did. It just happened.

I'm sorry, I whispered as Fab fell back into unconsciousness and Kristin and Elvin caught her.

9: Being a Bad Friend

Andalucia

I am a very bad friend, I thought, as Elvin and Kristen knelt down, holding Fab, and made her lie on the floor. I had used my calming abilities to, well, calm her a bit too much, to the extent that it made her fall asleep.

I had just sent my best friend into a coma.

Yeah, I was a really bad friend.

Oh my God Thor! What have I done? What have I done? What is *wrong* with *me*?

"What happened to her?" I heard Lyra ask.

I hurried over to them, guilt wracking me. Fab was lying on Kristen's lap.

I knelt down and looked at her and relaxed when I saw her chest rising up and down. She wasn't dead! I hadn't killed her. I gulped. Could I have?

Oh my God Thor.

This was the first time I had done something like this, and I wasn't exactly sure what would happen.

"Why did she faint?" asked one of the boys.

"Exhaustion?" I suggested weakly.

"She seemed fine before," Lyra said.

Ilatagite came and sat down next to her, his brows furrowed. He took her hand; it seemed he was checking her pulse. I hoped I hadn't done her any harm. I was pretty sure that I hadn't, I had just... made her unconscious. I groaned. Ilatagite glanced at me, one brow raised in question. I arranged my face to look innocent.

He turned to the boy with the glasses. "Elvin, you're a healer. What do you think it is?" Ilatagite got up. "Healers, take this as an opportunity to observe and learn something."

I was taken aback and unable to keep quiet. I said "But... I don't think that's such a good idea."

Ilatagite looked at me, his violet eyes flashing dangerously and I gulped. By Thor, he's so intimidating, like a megalomaniac.

99

He turned back to Fab but I had a feeling he wasn't done with me.

I heard Elvin say: "I can't figure out why she fainted."

The other healer, Josephine was a fragile looking girl with blonde hair. She too was sitting by Fab, holding one of her hands in her palm and frowning.

The werewolf was keeping his distance; he stood a bit away from everyone else.

"Is she going to be okay?" I asked. Shandre made way for me and I went through.

"I can't say," said Josephine. "I don't know why... so..."

I cautiously prodded Fab's consciousness. It was like she was sleeping.

Fab, sweetie, time to wake up, I muttered, panicking.

"I think she's getting up!" Josephine cried excitedly as Fab's eyelids fluttered open. She looked about in confusion with her baby blues and then her eyes found mine and they went wide in shock.

I am so going to hell, Thor.

"Are you okay?" Kristin asked her.

"Yeah," she said, very slowly. "I'm okay."

"What happened?" Ilatagite asked.

Fab shrugged. "I think I was just really tired professor, from the travelling and all. I didn't get much sleep last night either."

"You can go to your room and rest," he said. "I will tell Larissa to send your lunch there."

"Oh no," she protested sitting up. She looked woozy. "I'm fine."

"I don't think you are," he said firmly. "Andalucia, why don't you take her to her room?" His tone suggested that he was onto me and I should be worried.

I helped Fab up and she swayed uneasily. Had I done this to her? What was wrong with me!

She put an arm around me and I took her through the magic wall.

Fab waited until we were near the staircase until she exploded. "What were you thinking Ann?"

"I..."

"And I know it was you, so don't deny it!"

"Shush," I said, "the stupid telepath might hear us."

Her scowl was still intact, and directed very pointedly at me.

"I'm sorry," I said, "but I didn't know what else to do. And I had this weird feeling that you shouldn't, well, announce what you are."

She stopped midway and looked at me. "Couldn't you have told me? I wasn't planning on telling them I was a Sorceress!"

"But did you know what lie you would tell?"

"Okay," she admitted, "I was in a fix. But did you really have to... what did you even do?"

"I... knocked you out," I murmured, "I think."

She blanched. "You're impossible," she huffed.

"Well you've got to admit I keep your life interesting," I said half-jokingly. "So you just fainted?"

She glared at me, so I immediately looked sober. "In green. I fainted into some green light." My eyes widened and she narrowed hers. "You're evil. Now get me to my room, will you?"

"With pleasure," I said, trying not to smile.

Once Fab was back in her room, I slid down the banister and ran quickly to the magic wall-room, I had started to think of it that way.

I went through the wall, and then my heart stopped. A leopard stood in the centre of the room. I almost screamed, almost. My fists balled, I watched as the leopard changed back into Marcus. Then Cassius changed into an eagle and flew about the room before landing in front of me and transforming into himself. He grinned at me, as my eyes widened.

"Crazy, huh?" he said. He looked so young and excited. I nodded smiling.

"Andalucia, we're testing everyone's limits," Ilatagite said. "Join the group."

There were a few desks and chairs on which some of them were sitting.

Ilatagite was walking about, stopping in front of each desk and talking with them, asking them questions, testing their abilities.

He was with Irena now, who was moving her hand through a solid desk. Whoa. Creepy.

Aero was... well... leaping from one corner of the room to the other. He was standing on the right side of the room, then in the blink of the eye, he would disappear and reappear on the other side.

Wicked.

I went over to Kal who was reading a book. I saw diagrams of plants and flowers.

"Some of these can kill you! Look!"

Beresda, commonly mistaken for blueberry, can cripple anyone who
consumes it. It is widely used in making ammunition. An arrow
tipped with Beresda juice can cripple the body part where it strikes.
If the mixture is diluted it can cause paralysis for a few hours.

"Wow. Lethal," I muttered.

"Andalucia," Ilatagite called me. He was standing by one of the empty desks.

I grimaced at Kal and made my way to him.

"You're an animal Tongue," he stated.

I nodded.

"But you can shield your mind as well as others'?"

"Yes."

"I will try to break into your mind now," he said and then without giving me a minute to prepare, he attacked. I gasped, trying to maintain my barriers. It was much worse than the previous night's attack, I think the person who was trying had been at a distance; distance matters.

"Fight me," he said coolly.

My barriers were strong, but that was only because not many people knew how to break into another's mind, only magicians, besides which no one would try to break into mine. But Ilatagite was a Sorcerer with much more experience than me. He broke through and I fought back, panicking that he would see things I didn't want him to see. Flashes took hold of me, things I didn't want others to see.

He withdrew, but before he did he said *I want to see you in my study today.*

He strode away from me and I collapsed onto a chair. He had broken into my mind! So easily! I felt frustrated and I was sweating. How had he done that? How could I have let him! By Thor! What had he seen?

I was so caught up in trying to recover my breath, I hadn't noticed him come up to me.

"Andalucia, isn't it?" the Telepath said. I looked at his arrogant face with beady eyes, and scowled "What do you want?"

I know it looks like I'm hostile, but I'm not usually so hostile. Something about him irked me. Something glinted and I saw something shiny peeking through his tunic.

"Like the view?" he asked, smugly. I flushed.

He laughed. "You look frustrated. Perhaps I can help you. I am a Telepath after all."

I gave him an evil look before getting up and walking past him. I could almost feel Irena trying to burn me with her jealous looks. You can have him, I don't want the creep.

That evening Ilatagite let everyone go to the village. I didn't go. Fab begged me to but I was adamant. It took a bit of convincing Kal and Fab to make them leave me behind and go. Kal felt that I wasn't going because I was still upset about the Telepath. Fab felt that I wasn't going because I wanted to sit and mope around.

"Mope about what?" I had asked her. She just shrugged.

Now that they had left, I made my way to Ilatagite's office. I hoped I wasn't late. It had taken time to convince the girls that I was fine.

I stood at the bottom stair and frowned. I had no idea where Ilatagite's office was. There were numerous doors on either side of the staircase. I made my way towards the right side. There was a storage cupboard under the stairs, a big one.

There was firelight filtering from under one door, and I decided that this could be his room. I knocked.

I was right. Ilatagite opened the door.

"Good evening Sir," I said.

"Come in," he said, opening the door wider.

For some reason I felt like I had come into his room already. Wasn't this table towards the window? Ann, stop it! You've never been in here. Are you sure? I feel like...

I moved towards the bookshelf, looking at all the books. I was an avid reader but these titles were all strange to me. They were all about magic and history.

"How strong is Fabiana's magic?" It was an abrupt question.

I frowned. I felt wary.

"I don't really know," I said truthfully. "We've never been able to explore her magic in depth because well, she didn't have an instructor and we were worried it'd get out of hand. She can't do spells, Sir. We've tried once before but it didn't go too well."

"What did you try?" he asked, sitting on his plush chair.

"To turn our hair red," I murmured with embarrassment.

He didn't seem amused. "And the result?"

"She turned the leaves of the forest red."

"The whole forest?" he asked skeptically.

I nodded. "She can't direct her magic properly, but she has the ability."

"I know she does," he said and I felt chastised.

"Why don't you ask her directly?" the question was out before I could stop myself. He seemed taken aback by my question, but I was curious.

"I didn't think she'd do justice to the truth."

I had to agree with that. Fab could be infuriatingly modest about her abilities.

"Do you know the exact scenario in our land now, Andalucia?" I shook my head. "We lost eleven hundred men in the last two days." I felt dizzy. "We had a small victory. But that is nothing. Nothing at all compared to our losses." I stared.

"We aren't a very big population. Just about seventy thousand."

And that's not a lot? "No, it isn't." he answered. I hadn't realised I had spoken aloud.

"And now that we are losing so many... it seems a very insignificant number." Suddenly Ilatagite had me pinned with his eyes. "It was very wrong of you both to not step up before. Fabiana could be a full-fledged Sorceress by now, if it hadn't been for your misguided thinking."

My face felt hot, and I couldn't meet his gaze. It wasn't misguided! The Spirit told us not to! I think. It seemed so hazy now.

"But I shall not waste time and energy chastising you and your friend," he said. "That would be pointless. What we need to look at is the present and the future."

"I... er... I don't quite understand."

"You see, the situation is very delicate right now. One cannot say what will happen in the next minute. I hope I get enough time to train Fabiana."

"What?" I interrupted. "I don't understand..."

"There will come a time when I may not be able to oversee Fabiana's... purpose."

"What purpose?" I faltered. "Sorry."

He looked grim. "There will come a time when I may not be able to guide her. If such a time is to come, can I trust you to be with her at all times and make sure she fulfills her destiny?"

I could have argued that I didn't know what he was talking about, he hadn't explained anything to me, I knew nothing. What destiny? But I nodded, as always, like an idiot. Besides which, I had been with her before him. I was the one who was there for her always, yeesh, he didn't know us at all.

There was a silence and I wondered if I could leave.

"Tell me Andalucia, did you live in the Capital?"

I froze. Why was he asking me this?

He looked expectant. "When I was little," I whispered.

"And are you the only child?"

"No, I have a younger brother."

"Just one brother?" he asked, frowning.

"I had an elder brother," I said trembling inside, "but he's dead."

"How did he die?"

"I – I don't remember," I stammered. "He – was killed."

"Killed?" Ilatagite's brows shot up.

"He had an affair with the minister's daughter. Her brothers... they beat him up..."

"Was that how he died?" Ilatagite pressed. Was it? I was too nauseated to speak.

"You look dizzy, sit down." I did, gratefully.

"You saw his murder didn't you?" he asked, his eyes wide in recognition. "Don't you remember me?"

"Huh?" I felt so dizzy, and my head was aching like it would burst any moment.

"What are your powers, Andalucia?"

For the love of Thor, stop it! I feel sick. Stop talking!

"What happened the day your brother died? Think Andalucia, think."

I tried, I really did. But my head pulsed with pain. I saw red lights everywhere.

"Andalucia?"

There was a knock on the door and someone entered. My vision was blurred. I couldn't see who it was. What was happening?

"Oh, you've come early." Ilatagite said to the person.

"Can I go?" I asked in a daze.

"You look terrible," Ilatagite observed. "Wait, I'll get Larissa –"

"No, I'm fine," I managed to say.

"If you're sure –"

I nodded and stood up. I felt so woozy. My vision was blurring like I had tears in my eyes, did I? I swayed and a hand caught my elbow and steadied me. I couldn't see the person, just an outline of a giant-like being. I muttered thanks and left. I slipped out the main door. The others weren't back yet. Being in the open air made me feel better. I inhaled noisily. What had just happened? What was happening to me?

I sighed, taking deep breaths.

Keira?

No response. Maybe she was out chasing birds or something. I wondered if I should go back in, but I was still feeling uneasy. Ilatagite had rattled me. And I had no idea why or how or anything. I felt so lost.

The sun was just about setting when I saw a movement in the trees at the start of the forest. Something black. Keira? I screwed my eyes a bit more to see, it looked bigger than Keira.

Hmm…

The figure was retreating into the woods behind the Academy, so I ran behind it. I looked back to the Academy. It looked pretty creepy in the evening.

I wondered if it was some animal of the forest. And so I lowered my barriers, enough to communicate with them.

Hullo? Anyone there?

Again there was no answer. But then I saw the black shadow again. I moved towards it.

A black stallion stepped out of the woods, looking regal.

Oh.

Um… hi? I said slowly.

The stallion cocked its head, then said in a magnificent voice, *who are you?*

Um… I'm Ann.

How can you talk to me?

Uh… I'm an animal tongue of sorts. I said.

It shook its mane. *No, animal tongues are different. The way they communicate is different.*

I shrugged. *So… what's your name?*

Shadow, he said.

Ohh… and where are you from? I mean uh where's your rider?

I do not have one. I am a free, wild horse. Not some stable animal.

He sounded quite offended.

Oh... and do you, well, allow people to ride you?

He looked at me, yeah, like he was scrutinising me. Then he said: *Can you ride? Without a saddle?*

I frowned. *I've never tried... but maybe I can now? If you don't mind?*

He lowered his head, and I jumped onto him, holding him by the neck. Then we took off into the night. Every feeling of wooziness and unease left me. I felt free.

This is amazing! I screamed, both in my mind and aloud, clutching onto his dark, glossy mane.

He snorted.

So tell me more about you, I said. *Where do you live?*

In the forests. I roam free.

That's amazing. It must be nice to be so free.

It is.

I sighed, and then suddenly Shadow jerked to a halt.

What's wrong?

There's someone here.

Uh... so?

No, it's something... that shouldn't be here.

I got down. We were pretty much in the heart of the forest, and it was really dark. I wondered what the time was, I could get into a lot of trouble if I was caught out so late. But Shadow wouldn't move. He was convinced something was wrong.

My heart stopped. I had seen somebody move behind those trees.

Shadow, there's someone here.

Genius, he said, *that's what I said.*

Do you think we should go look?

He grunted, which meant: no way am I doing that. But I did. I slowly tiptoed towards the tree, and looked behind it. Nothing.

But then I saw movement again, and I turned. It must be an animal that moves very fast, I thought. What if it... eats humans? What if it was... a ghost?

Oh gosh Ann, don't be so dramatic. Ghosts don't exist.

Let's get out of here.

I managed to sneak into my room a few minutes before they returned. I saw the main gates open as I climbed into my room. I locked my room quickly and shut my windows. I was spooked out. I was sure I had seen someone, but who would be in the woods, that too, so deep inside, at this time? No one. Right?

But someone was there.

Question is, who?

10: Game of Lives

Fabiana

The trip to town was nice. Ilatagite hadn't taken many lessons, not that I would know, I had missed all of them. I had spent most of the time pondering how Ann had done what she had done. I hadn't known she could do that! I don't think she knew either.

Kristin kept me company, along with Kal. Kristin seemed really nice. She told me about her big family and how shocked they'd all been when she had Blossomed. There had been no magicians before. Her family, unlike ours, was glad to have her fight for Andoreya. They must be very patriotic, I thought. She also filled me in on what our life would be like for the next few months, with the help of Kal.

We would have classes till five in the evening. After that we could retire to our rooms, or sit in the lounge and talk, study, and so on until dinner time. And on Sundays we were free.

Today was a Tuesday.

Yesterday after the Limits class, as everyone called it, which had lasted for about three to four hours, then after the brief instructions, they were free. I don't know whose idea it was to go to the town, but I was glad they came up with it.

The housekeeper wanted to accompany us as we were a group of young boys and girls but Ilatagite said no. He said he wanted us to get to know each other and he trusted us and besides, he said, the rules for a chaperone were silly.

So we went. And it was different, and new, but nice. We all talked more openly than we would have with a chaperone along.

The town was a very lively and noisy one. The boys got caught up at the blacksmith's, while we went towards the only clothes shop in town. It was pretty huge, and Vandra practically wanted all the gowns in there. Then we all had a drink at the inn and came back.

Other than Irena and Vandra, I pretty much liked all the girls. The boys were... alright. Aero was nice, and so were the Webber twins and Elvin. Everyone else was a bit uptight.

During the evening I got into an awkward conversation with James, though I guess it was only awkward for me, he seemed very detached from, oh, everything.

"You never did tell us what your power is," he had said, while we walked back to the Academy.

"Uh…" what in heaven's name could I say? "Um… well, you'll see tomorrow."

"Will I?"

I didn't like the tone, it sounded like he was amused or something. I just nodded.

But other than that, the evening was good. Though the whole night I was weighed down by that conversation. What would I say? What lie could I invent?

The whole night I tossed and turned, not able to sleep. And that was when I heard a knock, not on my door but on my window. I got up quickly, and saw Ann standing outside. With a yelp I opened my window. "What in the name of heaven are you doing?" I said.

She grimaced. "I wanted to show you something. Come on."

"Come where? It's three in the morning, Ann!"

"I know," she said, "just come."

I raised my eyebrows but then pulled on my cloak and stepped out of my room through the window. I followed her cautiously, trying not to look down. "Ann? Can you just explain?"

Instead of answering me she jumped through her window. "Come on."

There was a lantern which threw a shadowy light on everything in the room. Ann sat cross legged on the floor, with a book open in front of her. I sat opposite her, curious.

She took a deep breath. "I wanted to talk to you… about something."

She looked so serious, I got a bit scared. "Sure, you know you can tell me anything."

She nodded and said not looking at me, "Okay… you know… the night when Ryan died?"

Ryan had been Ann's elder brother. She never spoke much about it, but I had a vague idea about his death, that I had concocted from the various tidbits

I heard while living with Ann and her family. He had been killed, that much I knew. How? I didn't know. She never spoke of it. But she had seen it.

I guess that kind of thing can cause a lot of trauma in a person, I mean seeing your own brother die?

The clothes Ann wore were his. That's why even though people teased her, she didn't care. Since the age of twelve she had taken to wearing his old clothes which she had found in the attic of her grandparents' house. She had gone there one summer and returned dressed like that. Her parents spent the next year trying to convince her to throw those clothes away and wear normal dresses like normal girls, but Ann didn't listen. She hadn't allowed her parents to destroy anything of his.

"Yeah..." I said softly.

"That was the same night the war started."

I frowned. "I don't understand."

She was flipping through the pages of a book. "I think it's somehow connected. His death, the war, the kidnapping of the prince..."

"How?" I asked, thoroughly confused, "And what book is this?" I lifted it up and saw the name 'Myths and Legends' written on it.

"Ann!" I cried. "Weren't you supposed to return this book to Professor Burns?"

She bit her lip. "Well... I sort of, um, couldn't." She quickly added "I couldn't give it away! It has so much important information in it!"

"No, it doesn't," I countered. "It's all myths, Ann!"

She shook her head, "I don't think so." She turned a few more pages, evidently looking for something. "See this."

These pages weren't printed, they were written in hand. And it was all about the Night Prowler, the war going on now, and such stuff. Recent stuff.

"And see," she said, showing me the first page, "it doesn't even belong to him! It belongs to someone called... Jonathan." She showed me the name written in calligraphy.

"Well... alright. So... you think all this is connected? How?"

"Er... I don't know." I rolled my eyes. "But we can find out! I mean we can, you know, solve it! It's like a puzzle."

"Well, if you want me to be able to piece the puzzle together Ann, you have to tell me more about... your brother's death. I mean why, what happened to him and all."

Her face fell, then she looked at me, her eyes welling up. "I wish I could Fab. But I'm not even sure what happened… I can't… I mean I don't really remember what happened." She sighed. "That's the funny thing about trying to suppress and forget memories, you actually succeed."

I frowned. Maybe like she said, it was all connected. But how? Her brother was killed the same night the war began. That same night the Night Prowler killed the Seer, kidnapped the prince and escaped.

But how was it all connected?

"Did… did your brother have any powers?"

"No."

The question that was irritating me was why was he murdered?

"Ann…" I said slowly, "why—why was he killed?"

She sighed, her head in her hands. "I don't know, honestly. As far as I know it's because he was involved with the minister's daughter."

"The minister's daughter?" I repeated in shock.

"Yeah…" she said. "So he was beaten up and killed."

"What?" I shook my head. "That doesn't make sense. I mean why would they kill him because of that?"

Ann got up. "I don't know, Fab. And I don't want to. This was a stupid idea. There's probably nothing at all. And even if there was, what can we do about it?"

She got into her bed. "I'm going to sleep; you can sleep here if you want to… or go back to your room. I'm sorry I woke you."

"It's okay. I think I'll stay," I said. Somehow I felt I shouldn't leave her here alone, "and read more of this book."

She turned her back to me. I heard her mumble: "They never found his body you know. Never."

I didn't know what to say to that. I felt really bad for her. Whenever the topic of Ryan came up she'd become like this. Moody, shut herself up. Maybe if she talked to someone it would help, but she refused to do so. She'd just clam up.

But who could blame her? Seeing your elder brother die in front of you… is harrowing.

I sighed, then took the big book on my lap. I sat on her window seat and placed the lantern on the table and started to read. I read from the beginning again, the part which Ann had read to me about the Four magicians of

Athanus. For a long time I found myself just staring at the word 'Sorcerer', before I dozed off, right there with the book lying open on my lap.

I woke up first, at maybe around six. I quickly scribbled a note for Ann, then slipped out through her window and slowly walked on the roof, back into my room.

I took a quick bath and dressed. It was as I was brushing my hair that I noticed a clump of strands were grey. What! My eyes widened as I leaned closer to the mirror. Grey hair? I was only sixteen! How could my hair be greying? By heavens! Was it the stress? Was *I* stressed? Well, yes, a little. But anyone in my place would be. Gosh, I needed to calm down or I'd even look like an old lady soon! I gulped then braided it in such a way that the grey was hidden.

Grey hair! Honestly.

I shook my head in disbelief before I picked up my notebook and stylus and left the room. Unfortunately, as I left Vandra saw me.

"Hey Fabiana," she said.

I cringed inwardly. "Hey," I said, forcing a smile.

"Are you going for breakfast?"

"Yes," I said.

"Great," she said, "I didn't want to go down by myself." We made our way down the stairs.

"So what exactly is your magic?" she asked me.

"Oh, you know..." I trailed off.

She looked expectantly at me. "You'll find out," I said coming off ambiguous.

She frowned, then sighed. "I wish my powers would develop faster."

"Heartsight, right?" She nodded. "How does it work?"

She laughed, "I have no idea, to be honest."

She seemed alright really. And I didn't understand why Ann and she couldn't get along. Except for the whole punching her brother in the nose, Ann hadn't done anything else to deserve her wrath.

As we entered the dining hall I saw Quinn finishing his breakfast alone. I wanted to say good morning but he didn't even look up.

"He shouldn't be here," said Vandra while she spooned her porridge into her mouth. Quinn had finished whatever was left on his plate at a speed that convinced me he didn't want to sit with us, probably because he thought we were repulsed by him. I felt bad for him.

"Why not?" I asked, as I spread some strawberry jam on my bread.

"Because werewolves are dangerous," she said. "If they bite a person, the person turns into one!"

I didn't know what to say to that, but I quickly ate my food and went through the wall as soon as I was done.

Surprise, surprise, James was already there.

Oh God, no.

Maybe I should turn and go back?

But he smiled at me; it would be weird to go back now. Maybe he wasn't so bad. Yeah and maybe Ann wasn't reckless and I wasn't a Sorceress. But I had to admit he looked handsome.

I sat in a corner of the room; luckily today there were chairs and desks.

We were the only two people in the room, and I was beginning to wonder whether I should actually leave and come back later when Irena marched in and went and sat right next to James, not before she gave me a disdainful glance.

I snorted. She was, not subtly, flirting with him. And he was flirting back.

I swallowed back my urge to gag. No wonder the adults thought we needed chaperones, look at them! Throwing themselves at each other like animals during mating season.

Ann walked in with dark circles under her eyes.

"You owe me," I told her.

"For that little thing I did?' she scoffed. "Well, alright, if you insist. I have the means to save you today."

"Ann!" I cried, shocked. "You are not doing whatever you did yesterday, again!"

She put a hand on her chest and tried to look offended. "Why Fab, you distrust me too much."

I narrowed my eyes at her and she grinned. "Truly! Tell me dear friend do you know what your fake power is?"

"No," I grumbled.

"Well, I do!"

"What?" I asked suspiciously.

"You, my dear girl, are a Fire Mage."

My eyes widened, "That's—"

"Brilliant, I know, I know." She looked sickeningly pleased with herself.

I hit her on the arm. But it was brilliant. Sorcerers could control the elements, well one in my case, and it was fire.

We settled down as Ilatagite came in. He leaned on his table and scrutinised each of us. Then with a clap of his hands he started our class, just like that.

"You all know magic comes from the Spirit world. But what is the Spirit world? Where is it?"

"Isn't it like heaven?" Aero ventured. "In a different dimension where mortals can't enter unless, well, they die?"

Ilatagite shook his head. "The Spirit world is our world."

What?

I wasn't the only one confused.

"How many worlds are there?"

"Seven," Ann answered. When I raised an eyebrow at her she mouthed, *what? I read.*

"Yes. And all these worlds are like the thread on a piece of cloth. They make the cloth just as the seven worlds form the Spirit world."

I leaned forward, my elbows propped on the desk to support my head.

"How many of you here are religious?"

A few people raised their hands.

"Aero, what do you believe in?"

"The Spirits," he said.

"As do most of us. Does anyone believe in something greater than the Spirits?"

"I do," Lyra said. I looked at her sitting diminutively in her chair.

"What do you believe in?"

"I believe there is a Greater Spirit. I've seen flashes of other worlds as well." Wow, that's amazing. That's…. unimaginable. "They call this Greater Spirit by different names. I believe this…. God created the universe, all the seven worlds. In some of the other worlds there is no magic. In some there are only demons, I think that's hell. I believe the seventh plane is Heaven and I believe the Spirit world is a constituent of every world but apart from every world. And I believe God is greater than the Spirits. I think He created them."

"Well said," Ilatagite said. "It is said that Someone, I suppose you can label this Someone as *God* or the Greater Spirit, created the Four, the Spirits to come down to *our* plane to help us."

"Because before magic we had a rule similar to that of the non-magical worlds, but war broke out."

Not another war, I thought, why couldn't people just live in peace?

"Who has heard of Athanus?"

"Isn't that a myth?" Kristin asked.

"It is believed to be now as we no longer have entrance there, but magic originated from there." Ilatagite paused. "Magic is everything on the sixth plane, it is their world, everyone who is on the sixth plane has magic. We are on the fifth plane. And everyone doesn't have magic in our world. Our world was separated into the People and the Beings."

I had never heard of this story until now. I listened in awe. Beings?

"Athanus is actually not part of our world. It is a banished island from the sixth plane."

"Our world is younger than the seventh and sixth, obviously. By thousands and thousands of centuries. The Athenians, for whatever reason, were banished here. They were wilder than our savages and the Greater Spirit sent four of his own to tame them. This was before the reigns of our kings and queens. It was in the very first years. Athanus was severed from Andoreya by magic, no Athenians could come to Andoreya without the permission of the Spirits, permission that would never be granted. The Spirits looked over the Athenians and disciplined them. And for a long time there was no contact between the People and the Beings. But then Andoreya was attacked by dark magic which could only have come from Athanus, though it is said that the magic wasn't from there, they didn't possess that kind of magic. Lycans, Jinn, Witches, Gremlins, Goblins were running rampant in our forests. They killed thousands. I suppose you all know the rest."

I nodded as did everyone else. We'd learned about it. So Athanus was the haven. Ann looked triumphant.

"The Spirits defeated and rounded up all the dark magic practitioners and exiled them to the Wastelands. The Wastelands were heavily guarded by our soldiers until, of course, recently." He sighed heavily.

"And Athanus was separated from us forever. So no doubts would enter the minds of the People. But it was too late. Magic had seeped into our land and taken over our existence. The magic that was once abundant, it seems, is now dying out, which is why we have fewer and fewer magicians every year.

There might come a time when Andoreya is restored to its former status, a land with no magic."

I shivered. No magic? I was so used to having magic in me I couldn't even imagine a life without it! It seemed so impossible.

How could we exist without magic?

"Lyra," Ilatagite said, "do you know what the difference is between magicians and non-magicians?"

She nodded. "We can draw from our Soulfire, which is essentially, linked to the Spirit world. It's what connects the universe."

"Exactly! And this is an ability you have to be born with!" Ilatagite clapped his hands together, looking charged. "This ability comes from the Beings. Those Beings who came to Andoreya along with the Spirits and stayed back. Elves and fairies and whatnot."

"Elves and fairies exist?" Cassius sounded sceptical. "Does Snow White exist too?"

"Snow White existed."

"What?"

"That's a fairy tale. Pshaw!" Aero rolled his eyes.

"Of course not, how stupid would that be?" Vandra smirked.

Ilatagite, however, smiled. "Yes, Snow was from the other side of our world. Of course I have met her daughter Crystal once, when I went there. The distance separates us but they too have magic of a different kind. Lana is where she lived. And Rounaq was her father before her stepmother killed him. Tragic tale."

We gaped.

"Rapunzel too?" Ann asked. "And Cinderella?"

"Yes, of course," Ilatagite said grimly. "Lana, Delphie, Hunwery, all part of our world Lenore, these tales come from there. Just as our tales go there."

"How?"

"Scribes," he said, and everyone looked at Kristin, who looked surprised.

"But that does not concern us," he said. "Back to our class... now, the four Spirits engaged in the lives of the People and Beings a lot, something which could be considered forbidden by the Greater Spirit. For the Spirits have knowledge that mortals don't and to share that with mortals was to cause strife and worry."

"The Spirits, Sir, are they still alive in Athanus?" Josephine asked.

His eyes lingered on me before he said, "We are not to know since we no longer have any contact with Athanus, in fact we don't even know where it is. Because the Spirits made the People forget, to ensure no further problems."

"But it's real?" Ann asked.

"As real as you and me."

"This involvement of the Spirits in our lives is actually famous amongst magicians. It's called the Game of Lives."

I felt Ann still behind me. Ann had once mentioned to me of a dream of hers, the one right before the Hounds came, where a Spirit (we still don't know who) had mentioned the Game of Lives to her.

I somehow didn't think it was just a dream.

"A game?" Ann asked, her voice shaky. "What do you mean?"

"Well," he rubbed his chin, "there is a belief among some of the older generations like mine that the Spirits like to play with the lives of mortals. According to this belief, it's a game like... like chess, we're the chess pieces and they're the ones who decide where to move us and such." He frowned. "However there is an argument that we are the players as well, as the Spirits do not have control over free will. Every once in a while people are chosen to become the amusement of the Spirits, to entertain them. Sometimes it's more than that; sometimes it's a game of power, of lives. Between the Spirits."

"That sounds harsh," Lyra said.

I didn't feel too fond of the Spirits anymore, they seemed cruel. I was seeing them from a different angle now. As tyrannical gods.

"Perhaps so," he conceded. "The Spirits control a huge amount of our lives even though we don't know it. For example, the biggest are the seers. Seers are basically puppets in the hands of Spirits."

Lyra paled. I imagined how terrible it must be to hear Ilatagite say you're nothing but a puppet. He could've been a bit more considerate. But he continued, regardless. "Magic is, to a large extent, controlled by the Spirits. Except for Sorcery." I brightened. "Sorcery is a direct link to the original Sorcerer who was a Spirit and therefore it isn't controlled by the Spirits."

This was too much new information. Sure, we had learnt history, but we had learnt nothing like this. We learnt about kings and wars, geography and taxes, dances and manners. They never taught us about the First Four in school, or about Soulfire or the Spirit world. I don't think anyone even knew this apart from, well, Ilatagite and probably whoever he had taught.

Apparently Kristen was thinking along the same lines, for she asked, "How come we were never taught such things in school?"

"Think of it this way," Ilatagite said. "It's like a secret between magicians, the history of magic. And anyway Soulfire can only be seen by magicians."

"Seen?" said Elvin. "We can see it?"

"Yes. You can see it. And in fact, the Soulfire tells you how long you will live."

"What?" said Dawn. "Is that even... possible?"

"It shows your natural lifeline. It could say that you will live for many more years and perhaps be murdered the next day. But apart from such external harm, how long you can live is decided at the time of your birth. But how you will die cannot be foreseen. I will show you one day. For now, today's class is over. You have a break of ten minutes, then assemble behind the academy and we'll practise Limits."

There was an audible murmur of resentment, I looked up at the grandfather clock in the room; we had been sitting here for four and a half hours.

It was twelve noon. Ann, Kal, Lyra and I walked together in the courtyard. Ann was silent.

"This is all so big, eh?" Lyra stated.

"Yeah..." I said quietly. Big wasn't exactly the word, I felt like whatever I had believed till now had been lies. It was like... suddenly the world was upside down.

I knew there was a Spirit World but I didn't know so much about it, not to mention the involvement of Spirits in our lives. In fact I had never given a second thought to the subject. So... I frowned, our magic was fuelled by our Soulfire which came from the Spirit World. And the Spirits thought of us as pieces on a chessboard?

I was dying to know what Ann thought about her dream now. And today Ilatagite had also said something about games... coincidence? I didn't think so.

"I can't believe our magic comes from the Spirit World!" said Kal. "I mean, is the Spirit World all of this?"

But Ann was looking somewhere else now and a slow smile spread on her face. "Look over there."

We followed her gaze, and even I started to grin. Vandra and Irena were literally fighting for James's attention. He, however, didn't seem to be paying any attention to either of them.

Irena and Vandra walked in front of him, boasting loudly about some dances and parties they had been to and such.

We laughed, making fun of Irena and Vandra. Even Ann looked pretty cheerful, but I knew her well enough to not assume that she had forgotten the morning's lecture. It was probably lurking at the back of her mind, just as it was in mine.

"So Fabiana," said Ilatagite, "demonstrate your powers, please."

Our outdoor class had started, and I had had to tell them that I was a fire mage. Somebody gasped when I did.

Imagine if I had told them I was a Sorceress then?

Ilatagite now wanted me to show how I did it, which was easy enough. Though I wasn't very comfortable doing it in front of others.

"Uh... now?" I asked.

"Yes," he said.

I nodded, feeling uneasy. Then I lifted my hands in front of me, like a cup. Concentrating, I muttered slowly, "Firai".

And lo, a fire danced in the cup of my hands.

"Oooh..." said Josephine.

The word I had said wasn't exactly some magic word that made the fire appear, it was a word I concentrated on to control the fire. It was the word Ann had said when she first saw me set the bush on fire. When I asked her what she had said, she said "fire." But I was sure I heard Firai. That word seemed magical, and that's what I used whenever I wanted to control my fire.

"Good," said Ilatagite, clapping his hands. "Now, Marcus and Cassius, can you change?"

It took five minutes, and Marcus turned into a leopard. I backed away with a gasp. And Cassius flew above us as an eagle.

"Okay now, try switching back and forth as quickly as you can."

Cassius tried, but it took him more than ten minutes to switch back into himself. It took Marcus more than that. Imagine if they couldn't ever switch back. Was that possible?

"Concentrate, boys," said Ilatagite. "You know I think it will be easier if you concentrate on your names. Why don't you try again?"

As they did, Ilatagite started going around, making everyone practise.

I had to make the fire bigger, smaller, make it move in the direction I wanted and such. Pointless. What I needed was to learn how to cast spells.

Aero was just, well, disappearing and reappearing in different spots. Once he came up behind me and scared me. Things here were certainly very different from home. I couldn't ever imagine interacting so freely with boys back home. I don't think even they were used to it. Except Aero, he seemed to be like Arni, young and innocent.

Irena was walking like a ghost through the solid objects which Ilatagite kept casting for her.

I watched in fascination as he did such things, I couldn't do such magic. Spells were beyond me. I had no idea how to cast even a single spell.

Quinn had disappeared into the woods; I guess he couldn't really practise being a Lycan.

Dawn, Kal, Lyra and Vandra were asked to focus their magic by meditating on something or someone. So they were sitting a bit away from us, cross legged and meditating.

James was also with them, but he sat away from them.

Elvin and Josephine were studying some book which Ilatagite had given them, together. Kristin was staring hard at a pen and board, I didn't know what it was supposed to do but by the look on her face I didn't think it was working.

Ann had managed to call birds and squirrels to her and she sat with them around her, reminding me strangely of Snow White. Hair as black as ebony, skin as pale as snow… her lips weren't the colour of blood though. But otherwise she was pretty much a real Snow White. Though, with her long hair she ought to be Rapunzel. I thought about what Ilatagite had said about them being real. It just sounded too bizarre. Even Belle was real? And she fell in love with a Beast? I shuddered.

I was making the fire swirl when someone put a hand on my shoulder, I yelped. But it was only Lyra. She looked disturbed.

"Something wrong?" I asked her.

She cocked her head looking curiously at me. "I saw something… about you," she said dazedly.

My heartbeat stopped. She was a seer. And she had seen something about me. My future.

"Lyra," called Ilatagite. She jerked. "Can I talk to you?"

She looked like a sleepwalker as she went towards him.

What could she have possibly seen? I caught Ann looking at me, worriedly. I shrugged, and then continued with my practice. But I couldn't concentrate much after that.

After that Ilatagite gave us each a different and thin book. It was for us to study, he said.

He also told me 'my' book was already in my room.

"Once you study your books, you will each give me a written summary on what you understood from the book and if it has helped you in any way. Then you will exchange books in turns and by the end of the year you will have studied all these different forms of magic. I will also give you other books, magic which we don't have in our Academy right now."

After that we had our lunch, which was rice, gravy and boiled potatoes. Then we retired to our rooms for an hour's rest. There was a fat book on my table. I flipped through it and saw the history of various Sorcerers. I yawned and plonked onto my bed and promptly fell asleep.

When I woke up, we were asked to go again to the Magic wall room as Ann referred to it, and start our summaries on our books.

By day I practised along with the others and by night I practised alone with Ilatagite. By the end of the week I was exhausted, sleep-deprived and welcomed any change in our routine. We went to the town once again. This time Ann came along, and I felt less tired as she walked beside me, humming to herself.

I recognised the tune, it was from last year's ball. I had got stuck with a horrible boy called Bradley. All he did was talk about himself. I remembered that dance.

"I think it's all rubbish," Bradley said, "this whole ball thing. Why can't girls and boys go hunting or something together?"

Hunting?

"Maybe because—" I started, only to be interrupted by him.

"And anyways balls are so boring."

"Didn't your father organise this?" I asked, feeling a bit annoyed.

"Yes, I told him it was a stupid idea. But he thinks it'll help me find a girl. As if I can't find one myself."

I stepped on his foot. "Ouch," he said.

"Sorry," I said smiling triumphantly. "I guess I was distracted."

Wrong thing to say, apparently, because he mistook my distraction to be due to his presence. Moron.

"Yes, that happens," he said. "You're a beautiful girl, Miss Mecatrus," he said, drawing me closer.

I resisted the urge to kick him. Balls were an excuse for the boys to fondle girls and the girls to flirt with the boys. I could see why Ann hated them.

"Mm," I replied, not looking at him.

"Do you like dancing with me?"

Not at all. But courtesy demanded a polite answer, so I just said "Hmm..." hoping that he wouldn't take that for a yes.

"I don't think the other girls can dance, but you have grace, like me. We're alike in many ways, you know."

Fortunately I was saved by a disturbance in the hall. Someone had fallen onto the drinks table.

Bradley who liked to be the centre of attention, wanted to go see what it was. I excused myself, saying my friend was calling me.

I quickly looked around the crowd for Ann, and found her sitting at one of the dinner tables on the side, her face as red as a tomato.

"Not too good huh?" I asked her.

She looked at me aghast, "I shouldn't have come. You dolt, it's all your fault!"

"Can't have been that bad," I said, grimacing.

"I managed to trip Mister Burns into the punch bowl," she said in horrified tones.

"Ohhh..." was all I could manage. "That was you then?" My eyes looked about until I found Gerry who was leaving the ballroom with one of his friends, dripping red punch on the floor.

I couldn't help grinning.

"I can't believe you're smiling," Ann whispered to me in furious tones. "I just embarrassed myself and him in front of everyone."

"It was an accident," I consoled her, trying hard not to smile, "and anyways Mister Burns is a nice person. He won't you know... hold a grudge or anything."

"Says you," Ann said in dejected tones, "and he was being nice too, not like the others. Ma is going to have me. And I'll be teased forever!" I giggled but stopped immediately when she glared at me.

"Be happy," I said "your, um, accident saved me from that brat Bradley."

"I am never, ever going to dance again, ever," she swore in furious tones.

I grinned at the memory of that night. Poor Ann, poor Mister Burns.

I can't believe you remember this!

Ann! I said shocked *why are you in my head?*

'Cause, it's my favourite place! she said sarcastically, *YOU are projecting your thoughts.*

I quickly tried to put my barriers up as I felt her withdraw from my mind. Funny, I never noticed her enter, only withdraw.

I remember when I last came to the town, there were crowds of girls, boys whistling about, children playing, sellers bargaining, but now, it was so... still. There were only a few people around, and they seemed tired and frightened-looking.

When we inquired, we found out that the war had taken a toll on their economy, also on their families. Boys of twelve were now forced to join the army; soldiers had come and taken them away.

Most of them died within two weeks of recruitment.

The war wasn't going well for us.

I sighed, another reason why I *should* give myself to the kingdom.

11: Gore and Guard

Andalucia

I watched as the clouds lazily drifted and formed shapes. Fab was studying, like a good girl, her legs stretched out. I was lying beside her on the grass, my hair tangled with the earth but I didn't care.

Two months were over since we had come here. It had been hectic and it had been monotonous.

A lot had happened in the past two months. Arni had lost his first tooth and my parents still refused to evacuate without me, why couldn't they understand? I had made friends with Dawn and even Irena, not Vandra though. Dawn was nice, Irena was tolerable. I had also gone on many rides on Shadow; he had become a friend too. Lyra admitted to fancying Aero. Both our healers were back from their small trip around Andoreya with Ilatagite, the only few days we were free, but even then he had loaded us with so much work, to visit reputed infirmaries and learn more about healing.

Fab had progressed a lot in her magic, and I was so glad, she had also turned seventeen, meaning she had Blossomed. If only she would trust herself more, she had so much potential.

We had started Herb-lore, studying poisons and antidotes. The war was still raging, and we were still in a miserable position. Too many people were dying. I couldn't let my barrier down at all because I was afraid I would be overwhelmed by someone else's memories. It didn't seem like we would be winning any time soon.

But today it didn't bother me.

I sighed, feeling content. It was after a long time I was feeling so peaceful. I should've known it wouldn't last.

Fab suddenly stiffened.

"Ann, sit up," she said.

I immediately shot up without asking her why. Her tone seemed urgent and for once I didn't question her. I'm glad I didn't.

A tall man, with broad shoulders, walked out of the forest. I stared. It seemed like he had just appeared from thin air which was of course impossible or maybe not.

Hmm, he seemed familiar.

He was dressed oddly. In a sleeveless tunic which showed off his huge biceps. A large tattoo was on his right arm.

We stood up quickly. Fab dusted her skirt.

He didn't even look in our direction as he walked past us. "He looks really haughty." I observed.

"And good," Fab said smiling.

I grimaced but I had to admit that he did. Like some dark prince.

"I guess," I said.

I lowered my barriers a little and tried to get a sense of who he was and what he was doing here. But I ran smack into a wall. I gasped, and Fab looked at me, alarmed.

Not many people had such strong walls. The impact of the hit was blinding. I gritted my teeth at my own idiocy. I should've been more cautious. Abruptly he stopped and turned his head in our direction. Fab dropped her gaze, blushing furiously. I looked away quickly and back again because I didn't want him to think we had been admiring him or something. He seemed like the kind who would think exactly that. He must've sensed the intrusion. Which meant he knew something about magic, or maybe was a magician himself. Darn it. Darn it all.

But I didn't stop staring and neither did he. It was like a competition of wills except that we didn't know each other, at all.

"Can we help you… Sir?" I finally managed.

Fab was pinching me but I shrugged her off. I hadn't meant to sound so… defiant.

His mouth twitched as though he was about to smile and then he said: "No. I don't think *you* can really." And with that he walked away.

I glared at his back until Fab broke my reverie. "What was that all about?"

"Don't know. Bloody haughty… arh stranger," I muttered. "Pfft. I hope the hounds bite his head off."

"Ann," Fab said sitting down and rolling her eyes, "you don't even know the man."

"Fifi, Fergus?" I mimicked calling, my palms cupped around my mouth, "Babies, go chew the Giant."

"You did not!" Fab said looking at me with wide eyes.

"I'm tempted. But Fifi and Fergus may end up biting me, they're a little weird."

"Wonder why he's here..." Fab murmured.

"Hmm," I frowned, "let me see if I can find out."

"Ann, no," Fab said quickly, "absolutely not."

"I'm just going to see," I said, knotting my hair back into a bun. I slowly walked towards the institution, looking back in between at Fab, who was glowering and shaking her head at me.

But as soon as I went inside I was caught. "I've been looking for you," Dawn said, coming down the stairs.

"Hmm?" I asked distractedly, looking for the tall stranger. Dawn was blocking my way. I looked at him. His long brown hair was in a pony today. Funnily, it reminded me of a pony's tail.

He hesitated. "Ann, I think something bad is going to happen soon."

I raised an eyebrow and snorted, "Since when have you become a seer Dawn?"

"It's not..." he sighed, "it's not me, it's something Lyra said."

"What do you mean?"

He looked around fearfully before he whispered "I was in the library yesterday when she came in. She was just looking through books and then she came over and we were just talking you know. About our powers and stuff, when..."

"When?" I pressed. Lyra was a seer, had she seen something?

"When she went all weird, like her voice. And then she said... that someone was going to die soon."

I blanched. "What?"

He nodded. "Yeah... but that's not what, I came to tell you... that... she also said that she's going to die too, soon, because of her powers. And that she's... going to be..." he shuddered, "murdered."

"Don't be silly," I said slowly. "She was probably playing a prank on you."

He shook his head. "I don't think so." Then, with a sigh he said: "You'll probably find out soon. A girl from town has been found, murdered."

I felt my insides go cold.

Then hesitatingly he murmured, "There's blood in your past."

"What?" I said, as my heart beat faster.

"You've witnessed a murder before, haven't you?" he asked.

"I told you never to read my past," I said, my fists clenched.

"I haven't," he said quickly. "I haven't seen your past. But my powers gave me a gist of it when I first saw you."

He avoided looking at me. Tears welled up in my eyes.

"For your information," I said shakily, feeling lightheaded and heavy at the same time, "the murder I witnessed was years ago. And— it was my brother who got murdered."

He looked aghast. "Ann—I didn't know—"

I didn't hear the rest. My blood was boiling and my eyes were burning as I tried to push down those memories. I did the only thing I was good at, that I always did. I ran.

I ran as fast as I could into the woods. I could hear Dawn calling me, but I didn't listen. Fab might've seen me. But I didn't care. I ran past the trees whose branches raked at me as I ran, I ran until I tripped and fell. I lay there and cried.

How could I explain, that I didn't remember the most important thing that had happened to me? That I couldn't, that... even if I wanted to believe what had happened I couldn't.

Three murders...

One after the other.

Can the dead walk?

My heart stopped, someone was coming. But even as I formed that thought, the person was already there.

It was Aero.

"Ann," he said, sounding relieved. "Everyone has been looking for you."

I let my hair fall as a curtain between us, so I could wipe my eyes. "Why?"

"Soldiers from the kingdom have come, they're raiding the Academy."

"For what?"

"Someone's died Ann. And... will you come? Everyone's worried."

"Someone died?" I asked, shocked.

"Some girl from the village."

I relaxed, then got up.

"Ann," he said, "promise me you won't come here again."

I looked at him with a frown.

"It's not safe," he murmured. "This isn't the first time this is happening. I heard Ilatagite tell Larissa two weeks back maybe, that a girl had died. And just like this girl, her body was found in the woods, the woods which you keep sneaking to, alone." I'd never heard Aero sound so serious, almost like Nick.

I sniffed. A girl had died? Two girls, not one and their bodies had been found in these woods? I shuddered.

"Ann… if something happens to you," Aero said slowly, "I won't be able to face anyone back home again."

I gulped and looked at my feet.

"Are you okay?" he asked giving me a hand. I nodded.

We had to go through the front entrance, because the back door was locked. There were around fifteen soldiers in the front, who eyed us suspiciously.

"What were you doing in the woods?" asked one soldier, barricading our way.

"I was," said Aero, "looking for her, because the professor told me to."

"And what were you doing in the woods, miss?" the soldier asked me. He had a big moustache and beady eyes.

"I was… I was," I looked past him and inside the Academy. Everyone was there, and they all looked very nervous.

"I was crying my eyes out," I said finally with brittle cheer. "You know adolescent issues," I waved my hand dismissively. "I didn't know what was going on."

He looked taken aback, but he let us through. Everyone was staring at us. Ignoring Dawn trying to catch my eye I walked over to Fab.

"Are you okay?" she asked.

"Yeah, I'm fine," I mumbled.

She didn't say anything. "Why are there guards?" I asked.

"A girl died," Kal answered. "She lived in the town. Her body was found… near the Academy's woods."

"What was her name?"

"Rose," said Lyra. "Her name was Rose." Lyra looked tired.

"Oh, did you know her?" I asked casually.

She shook her head, tears streaming down her face. "But I saw her, I saw her dead body in my vision."

No one said anything; it must be so hard to see what the future holds and not be able to change it. I patted her back clumsily, trying to keep my tears at bay when she suddenly threw her arms around me in a hug.

I was so shocked, I didn't move for a minute before I whispered, "Shh, it's okay, it's okay."

I had never been too fond of Lyra but now, as she wept on my shoulder, I felt responsible for her. I don't know why. She looked so innocent, and fragile.

I looked at Fab who sighed.

"Lyra," called Ilatagite, coming into the room, "come with me please. You too, Dawn."

Lyra let go of me, and went behind Ilatagite. Dawn followed her, and they both went into his study. The door shut behind them.

Immediately everyone broke into whispered discussion.

Irena came over to us, and demanded "What happened to her?"

"She saw a vision," Fab said, "a vision about the dead girl."

Irena shook her head angrily. "She should've kept her mouth shut. Never should've come. The stupid girl." And then she just stomped off and went up the stairs into her room. The door slammed.

I sat on the steps; Josephine sat next to me patting my knee. Fab leaned on the banister, her hand on her forehead.

Shandre came and stood next to her. "Apparently this girl was involved with someone," she said. "Her family warned her against him, everyone suspects he murdered her."

I shut my eyes. Of course. A boy would have to be involved.

"He probably ruined her before he stabbed her in the back and killed her," I said with surprising vehemence.

Everyone looked at me, surprised.

I had heard too many tales about girls being raped, and killed brutally. And felt the pain of one victim too. I shuddered trying to forget that memory. I had been thirteen. I hadn't been able to sleep for nights after that. I had lost control of my barriers and they had crashed, it used to happen a lot when I was younger. But that time was the worst. There was a girl who lived in Gondon with her Aunty and Uncle, her father was fighting and her mother was a magician. She used to be raped every day by her uncle and her aunty didn't know. One day it got too much. She committed suicide, hanged herself in her bedroom. Everyone believed her to be a maniac, some whispered she had a secret lover who betrayed her. If only they knew.

I developed a high fever and was in bed for a week. I hadn't talked to anyone.

I jerked back into the present, shuddering. That was before I learned how to shield my mind. Learning to shield my mind was necessary for my sanity. It was my grandpa who taught me how to do it. He had slight telepathic abilities. He had helped me get through it and learn how to protect my mind, and I had taught Fab. He died soon after.

I wrapped my arms around myself. Ilatagite came out of the study. Dawn and Lyra did not come out with him.

One of the soldiers said: "Does the seer know—"

Ilatagite interrupted, "No she does not," Ilatagite said loudly. "She doesn't know who committed the murder. I would much appreciate if you soldiers would leave now. There is nothing you want here. We do not have the information you seek."

"We have to question them," said the soldier. "If any of them has seen anything strange…"

Ilatagite looked at each one of us, but no one said anything.

"You see," he said turning back to the soldier, "they do not know anything."

The soldier bowed. "Meaning no disrespect, Sir, but the dead girl's family said it was a boy of around seventeen to twenty who they suspect. And we have questioned all the boys in town. We would like to question the boys here as well."

I looked at the boys, they all looked taken aback. Except for one of them. James.

"Has anyone ever seen this boy?" Ilatagite asked his voice harsh.

"No," said the guard.

"Then how have they assumed it is a boy?"

The guard looked uneasy, and I knew what he was about to say. "She was… ruined sir."

My breath caught and a wave of nausea overwhelmed me.

Ilatagite didn't even flinch. "I see. Well, if you must check the house, question them. Just get it done with quickly. I'd like to talk to my students in private."

In a trice the soldiers were running about the house, searching all the rooms and halls. Two of them were questioning the boys. I listened carefully when one of them questioned James. "And you say you've never met a girl of this description?" I saw him look in our direction, at Fab, with a hungry look. He caught me looking at him; I glared until he looked away.

"Never," he said coolly.

Once the soldiers left, there was a meeting. Some of us sat on the steps, most of the boys just stood there.

"The girl did not die an ordinary death," Ilatagite said. "She was not only murdered, but her body was found without a drop of blood left in it."

Pin drop silence followed this statement.

"Do you know how that is possible?" he asked. No one said anything. "Has anyone heard of creatures called Jinn? More commonly known as Vampires or Blood-drinkers?"

Some said they had, but most of us hadn't. I had a vague memory of reading something about them, but I couldn't recall it.

"They were the first supernatural creatures in Andoreya. It is because of them that the First Four even came into our land. They are immortal."

There was an excited murmur. Being immortal was obviously something exhilarating.

"But, even though they are immortal they are only so if they feed on blood."

Shandre gasped. Everyone was looking at each other, nervously. There was no excitement anymore.

I felt nauseated.

"The king does not want anyone to know, but as magicians you ought to know. It is these creatures that we are having a war with. And we are losing. The king needs magicians."

At this, his glance paused on Fab for a minute before sweeping over the rest of us.

I saw Fab turn pale.

"In a few months, your studies here will be over," he said. "You will help the kingdom fight the war." He paused, letting that sink in. As if we had any say in the matter, I thought sourly. "You can all go to your beds now. Tomorrow we will have class as usual."

Saying this he went back into his study. I saw Fab linger for a minute, when I caught her eyes she mouthed *I want to talk with him.*

I nodded. Kristen and Shandre were helping Lyra up the stairs.

"Ann," called Dawn as I climbed up the stairs. I stopped. I saw James watching us. "I'm sorry…" he said. "I didn't mean to…"

"It's okay," I said quickly, not wanting James to understand our conversation. "I just got mad, it's not your fault."

"Yes, it is!" he said insisting, "I shouldn't have ever said anything."

"Probably," I said. "It's okay though. We can't change the past."

He nodded, it looked like he wanted to say something more but then he just shrugged and said, "Goodnight."

"Goodnight," I said.

Though I didn't have a good night. I had nightmares. There was blood everywhere. So much blood.

12: Attacked

Fabiana

"You have to believe in yourself!" Ilatagite said angrily.

"I do!" I cried, as sweat beaded my forehead. "It's just not happening!"

"Because you don't believe in yourself," he shouted. "Try again. You are not leaving until you do this tonight."

I gritted my teeth, why couldn't I do it? Why? I was such a pathetic Sorceress. I shouldn't even be one.

I was furious with myself, livid as I bellowed: "Move!" and the furniture, as though it had been waiting for this command, just slid across the room and hit the wall with a CRASH and then it vanished. Just vanished.

I collapsed onto the floor.

"Good," Ilatagite said, bringing back his furniture from wherever I sent it. "That was good."

I didn't say anything. Tears started welling up in my eyes, and I blinked them away.

"Do you remember?" he said suddenly, "the story of the Spirits?" I nodded, wondering how it was relevant to what we were doing now. "What if I told you that you were one of the Four Spirits?"

"What?"

Had he lost his mind?

"What if I told you I knew a Warrior?" he said his eyes fixed on me, "and a Shape-Shifter?"

I shook my head in disbelief. "But, the four are dead or stuck in that Haven place. And I'm not one of them. The Sorcerer's name was… Lucifer or something."

"You can go now," he said abruptly. "Go take some rest."

I got up, confused, but Ilatagite opened the door for me and I walked out, because I didn't know what else to say.

I snorted; yeah I'm one of the four. I can't even cast a spell.

When I reached my room, Ann was already sitting on my bed.

I plopped down. "Ilatagite's mad," I said.

"I already knew that," Ann said with a grin.

"No, he's really mad!" I said sitting up. "He thinks I'm some myth! That I'm one of the Four! Me? Ha!"

Ann frowned. "What? But—that's crazy."

"I know," I said.

"No," she said, "I mean, what if it's true?"

I stared at her. "Are you crazy too? Me? Me? One of the most powerful beings ever? I can't even cast a spell."

She didn't say anything, but I knew she was thinking about it. I was too.

"Fab," Ann said sitting straighter and staring at my head. She leaned forward and lifted a few strands. "Your hair! What happened? Did you try some spell?"

"What?" I cried.

I scrambled to my feet and dashed into the bathroom. My eyes were like blue orbs in my face in the dim light of the lantern. I cocked my head and looked at the mirror with my peripheral view. A section of my hair had turned the colour of snow. I frantically spun on my feet, keeping my eyes trained on the mirror to see the back of my head, where strands were sparkling white as I checked if more was greying but it seemed not. I even checked for wrinkles.

"You think you're turning into a hag?" Ann asked me from the doorway. She was leaning on the doorframe, her arms folded, and a frown on her face.

"Maybe I am," I said blinking at the white in my hair.

"You could try changing it to your natural colour." she suggested.

"Huh, there's a thought." I frowned then tried. I concentrated on the image in the mirror and my greying hair. I inhaled and imagined as I exhaled, power washing over my whole body from head to toe, and reviving me, washing away any weariness. I opened my eyes.

"You did it!" Ann cried excitedly.

My eyes glowed with warmth, there was colour in my cheeks, I looked much better and my hair was its natural brown again. I double checked but there wasn't a single grey hair. I grinned at her.

My classes continued, but it didn't seem like I improved much, or was it because I was slowly improving at a snail's pace?

Ann was getting worried. Most nights she would visit my room, entering through the window. And I would yell and scream and vent my frustration, and she would quietly listen. Encouraging me, consoling me, then I would fall asleep. When I woke up she would be gone. Sometimes we would discuss the Four, and she would look at me weirdly. And whenever I asked her, she would change the topic and try to distract me, successfully.

Today Ilatagite had left me early, it was only nine. I plopped onto my bed and closed my eyes. Deep breaths. Inhale, exhale, in, out, in, out. Relax. I let my shoulders drop. I took deep breaths, feeling at peace, just listening to my steady breathing. I felt better.

Then slowly, I let my guard down. And I let my mind probe into the centre, right near my heart. I could feel the presence… of my fire. And that giddy excitement came back to me, like it always did whenever I did this. It had been a while since I had looked into my Soulfire. Ilatagite had taught me how in one of the earlier classes. But I had done it only once, it was easy.

The beautiful blue engulfed me. It was blue like the sky, blue like the sea. So beautiful. I waltzed peacefully in the blue. Then slowly, I moved to the core, where the fire was. It blazed blue.

I still had time I thought, relieved. Lots, apparently. I wasn't going to die soon. That was nice, I was always worried that, being a Sorcerer, something would happen and someone would kill me.

Silly thoughts really.

The fire was so attractive. I felt like walking right through it. In fact, that's what I did, though it wasn't a conscious movement. I just glided towards it. And then, I was right in the middle of the fire. It raged around me, but I didn't feel the heat, only warmth, pleasant warmth.

Abruptly the fire faltered and then – Oh! Suddenly it burned a dark red colour. And now I could feel the dark heat around me, panic bubbled in me. It burned me, and I screamed. What was happening? I didn't understand. I could feel the heat biting at my skin, blisters rose on my skin.

And then as suddenly as it happened, it vanished, the dark red colour left and my blue came back. I knelt on all fours and let the blue fire embrace me. What had just happened? I couldn't comprehend it. And I let the fire hold me and cool my blisters, but my mind was still in pain.

"Mental assault, I can't believe you let your guard down you dolt!" I heard someone say dimly. Like a voice that was cracking, I couldn't hear it properly. But I understood all the same. "Snap out of it," the voice ordered.

I jerked back to reality. I was lying down on the bed, and Ann stood over me like a disappointed teacher.

"Honestly Fab, I thought you knew better!"

"What'd I do?" I croaked.

"You don't just let your guard down like that!" she chastised.

"But if I had to look at my Soulfire...?" I mumbled confused.

"You're supposed to relax, that doesn't mean you completely let go of yourself. And I thought Ilatagite had put some spell over the Academy so such things never happened." She looked troubled.

I felt really embarrassed, and then, to add to my embarrassment, Larissa came in. She never came to our rooms ever. And certainly not like this. She had just burst in.

"Are you alright dear?" she asked concernedly.

"I'm fine," I mumbled.

"I heard what you were shouting about, Andalucia," she told Ann. Ann was taken aback. "She's right you know dear, you should never let your guard down. Dangerous times."

I blinked.

"Dangerous times, Larissa?" Ann repeated with a cocked brow.

Larissa nodded "I can feel something bad is going to happen... dark times. They are rising." And as she said this she looked at me and her eyes glinted. Then abruptly she said: "If you have any laundry, then you should give it to me now."

Such a leap in topic.

"What do you mean by they are rising?" Ann asked.

Larissa looked confused. "Who is rising, dear?"

"You said bad things are coming and that they are rising..."

Larissa frowned, looking confused. "Really dear, I said no such thing," and she bustled out of the room.

Ann and I stared at each other for a few minutes.

"Maybe she's losing her mind," I said finally. Ann huffed. I got up and took my hair brush to brush my hair when I heard Ann gasp.

"What?" I asked turning to face her with wide eyes, "What happened?"

Her hands were over her mouth and without her telling me I knew.

I moaned, "It's back isn't it?" I brought my hair to the front and saw the white.

"Fab! It's even more than last time!" she said, horrified. She took my hair and touched it gingerly as though afraid it would turn her hair white too.

"I don't understand!" I cried. "How can this be happening? Even my father's hair only started greying recently!"

"You must really be stressed," Ann said, looking at the white hair in awe.

I let out a wail. "What do I do? My magic isn't helping! And it's more than last time! Oh my God Ann! What if the whole thing turns white?"

Ann laughed. "What? No! That's ridiculous Fab!"

"At this rate it could!" I cried.

"No!" Ann said shaking her head. "Just... stop stressing."

"Ann," I said seriously, "I am stressed but not enough to turn my hair white!"

Ann frowned. "Well... I don't know then. Maybe..." she shrugged.

When Ann left, I lay down on my bed. Wondering what on earth was going on, I fell asleep.

It was only a week later that I was able to summon objects, but I needed to know where they were, in order to do it. Once I did it, it became very easy to do it again and again. In three more days I learnt how to cast spells to make things lighter and heavier, to create false images, to protect a place or person, to cause pain, blind someone, to injure them, as well as spells that made me invisible. Some of them seemed so cruel, some required a lot of concentration. Most of them didn't need words, some did, and some needed actual incantations which were difficult to pronounce.

"It's the language of Old," Ilatagite said, after teaching me one really hard incantation that would summon a memory "Of the Beings."

As I developed my magic, my hair started to grey faster until I started to fear that it was my magic's fault, I was pushing myself too much. I was constantly using my magic to hide the white hair but it was spreading too fast.

Nevertheless I was in a very good mood that morning when Ilatagite announced that he would be teaching us a few things in potion-making and identifying poisons.

"I thought I should teach you a bit of potion-making," said Ilatagite, as he entered the room. "There are only two months left, but I think it'll be enough to learn a few basic things, since we're done with our magic lessons. I have taught you all I can on that matter, so now a bit on important potions and herbs, how to identify poisonous plants and such. I will also teach you how to make a potion to heal wounds, fever and so on."

"We don't have any ingredients or anything," Irena said.

"I shall provide that," he replied. "Everything you need is in that cupboard," he said as a huge cupboard appeared next to the blackboard. On the blackboard, ingredients and instructions were listed.

Everyone filed past, taking weird apparatuses and phials out of the cupboard and then went and sat at their desks.

I was the last one. "Fabiana," he said. He had just got back yesterday; it had been two days since our last practice session.

"Yes sir?"

"Tomorrow, same time and place."

I nodded and started to search through the cupboards for the things I needed. There were lots of phials, one of which looked like blood. I shuddered.

I sat at my desk; I was in between Irena and Elvin.

I saw Ann standing at the farthest side of the group, looking lost. I also noticed with a jolt that James was looking at me, *again*. I'd seen what he and Vandra had been doing near the woods the other day, ugh. Vandra seemed to be dazed after that. I hoped she wasn't in love or anything, he didn't seem like the kind to fall in love with.

I quickly focused my attention on Ilatagite who was standing by a row of weird looking potted plants.

"So does anyone know the first one here?" he asked, pointing to a plant with leaves that were a fierce orange. It had a cluster of silver balls and a blue stem.

"Looks poisonous," Marcus said.

"Not edible for sure," Aero stated.

I didn't think it was poisonous… but it was definitely not edible.

"It isn't poisonous," Elvin said voicing, my thoughts. "I can't remember its name," he continued. "If I remember right it's one of the main ingredients in a potion to cure fever, body aches and such."

"Rightly said, Elvin," Ilatagite said, "it's name is Aurnet. Well, Aurnet here, as he pointed out, is not poisonous till it's fully mature, when its leaves become red."

Then he gestured at the second plant, a green plant with little green leaves that looked quite ordinary.

"What about this?" he asked.

"Is it Chitup?" Vandra asked.

Irena was seated next to Vandra, they had become really close friends. Guess it's not just opposites that attract, I thought.

"No it is not. Chitup is a salve used to ease headaches. Andalucia?" he said suddenly, turning to Ann.

I saw Ann's surprise. She hadn't been paying attention.

"I'm sorry sir, what did you say?"

"Andalucia please pay attention." Vandra smirked. "I was asking whether any of you could identify this plant?"

After a pregnant silence she answered quietly, "Um... no."

"This is a very rare herb known as Ryptos, its leaves will turn blue in about a week, then it is ready to be used in potions. Ryptos is a component in many potions, but rare to find. Also in its raw form, it is used as an anesthetic."

Then he turned to Ann. "I expect you to pay attention in class. Herblore is a very important science, either you pay attention or don't attend my class. Do you understand?"

"Yes sir," Ann mumbled, looking downcast.

Ilatagite continued identifying and telling us the properties of the rest of the plants. A few we guessed. Ann remained quiet throughout the class. She just sat like a statue. I felt bad for her, I wanted to go talk to her, but we were seated too far apart.

James was sitting right behind her. I looked at him. He was now watching Ann. What was his problem? Why did he keep staring like that? As though he wanted to... eat us for dinner or something? I shuddered.

"Fabiana... hello?" I snapped out of my reverie. Kristin was peering at me, looking concerned.

"Uh sorry... daydreaming I guess," I quickly said.

"Oh. Is that why you were staring at James?"

"What?" I asked, appalled. Had I been staring at him? Kristin laughed.

I couldn't have been staring. Oh god, what if I had been staring? He must've heard us, though I don't know how he could have, but he looked at us, haughtily. I looked down into my cauldron. Ilatagite had provided us everything from tiny silver spoons to three different sized knives.

"Making a potion is simple and straightforward," he said. "It's just a matter of proper measurements. You have your ingredients, and the instructions are on the board. I will be doing the rounds and will provide help whenever needed, but otherwise you're on your own. You have half an hour."

I immediately glanced at the board.

Flaxfern powder – 2 medium sized spoons

Jujune – 1 medium sized.

Polymefrald— 3 large spoons

And the list went on and on, fifteen different ingredients! I had taken all of the phials and bottles with the given names on them, but how could you remember so many ingredients?

"No newt's eye?" Irena muttered.

"Newt's eye is a witch ingredient," Ilatagite said. "We make all our potions from herbs and plants."

Witches. They were the dark magic practitioners. Most of their powers were unknown, but anyway they were exiled to the wastelands.

Witches were apparently a Sorcerer's mortal enemies. I gasped.

Kristin looked at me, questioningly. I gave her a weak smile, before looking down at my cauldron again. She had already started. I bent down quickly, searching for the ingredients. They were stored in small crystalline bottles. I grabbed them and placed them on the counter and then proceeded to dice the orange beans – Dehyu beans.

Witches. Oh my god. We had ruled out every possibility of Ann being a Sorcerer, but maybe she was a witch! Or maybe something else. Something that we didn't know about, or something that people said didn't exist but did. So maybe... Ann was something like that. I shuddered.

If she was a witch... and I was a Sorcerer, weren't we supposed to be mortal enemies?

She couldn't be a witch, no, she couldn't.

"Fabiana!" Kristin hissed, "That's mine."

I was holding her bottle of Flaxfern, mine was sitting on the desk, untouched.

"Sorry," I mumbled, giving it back.

For the rest of the class I forced myself to pay attention to my work, and by the end of the class I was feeling pretty good. My potion was simmering, giving off a faint peppermint smell. It was a translucent blue colour, just how Ilatagite said it should be.

I felt a surge of delight as Ilatagite declared my potion the best, which deflated a little when he declared Ann's the worst.

It was giving out a strong smell of... I don't know what exactly. I watched as Ilatagite took her aside with a frown on his face saying something to her in a low tone. I saw Ann mumble something. I couldn't hear that either, I stomped my foot in frustration.

Later during lunch, which was rice, chicken and salad, I asked Ann what happened.

"Uhh... my cough potion wasn't right," she replied quietly.

"What went wrong?" I asked.

"I think I added too much Flaxfern or was it that red berry-like thing..."

"Curin?"

"Yes, that," she said frowning, as I heard something that stopped me from asking her if she was alright or not.

"Yeah, a girl," said Elvin, "a little one, don't know how but they found her body near the woods."

"She died?" Shandre was asking.

"Who died?" I asked.

"A girl from town," Marcus replied grimly.

"How did she die?" Kal asked.

He shrugged. "Same way the other girl did, I suppose."

I didn't feel so good anymore, I felt kind of sick. For the rest of the meal, I pondered over these murders. Who would murder them and why?

I was flummoxed. I wanted to know. I wished I could do something. Use my magic, my powers to help. But fear gnawed my stomach. What if I wasn't able to do it?

I had to leave everything behind if I wanted to truly help.

Ilatagite already knew I was a Sorceress, he would tell the king sooner or later. Maybe he had already informed the king, how was I to know? Why should he, the Royal Sorcerer, keep his word to two young girls? He had been on the warfront; he knew how dire the situation was. And they needed magicians; that much even I knew.

I wondered what I would do if he took me there by force.

I shuddered just at the thought. I wasn't ready to serve the kingdom or fight for my world yet, but what if I didn't have a choice?

13: Alive

The king walked slowly through the corridors until he reached his study. What was the point of this war? To win a kingdom that had no heir? To continue living this miserable existence?

He sighed and sank into his chair.

He could still see them so clearly in his mind—his beautiful wife with her long, golden hair and wise hazel eyes. She always knew how to make things right. And their little boy, Edwin, with his curiosity and innocence. All lost.

He had never expected it. It was a blow directly aimed at his heart. The loss of everything. He had never even thought it possible. How could the castle be attacked? How could one man, just one man, destroy his world and get away with it? And *who* was this man?

The Sorcerer had told him that it was Him that had taken his son. How could He even be alive? What kind of dark magic was it? These were things beyond the understanding of the old king.

How much longer could he hope? He knew there was no point. They were losing the war; he had lost his world.

He sighed. What they needed more than anything was an intervention. The Spirits had helped before, would they not help again? He had already dispatched men to find Athanus but none had returned alive. The other ten kingdoms could only help so much. They were parted from Andoreya by seas and seas, there was no way to get here even with the help of magic.

Before, long back, exchanges between the kingdoms flowed easily, but after the entrance of the Beings into Andoreya back then, the kingdoms were separated by a stronger force. And with the Beings, the flow of magic spread, but now, centuries after their arrival, the tide of magic was ebbing.

The king sighed heavily. He had lost his world but he could not lose his kingdom too. He knelt down to pray for an intervention. If the Spirits had saved them once they could do it again.

Miles away a son heard the prayer and woke up.

143

14: The Dying and the Dead

Andalucia

I felt this weird feeling in the pit of my stomach as Ilatagite started our class on Soulfire.

"Soulfire is, like I told you once before, our life force. It fuels our magic." He clapped his hands together, "And today I'm going to teach you how to perceive it."

We were sitting outdoors, cross legged on the ground. It was a cloudy day, warm and pleasant. I wanted more than anything to roam the woods, ride on Shadow, maybe climb a few trees... but I was stuck here with lessons.

I sighed.

"First, you must relax. Clear your mind," he said. "Let go."

Not very likely, I thought, there's a telepath, that too a creepy one. Letting go would mean letting down my barriers. No way was I doing that.

"Come on," he instructed us, "all of you, close your eyes. Breathe slowly. Relax."

There was a bit of commotion as everyone tried to get comfortable, then closed their eyes.

I kept mine open, until Ilatagite caught me staring at the head of Elvin who was sitting in front of me.

I quickly shut them.

Ilatagite had come behind me. "I said relax, Andalucia, don't tense up."

I bit my lip.

"You can't do it if you don't relax."

Urgh. I didn't want to do it anyway, not when haughty telepath James was around.

But I decided that I'd pretend to, since Ilatagite was standing behind me.

I let my shoulders sag a bit, and started taking deep breaths.

It was somewhat peaceful, the silence. I could hear the rustle of leaves, the flow of water over the pebbles, the birds twittering... it was beautiful. I could hear the soft breathing of the person next to me, Josie?

"Now try to look into yourself" Ilatagite's soft murmur came, "I don't expect you to be able to do it by today... but try. Concentrate on the place where your heart is."

Maybe I should do it too.... I mean what's the harm? It would be fun. And I would only let my guard down for a second.

I relaxed more, letting go. And then, I let my guard down. Nothing that I expected happened, everyone was peaceful now. No one was thinking much, their thoughts were, in a way, lethargic. Once I heard someone's mind I could identify them... it wasn't Josie next to me. It was Dawn. Dawn had recently taken to being beside me all the time. During breakfast, lunch and even dinner he would somehow always end up seated next to me. If I went out for a walk he would be there, if I was trying to read quietly in the library he would be there too. It was just crazy; I hardly had a moment to myself. Unless you counted the times I was in my room, or went for night time strolls. I was beginning to suspect that he liked me, but then that was a stupid idea. But it was still very unnerving.

"Now try to look further into yourself, right to the place where your heart rests," said Ilatagite, "where your Soulfire rests. Everyone has a different colour, it reflects your personality. The bigger and merrier the fire, the longer your life..."

His voice sounded so far off.

Colours. Mine was a green colour.

I meditated, or used to at least. Ryan always said it was good to calm your nerves. And once while meditating I had stumbled upon my Soulfire though I hadn't known what it was then. And not being able to explain it I had kept it to myself. Overcome by the heady calmness I decided to look.

I concentrated slowly on the place in the centre. And very slowly I saw it, a light... green. Green like the forests, green like my eyes. It looked even more beautiful than before.

I tried to see more. Expecting to see the crackling bonfire, enormous dancing flames...

Instead I saw a stuttering fire. Dying embers in a multitude of green shades. It was a breathtakingly beautiful fire but unquestionably dying. My head suddenly felt light, my eyes felt heavy like someone was pressing them down.

I couldn't do anything, as I fell back into the darkness.

'Andalucia,' said the voice.

I wanted to say something but was unable to.

'The game has begun. The wheels are in motion. Do justice. Bring honour. I chose you. Do not fail me.'

And I jerked back to reality, as someone splashed water on my face.

"Ann, wake up! Ann?"

I turned my head and blinked a few times. The sun hurt my eyes, and I immediately shielded them.

"Ann? Are you ok?" someone asked. Kristin? Josie?

"No I'm blind," I mumbled. Had I lost my sight? What had the Spirit warned me of? Was it this?

But I found my vision slowly returning and I relaxed.

"Blind? Blind?" I heard other voices say.

"No she said find, find what?"

"I thought she said kind."

"Andalucia, are you alright?" asked a voice, a more sensitive and sensible one.

"Anda— who?' I said dazedly. Oh wait, that's me.

"She doesn't remember who she is," a girl said, shocked. I'd heard that voice… Josie?

"Ann? Are you okay?" another voice, a less shocked, calmer voice. Fab.

"I'm okay," I mumbled.

"How many fingers am I holding up?" Aero asked, as I sat up.

"I don't know."

"Three? Four?" he asked again, waving his hand in front of my eyes. My head felt heavy.

"I'll chop your fingers if you don't leave me alone," I mumbled annoyed. He pulled his hand away quickly.

"Andalucia? Are you okay?" Ilatagite asked.

"Yes," I said, though I wasn't so sure. How many times had I been asked that question now? And how many times had I lied?

"What happened?" he asked.

"I don't know," I answered truthfully.

Ilatagite watched me for a long time before saying, "Alright, class is over for today. Andalucia I suggest you take some rest. We will meet again on Monday." And then he left.

"What happened?" I asked them. All of them were crowded around me, James was looking at me intently which made me uncomfortable.

"Well, you fainted," Aero answered. He sat on the ground next to me, looking worried.

"I know that," I snapped. "How?"

Everyone looked at each other. "We didn't see. We didn't realise until you fainted. Lyra was the one who noticed first." I looked for her, she wasn't there.

"And where is she?" I asked. Kristin shrugged. I tried to stand up, my legs were wobbly and I was trembling all over. Fab gave me a hand, I gratefully took it.

"Are you okay?" Dawn asked, and I could sense his worry. I nodded, not looking at him.

"I can't believe you fainted," Fab said, laughing quietly.

"Why?" I asked as we went inside the Academy.

"Because... well, that's kind of girlish? You know damsel-in-distress sort of thing."

I glared at her.

"Okay maybe not... but that's the first thing that came into my mind," she said, still laughing.

There was nothing whatsoever girlish about it. It was a completely weird and horrifying experience. Weird because I had had a conversation with a Spirit. Horrifying because now I knew one thing.

I was going to die.

Soon.

On Sunday morning, I sat in the library with a novel. But my mind was too disturbed, and kept dwelling on my... imminent death.

Maybe I had been wrong, maybe I wouldn't die. After all, come on, Soulfire? Lifelines? Pshaw.

"And have you seen anything of my future?" I heard someone ask in a silky voice.

The good thing about the place where I was sitting was that people couldn't easily spot me. I had drawn the curtains over the window seat I was sitting on, so I wasn't exactly noticeable. I was hidden from view.

But I could hear them from my spot. They were probably standing behind the shelf. I peeked through the curtains, I was right. They stood behind the shelf. I could see them now.

It was James and Lyra.

"It doesn't work like that," answered Lyra, looking a bit tense. "I can't see what I want, I just get random glimpses."

"Lyra," he said softly, "you have nothing to be afraid of."

I frowned, they sounded like... lovers. Well James did. But, James and Lyra? James seemed like the type who would go for people like... well, Irena.

But what he said next unruffled me even more.

"I need you to tell me what you saw in your vision, the night that girl died."

I squinted, trying to see Lyra's expression. She looked dazed.

"I saw her dead body, that's all."

The girl had died weeks ago, why was he so interested to know, now?

"Did you see who did it?" he asked.

"No."

"Have you seen any other visions about deaths?"

I saw Lyra's face crumple. "Yes, I saw... mine."

I flinched.

"And who killed you?"

What? Kill Lyra? Why?

Suddenly the dazed look on Lyra's face changed into one of suspicion. "I didn't say anyone killed me."

For a brief minute James looked surprised before his face became impassive again and he said "My mistake."

But she still looked suspicious. "What – what's going on –?"

Suddenly he held her by her shoulders and stared into her eyes. She looked shocked, was he going to kiss her? I didn't want to see *that*!

But apparently not. "Forget this conversation ever happened. Now go. And if you ever see any more visions come and tell me," he said firmly.

Lyra nodded, then she walked away slowly. James stood there, looking thoughtful. He took a deep breath, that reminded me of a predator sniffing for its prey, and then his eyes suddenly focused on my spot and I quickly let the curtain fall.

Oh my God Thor, he's seen me. Or rather sniffed me out. How had he – ugh, not now Ann.

From behind the curtain I saw his form move towards me, I quickly opened the window and jumped out of it and scuttled down the roof. By the time I reached the ground, I was breathing hard. Had he seen me? I didn't think so; he probably saw my form but didn't know who it was. What had I just witnessed?

I felt confused, it made no sense.

James wanted to know about Lyra's visions, but why was she even telling him? And… she had seen her death? Hers? And he had asked who had killed her, but why would anyone kill Lyra? Because, she's a seer, I thought slowly. But even so, there are so many seers, why would you kill her? Maybe because she had a vision which… somehow threatened somebody. Who? James?

My head hurt with all the questions.

I bounded up the stairs, trying to make sense of what had just happened when I crashed into him. James.

I swallowed.

"Hello Andalucia," he said, smiling.

"Hi," I said shortly. "Would you mind? You're blocking my way," I said with surprising composure.

"Of course," he said, moving and giving me way.

I climbed up, feeling relieved, when he called, "Oh and Andalucia…" I turned my head slightly. He smiled. "I know it was you in the library."

My breath caught. "I… I don't know what you're talking about James," I stammered, trying to look confused.

"I think you do," he said, his smile widening, "and you should know I'm onto you."

"Sorry?" I said, my heart pounding so hard, I thought it might pop out of my chest.

"Good day, Andalucia," he said, walking towards the entrance of the Academy and stepping outside.

My hands held on to the railings, as I felt my heart slowly resume its normal speed. My mind was spinning, as I tried to take in what had happened. I scowled at his retreating back, my courage returning to me now. I did a cruel impression of him and murmured, "Good day Andalucia," in varying degrees of intensity and ridicule until I got the fear out of my system.

I should become a comedian, I thought with a snort.

One thing was sure though, James was NOT a telepath. I knew that much because of what my mind-reading skills had told me. I didn't know how he had managed to fool Ilatagite, or was it something like I had done. Was Ilatagite covering up for him like he was doing for Fab? Did Ilatagite know what he was?

Which brought me to the most disturbing question. What *was* he?

I was ambling around, trying to figure out if I should confront James or ignore everything, when I heard footsteps. A soldier entered, looking unsure of himself. His uniform was stained with dirt and blood, and he was wearing a haggard expression. He looked utterly lost.

"Do you need some help, Sir?" I asked.

"Ann," he said, and I stared. How did he know me? "It's me, Nick."

"Nick?" I repeated aghast, staring at my cousin, who looked about thirty.

He stood there staring at me. And then he moved towards me, slowly, like a sleepwalker, as if each step he took would bring him down, and then he was in front of me and he looked torn and lost before he engulfed me in a hug. I was so shocked I didn't move. This was Nick! Upholder of rules and believer of norms! What was he doing hugging me in the middle of the hall, all covered in blood and sweat?

"He's dead," Nick murmured and I could feel him shaking. "Ann, he's dead."

"Nick, what –?" I said into the dirty coat. The stench of blood overwhelmed me. I felt sick.

"Nellie's dead."

I froze in his arms.

"I'm going home. I was on the way for – for the funeral. He's – he's gone."

He pulled away, shaking with sobs. "I couldn't save him Ann. He saved me and I couldn't save him. If I was – if I hadn't been such a dolt –"

But nothing made sense anymore, I didn't understand. How could Nellie die? How could he? Nellie… so strong, brave and cheerful. How could he die?

Just like how Ryan had died.

I sniffed, oh Nellie.

I don't think both of us noticed the others come down for dinner or them looking and whispering in shock at a boy and girl sitting together, so close, their hands held. But we were so consumed in our grief.

"Nick?" Aero said, "Is that you?"

Irena and Kristin were looking at me in shock but I didn't care. I sobbed and sobbed into my hands. I felt Fab's arms around my shoulder. I heard Aero murmuring "No, no" over and over again, but nothing registered in my head except for one cold fact: Nellie was dead.

We were allowed to go home, Aero and I, along with Nick and Nellie's… body. There were pallbearers who took him ahead of us. On any other occasion I would've been ecstatic to go home and my family would've been ecstatic to see me. Ma made a comment that I had lost weight but nothing else. No one talked. A dreary silence filled our home. Nick's home was even worse. But it wasn't just our families. The whole town seemed to mourn. Everyone loved Nellie. It wasn't just that though. There were hardly any people left in Gondon, what with the war and the magicians. And the evacuation. Father told me about it the night before the funeral.

"The King has arranged a place for all the citizens to evacuate to. It's supposed to be an island protected by magic. Many people have been leaving. Your professor, Mr. Burns and his family left with the exception of his son… Gerry was it?"

I nodded, tight-lipped.

"He's fighting."

Great, the one boy I like and who is nice to me, goes off to die.

But I was tired and exhausted and out of tears.

Who needed beaus and love anyways? Not me. I didn't even need people. I'm a magician. I have… superpowers. Let everybody die, who cares?

And though I did think I was out of tears, my vision blurred with them. Luckily my father didn't notice and I blinked them away quickly.

"We thought about evacuating…" my father murmured, so softly that I almost didn't catch it.

"But that's a great idea!" I said.

"Except we'd be leaving you behind so we decided against it."

"But I'm in Rivendell! I'll be fine! You must, absolutely must go to this place. It's safer! Better."

"Your mother and I have discussed this already. We cannot leave you and hide."

"But you don't see me anyways. I'll be going to the castle."

A silence followed in which my father looked at me, his expression sombre. I took a deep breath.

"Father, please. I'll be fine."

"No Andalucia." And I knew nothing I said would make a difference. I felt angry and frustrated.

"What about Arni then?" I asked, trying to keep the anger out of my voice. "Send him at least with someone we know. Why does he have to suffer for this? It'll be safer for him. Please."

My father was silent for a long time.

"We could send him with your Aunt Rose."

I felt myself sag into the couch with relief.

I got up slowly, said goodnight to my father and went up to my room. My mother was with Aunt Jennifer.

It was a cloudy day. And it rained during the funeral service. People spoke a lot about Nellie, about how he was always nice and funny and the life of a party. Aunt Jennifer had been sobbing the whole time. Nick just stood there, his eyes glassy. I don't think he heard anything much. His speech had been short.

"Nelson has always been.…. always been a better man than I ever will be. He's always been a source of inspiration—" and then he had looked down at his shoes and said no more.

My speech had been short too.

"He was a brother to me, almost a replacement for the one I lost. And… Nellie, wherever you are I know you'll be laughing at the chaos you've created by leaving us. You've always.…. I hope you're happy where you are now." It's a good thing it was raining because I couldn't stop crying.

I was the last to leave the funeral place. I sat there near his grave until the sun set. Someone called me. I got up slowly and walked away from his grave. I turned back to look and saw someone.

A person in black robes and a black hood, looking like Death himself.

My heart froze. From where I was standing it looked almost like Nellie from behind. The person knelt next to the grave.

"Ann!" Ma called.

The person laid flowers, then turned to face me slowly. I couldn't make out his face because of the rain and the hood… and the dark shadows. But I was trembling.

And then he walked away. I was shaking for a long time afterward.

I returned the next morning. Father arranged a carriage to take me along with Aero. We didn't talk.

The death of Nellie weighed on us, suffocating.

15: Prophecies of Doom

Fabiana

Aero and Ann returned in two days. I'd never seen Ann so gloomy. She had dark circles around her eyes, every morning she came down with red puffy eyes. I tried to console her as much as I could, but I couldn't get through to her. She spent hours staring blankly at the walls.

The weather matched Ann's mood. It was raining heavily and continuously. If the rain kept at this, we'd all be drowned. And therefore it wasn't a surprise when most of us fell ill.

"I don't need to be in the sick room," I tried telling Kal, as she dragged me into the room downstairs where Ann, Kristin and Cassius were already being looked after.

"You have a red nose, Fab," she said, "and eyes. And you're talking like you're drunk."

I grumbled. The sick room looked sick to me, I could hear sniffles and sneezes everywhere. Kal and Elvin were tending to everyone along with Larissa.

By nightfall I had a fever and with the fever came the nightmares. One stood out amongst all others, the only one with no blood and gore in it, but much more heart-breaking.

Tears blurred her eyes as Sylvia finished off the letter that would change their lives. She couldn't do it anymore. And for the sake of her child, she knew… she had to do this. If she was alive her child would be in danger. How long could she keep hiding her illness? What if it came out when she least expected it and… did something unspeakable? No good could come out of her existence…. nothing but harm to the people she loved who knew nothing about her deplorable state. Besides He would always be after her, shadowing her life as He always did. She wouldn't let Him shadow her daughter's life as well. Sylvia angrily brushed away her tears, sealed the letter and placed it on the table where her husband would see it. Good thing he wasn't home. By the time he came, everything would be over. She would never see him again. And all the man had ever done was fall in love with a girl like her. *A girl whom he knew nothing about. Sylvia rose and went into her daughter's room. The little girl was snoring gently, her small hand curled over her chest.*

"My little angel," she whispered. The girl was special, she knew. She had been told. But she would protect her child as long as she could, even in her death. Her child would not live under eternal fear. In a stronger voice she said "You will not live the same lie as mine. He will not touch you. Ezrae tal garde si rect. Ezrae tal garde si rect. Ezrae tal garde si rect."

She kissed her daughter gently on the forehead, transferred every bit of power in her to the little girl and slipped out of the room.

In the evening when her husband returned he would find his daughter awake and bawling, and his wife on the floor, cold as ice. In her daughter, however, Sylvia left a gift and a curse, the girl was doomed to her mother's same destiny but she was the Chosen, and unknown to the infant, Spirits watched over her, waiting for her to fulfil her destiny or meet the same fate as her mother.

I woke up, breathing hard.

"Hey, are you okay?" Cassius asked me in a whisper.

I nodded. I took the glass of water near my bed and gulped it down eagerly. I tried to remember what I had just seen but the feeling of terror overwhelmed me, making it difficult to think.

When I had calmed down sufficiently I tried to recollect it. But all I could see in my mind was my father crying on the floor.

Cassius was still peering at me anxiously. He looked so young.

"How old are you?" I asked him.

"Fourteen," he said shyly.

"You must miss your mother."

"Yeah," he admitted. "I think it's harder for her though."

I sighed.

"This war… it's just destroying everything," he said quietly.

"Yeah."

I recovered quickly under the watchful eye of Kal. I was worried about the two days' class I had missed with Ilatagite. I was doing much better than before. I thought about what Ilatagite had said about him knowing a Warrior and Shape-shifter. He was joking right? I mean he did say what if. How could they possibly exist? I mean… they couldn't.

Irena had asked Ilatagite if we could go to the town in the evening and he had agreed. What was the point of going to town? There were hardly any people left, only dead bodies and mourners. I cringed at my harsh thoughts. When Lyra asked me to join them, I declined. I didn't even feel like it. I was still pondering what I had seen. I couldn't make head or tail of the dream. It felt important, if only I could remember it.

I was climbing the stairs, lost in my thoughts when I crashed into James.

"Hello Fabiana," he said. "Aren't you coming to town?"

"Uh…" I swallowed, why was he so handsome? "I can't, I have some work to do."

"Ah," he said smiling, "always working aren't you Fabiana? Late into the night…"

My breath caught. What did he mean by that? Had he seen me returning from practice late in the night? But no, that couldn't be, I would've noticed, wouldn't I?

"I was hoping," he continued in his silky voice, "that I'd be able to talk to you, alone."

"Alone?" I repeated, my insides going cold. "Why?"

He shrugged. "Just to talk. You aren't scared to talk to me, are you, Fabiana?" he asked, extending his hand, almost touching my face. I backed away so quickly, he pulled his hand away.

"So you are scared," he said with a smile that made my heart pound.

"No," I said shaking my head. "I just… um…"

Ilatagite's voice cut through, sharply. He came from his office and looked at the two of us. "Is something wrong?"

"No, Professor," James said smoothly, "I was just asking Fabiana why she wasn't coming to town. We are all going you see."

"She's only just recovering and too tired to be prancing around," Ilatagite said.

James bowed his head and left without even glancing at me. I felt relieved now that he was gone.

"Are you better?" Ilatagite asked me.

"Yes," I nodded, though I wasn't.

I suddenly realised Ilatagite wasn't alone. There was a huge person standing next to him. I saw a sword hanging from his waist. I couldn't see his face because he was wearing a cloak and the hood covered most of his face. I made out high cheekbones, and stubble marked his face. He seemed familiar. Oh. It was the man Ann and I had seen a few weeks back. Why did he keep coming here? I frowned, was he a soldier?

I thanked Ilatagite and ran up the stairs, my heart pounding. I thought I heard Ilatagite say something but it was probably to the man, though I was sure he had said my name.

I entered my room and shut the door behind me. I was about to collapse on my bed when I saw the tiny, bound book on it. I picked it up. I knew Ilatagite had left it there.

I picked it up, lay down and flipped through it, trying to cool my mind until my attention was arrested by a sentence.

There are not one but numerous worlds, the Spirit World being one of the most evolved worlds. The different worlds are like threads to one tapestry. Some are more colourful, some dull, and so on.

What? Dull? Colourful? How does that even apply to worlds?

The Lake of Life is believed to hide the entrance to the Spirit World, but entering the lake itself is a feat no mortal can achieve. Also without the proper magic, the lake will not yield the entrance. It is also said that if a person bathes in the water of the lake, they will be healed completely from any ailment.

I slammed the book, what a load of nonsense. How stupid, such things can't exist.

Lake of life, lost cities and indestructible beings, God!

If such things existed shouldn't life be easy? A walk through a rose garden?

Yeah, *if only* my life was a walk through a rose garden.

I slept fitfully that night. I dreamt of my mother. I dreamt of her crying and talking to me, but I couldn't make out her words. I tried to tell her that. I tried to tell her that I wished she hadn't left me, hadn't died, hadn't killed herself. Because I knew with sudden certainty that she had done it. She had taken her life and left me and my father alone. I tried to ask her why she had done it. But she didn't answer me. She just kept saying over and over again that she did it for the best. And one day I would understand.

I woke up crying. The tears wouldn't stop, so I let them flow. I wondered how different my life would've been if my mother had been alive.

My father was a good parent, he had tried his best to raise me right and give me all the comforts he could. But he was never around. I had mostly been raised by Lina and Ann's family. I loved them all, but sometimes a girl needed her mother. Right now was one of those moments.

"I see…" giggled Vandra, her hands on either side of my forehead, "ooh! A handsome, tall, dark stranger with the most beautiful blue eyes."

"Anyone we know?" I asked, anxiously.

"No," she said with a grin. "Here I'll show you."

I hesitated. What if I didn't like the person I saw?

We were sitting in the lounge, Vandra, Kal, Kristin and I. Vandra had advanced a lot in her Heartsight abilities and so she was prophesying our future husbands or soul mates or something.

I know, stupid. In our defence, we were bored.

Without waiting for my approval, she decided to go ahead and show me.

My mind was flooded with the face of a young man. He had dark hair and high cheekbones, and sparkling blue eyes. He was one of the most handsome men I had ever seen. I didn't know him but he seemed familiar. I felt dizzy.

I wish I knew everything but I don't, all I know is I love you now and forever.

I frowned, trying to get rid of the handsome man's face and the words that didn't belong to me.

But with his face merged another one. I heard Vandra gasp. A boy with a tumble of fair hair… and…

Vandra pulled away frowning hard.

"Vandra? What was that? Who were they?"

"They? How many soul mates do you have?" someone teased.

"I don't know," Vandra said. "I guess I messed up or something. Do you know either of them?"

I shook my head. "I've never seen them before. How—how does your power work? What relation do they have to me?" I asked, trying to rid my mind of the faces she had shown me.

"I don't know exactly how it works," she said. Everyone was listening.

"It's… the person I showed you, he's the one person you'll love no matter what, uh your soul mate! But I can't say when and where you'll meet or if you'll ever meet or… or if you will end up marrying each other. I see the people you love and will love. I don't see the stories of these people, I don't know who they are or anything. I just know they mean something to you or will in the future." She shrugged. "I don't know why there were two. I guess maybe my concentration faltered."

"It's interesting," I said, as I pulled back.

"It's rubbish," Kristin said, yawning. "Soul mates. Hmph."

"It's not rubbish!" Vandra said angrily.

I quickly slipped away, not wanting to get involved in another cat fight.

"Where are you going?" I asked Ann as she slid down the banister.

"To see Shadow. Coming?"

"I have work," I said gloomily.

She grinned. "Aw, poor miserable you. Stuck inside on such a glorious day."

I stuck out my tongue at her, then I remembered what I wanted to ask her. "Ann, is it possible to have memories of someone else?"

"What?" she scoffed.

I shifted uneasily. "Like have memories and thoughts that aren't yours?"

"Then whose would they be?"

"I don't know," I said honestly, "but is it possible?"

"Right now," Ann said, her eyes darkening, "anything is possible."

I sat at my writing desk. I've always had this déjà vu sort of thing where I saw two images at once, one from the present and one, I think, from the past. It had happened more often over the last year. But whose memories and thoughts? And what connection did it have to me? I shook my head. Maybe I was working too hard.

Okay, let's see… healers. I wrote the heading on the parchment.

Hmm…

I riffled through the pages, how to start, how to start?

Healer magic is rather unique, I thought, writing it down. Unlike other magic, what they do is actually take the patient's illness, absorb the discomfort and dissipate it.

I stared at it, it sounded stupid. I crumpled the parchment and took a fresh one.

I wrote the heading on it again.

I stared at my handwriting. I knew it was similar to my mother's from one letter she had left for us just before she had died. She must've known she was going to die. My father didn't know I had read that letter. I had well… stumbled upon it in his private study that I was not allowed to enter. I hadn't meant to pry, I had been searching for the only photograph we had of my mother. I thought he might have kept it there. He had, along with the letter.

Once I had read it, I spent a good few hours crying. I wanted to keep it with me but I figured he would probably notice. And I had a feeling he had kept it away from me because he had thought it would upset me. It did. So I kept it back. But I did sneak in a couple of times to read it again until I had every word etched in my memory.

Dear Manzeria and my beloved girl,

I wish I could stay with you and be content in your love. But I can't.

Manzeria, I thought our love would cure me. It did cure me for a long time. I felt better; I thought I was almost cured.

But I haven't been cured.

I won't live long enough to see you grow and become a beautiful young lady, darling. I've tried to give you as much as I can of myself. I know one day you will find out why I died. And I hope you can forgive me for it.

But always know that I had no choice. I could not fight my illness.

Be strong my little flower.

My love, I'm sorry I could not love you the way you loved me. I know I can blame it on this sickness of mine, but… that would not be right.

I did try. I want you to know that.

Always,

Sylvia.

I felt anger flood me, and sorrow in equal measure. She had no choice, I thought, she was ill. She couldn't be cured. I wondered what sort of illness she had, sounded terrible.

Someone knocked, and I jumped. Shaking my head at my reaction and quickly wiping my tears, I got up to open the door. It was Lyra.

"Hello," I said opening the door.

"Hi," she mumbled. "Can I come in?"

I opened the door wider to let her in. She seemed tense. She sat down on my bed, as I shut the door behind me.

"Are you okay?" I asked. "You seem… nervous."

"I am," she said with a sigh. "I have to talk to you."

"Sure," I said sitting on my chair. "You can tell me anything."

She nodded fervently. "Yeah, but… I don't think you'll like what I'm about to tell you."

"Uh… alright," I said slowly, "you can, uh, still tell me, if you want, that is."

She looked at me, her blue eyes looked worried.

"I had a dream last night," she said, "about you."

"Oh," I said "and?"

She hesitated before blurting: "You're a Sorceress."

I'm a Sorceress. Mother! I'm a Sorceress!

I froze.

You can't be darling, there are no Sorceresses. Only Sorcerers, love.

"I mean," she amended, "in my dream you were."

I relaxed. "Uh, right," I said with nervous laughter. "Like that's even possible."

"Yeah," she said laughing too. But the worried look didn't leave her eyes. "There was something else I wanted to tell you Fabiana but Ilatagite doesn't want to –"

Suddenly she froze, her eyes went unfocused.

"Lyra?" I said, "Are you alright?"

She suddenly started to tremble, her eyeballs rolling in their sockets as she said in a coarse voice:

"When all else fails

Sorceress shall cast spells of forbidden power,

Open she shall door to unknown.

Strength be the key to lead in the dark,

Wield the old, wield the forgotten, to leave the mark.

Blue blood shall be spilled to shift the lock,

Blue blood shall commit the final act, and avenge life lost.

Guardian must cross threshold of life

For only she can, spirit that she be.

Should they succeed

We shall be freed forever so

From abyss of life, end of the world.

But failure if be

Into the darkness forever we plunge.

One way or another

Life will be lost

For price must be paid for power so great." Lyra choked but still her grasp on my hand was tight, drops of blood were forming where her nails had dug into my wrist. *"He searches the land to find the Four. One is already his prisoner. One is under his watch, One he shall soon have, One more to find. He knows. He knows where you are. Run. RUN!*" The last word was a scream, her grip on me loosened, her head fell back and she started to shake violently.

"Professor!" I screamed, blasting my door open with my magic. "Larissa! Somebody, help!"

Spit was dribbling down Lyra's mouth, "SOMEBODY!" I screamed, tears streaming down my face, "HELP!"

"And what exactly did she say?" asked Ilatagite, once I had calmed down.

Larissa was wiping Lyra's face with a wet sponge; she had sent out all those who had rushed into my room after I had yelled, and moved Lyra into her room. For a small woman she had lots of strength. Irena sat next to the bed, her face white. I was sitting on a chair in Lyra's room.

Only one person wasn't amongst those who ran into my room. Ann.

"I don't know," I sobbed. "Something about... something about spells and death. She said... she said... a prophecy, and then she... said someone was coming. He was searching for..." I sniffed, "the four or something. And... and then she told me to run. She looked like – she looked so scared!"

"I need to know what exactly she said," he said hushing me. "Don't cry now."

"I'm sorry Professor, but can I come in?" said a voice. It was Ann. Her face was distraught as she entered, her hair dishevelled.

"I am so very sorry Fab," she said kneeling next to me. "Are you okay?"

"No, no I'm not," I cried. "Lyra – something happened to her. She had fits!"

"I heard," Ann said grimly.

"Where were you?" asked Ilatagite.

"I had to go to the town sir, to send a letter to my parents," she said.

Ilatagite put a hand on his head, tired. "I need to know what exactly it was she said to you, Fabiana."

I sniffed, "I can't remember the exact words. Something about the end of the world..."

"The end of the world?" repeated Ilatagite, looking pale.

"She says that a lot," said Irena suddenly. "She always used to talk about the world ending, and everyone dying. She used to have nightmares."

Ilatagite nodded. "I see." He stood up. "Maybe we should leave Lyra to rest. Why don't you both come with me?" Ann helped me up. I was shaking.

"I think maybe we shall sit in your room, Fabiana," said Ilatagite.

I nodded, wiping my tears away.

My room was a mess. The bedspread was all rumpled and lay on the floor. There was water on the floor, I didn't even know where it came from.

Ilatagite sat on the chair. We sat on the bed. "Fabiana, please... try to remember what she said."

I sucked in my breath. "I told you she said something about the world ending, and a Sorcerer casting spells. She said something about the ... about the Four."

"Sir?" said Ann, "I can... I can look into her mind and tell you what she heard. It will be there, recorded in her mind."

Ilatagite looked surprised. "Is that a power of yours, Andalucia?"

"Sort of," she said quietly.

"I do not have time to ask you why you never told me this before. I am supposed to leave for the Capital soon. So if you can, please do it."

Ann turned to me. "Fab, loosen up a bit. I want only that memory, trust me."

I was too tired to argue. I closed my eyes. "Do whatever you want."

I felt her enter my mind, I didn't say anything. I just kept quiet as she searched my mind. I could feel her mind. Her nervousness, her worry, concern... and I could tell that she was hiding something.

She heard me because she said *I'll tell you later.*

Then the memory started to play in my mind, I cringed seeing everything happen again.

I can't, I said.

Just once Fab, once.

I resigned myself to my fate, as she accessed the memory.

Don't worry, you'll be okay. As she withdrew she granted me a calm mind. And I relaxed.

I opened my eyes, as Ann started to recite:
"When all else fails
Sorceress shall cast spells of forbidden power,
Open she shall door to unknown.
Strength be the key to lead in the dark,
Wield the old, wield the forgotten, to leave the mark.

Blue blood shall be spilled to shift the lock,
Blue blood shall commit the final act and avenge life lost.
Guardian must cross threshold of life
For only she can, spirit that she be.
Should they succeed
We shall be freed forever so
From abyss of life, end of the world.
But failure if be
Into the darkness forever we plunge.
One way or another
Life will be lost
For price must be paid for power so great."

"She also said something about someone searching for the four. That this person had found one of the four, one he was uh… watching and one he would have soon and there was one more to find. Then she told Fab," Ann paused before saying, "she asked Fab to run."

Ilatagite was frowning.

Ann petitioned to Thor.

Ilatagite was quiet but I knew what it meant. "Someone's after me."

Ann looked at me.

I knew it sounded stupid, but I was also sure that what I said was right.

"Lyra had come into my room to warn me about that. And the prophecy or whatever it was… it says Sorceress."

Ilatagite's brow furrowed. "Yes it does."

"Why would they be after you?" Ann asked dubiously.

"I don't know… maybe because I'm the last Sorcerer left?" I felt like crying, the words hit me so hard. I bowed my head so that Ilatagite couldn't see my face.

"Your hair…" Crap! My head shot up and I looked at him with fright.

"Your hair is turning white?" he asked in disbelief.

I tried to be nonchalant about it. "I guess it's the stress."

But Ilatagite wasn't listening to me. "How long has it been happening?"

"Um what, professor?"

"Since when did it start turning white?"

"A few weeks back," I answered confusedly. I looked at Ann who seemed as clueless as me as to why Ilatagite would be interested in such paltry, well, not that paltry, issues.

"That would mean…." Ilatagite said, and we waited for his next words eagerly, there was an explanation! Had his hair turned white too? But his hair was auburn as always with few, very few strands of grey. I wondered vaguely how old he was. Sorcerers aged twice as slow as magicians.

But he didn't complete his sentence. He got up, coughed, and said, "Very well, I have to leave. Fabiana don't worry about anything, I assure you nothing will happen to you while you are under my roof. No danger will come to you. Andalucia, I want to speak to you," he said, as he left the room.

Ann and I exchanged looks. "That's just it, what if the danger is already under the roof?" she said softly. More to herself than to me, I think.

She sighed "I think you better sleep Fab."

"Ann—" I said, before she shut the door.

She stopped and her head peered through the door.

"Don't leave me alone please," I said, almost pleading.

"I'll be back as soon as I can," she promised.

I was standing on a cliff, looking down on a glittering sea that looked like it went on forever.

It was beautiful.

Then I heard someone's voice.

A silky, velvety voice.

I turned and saw a boy of about nineteen or twenty standing there. He had jet black hair and light blue eyes.

He looked oddly familiar.

"So you are Fabiana," said the voice.

I frowned, he looked so familiar, but I just couldn't place him.

"I've been searching a long time you know," he continued. "I thought the only Sorcerer left was that old man but then I found out about you. Do you know how?"

I shook my head. Who was he?

Whoever he was, he made me tremble.

"One of my men told me, he found out about you. At first he wasn't sure which of the two it was. And I was dearly hoping it wasn't her. It wouldn't be very nice if it was her." He shook his head as though to clear it. "But then one day he caught you going into the Sorcerer's study at night, and then many days after he watched you and the same thing kept happening. So he tipped me off, told me he had a feeling he had found the Sorceress."

He said Sorceress, stressing on the 's' sound. It sounded like he hissed the word. Sorceresssss….

I licked my lips.

"Don't worry I won't harm you. Not yet anyway. I'm still wondering what I should do, you see. My brothers and sister think they can outsmart me, how delusional they are."

He laughed, a blood-curdling laugh.

Finally I managed to stammer: "I—you—who are you?"

He laughed again, but this time, as he laughed, the waves rose and came to my level. "You don't know?" he asked, his blue eyes like shards of ice, darkening on blue, becoming black like coals. Then the waves crashed over me and I was pulled down into the depths of the sea.

I was drowning, kicking my legs to reach the surface. But there was something that was pulling me down, with horror I watched as a slimy green tentacle wrapped itself around my leg and pulled me down.

I woke up drenched in sweat, and breathing hard. There were goose bumps all over my arms, I was shivering.

I jumped when I saw the figure on my chair. It was Ann. I relaxed. Her head was on a book and her body rose and fell with each breath. She must've fallen asleep while reading.

I turned back to what had wakened me. What kind of nightmare was that? Or was it even a nightmare? It seemed so real… I still felt the horror as the creature pulled me down into the depths of the sea.

I took a deep breath and told myself: It's just a dream Fab; nothing more. But in my hand I was clutching a black feather and it didn't seem like a dream, it seemed frighteningly real.

The inexplicable feeling that I was in danger only increased.

16: More Than a Freak

Andalucia

When Fab screamed for help, I was in the forest talking to Rose.

The first time I met her was the day after I heard about the girl who had been killed. But then I hadn't known that she was a ghost when I met her.

Shadow had got pretty spooked by her, but I thought she was nice. She was really pretty, and petite. Like a little angel, an angel who couldn't remember her own name.

At first I thought maybe she didn't want to tell me her name, but later – when I kept seeing her every time I came riding into the woods, always in the same place, under the same tree – I started to feel that something was definitely wrong.

Slowly she did tell me that her name was Rose. When she did, my heart stopped.

But hey, I was being stupid, she couldn't be the same Rose who was murdered a week before, right? I mean no, that was silly; I wouldn't be able to talk to her then.

For a while I lied to myself, making excuses for her memory loss and such, but soon even I couldn't come up with a good enough excuse.

After the death of Rose, two more girls had died, and their bodies had been found in these very woods.

But I couldn't not go there. I had to know, had to know if she was the same girl… who died a week before.

So when I saw her next, I asked my stranger friend questions about where she lived, why she was always in the forest, where did she go when I wasn't around and such.

She had no answer. She said she couldn't remember.

By then it was getting really difficult to ignore the fact that I could see, partially, through her.

My excuse before was, hey, maybe she's a dryad. Though they didn't exist, of course. Not in Andoreya at least.

Now I had to face it, and the truth hit me right in the face. Of course, she wasn't alive. She couldn't be. She was always here, she never left this place. It was like… her soul haunted the tree! She couldn't remember the last time she had eaten or drunk something, and I could see through her!

She was dead alright.

Now how do you break such news to a person, or rather, a ghost?

This is what I did. I took a deep breath and said "Rose, I think… that um you might just be, well… you are… you know… dead."

Her eyes widened so much I thought they might pop out. If she was alive that is. And even then eyeballs don't pop out do they? But Rose's looked like they would. Okay, maybe I shouldn't have told her. What have you done now, Ann?

"Rose?" I said in a small voice, feeling extremely guilty. I'm a heartless idiot. No wait, I'm a heartless freak who sees dead people.

"How?" she asked after what seemed like hours to me.

Oh thank Thor.

"I think… you were murdered…" I said slowly. "In fact… I think you were murdered right under this tree," I stated.

"This tree?" she repeated, looking dubiously at me.

I nodded, "I always meet you under this tree, never anywhere else."

I examined the tree. Nothing whatsoever would suggest that someone had died right under it and was haunting it now.

I admit I didn't know how to break bad news to a person. But after I explained to her, and comforted her she accepted the fact that she was indeed dead. Well, she didn't accept it aloud. But the next question was why she was still here? Why hadn't she gone to… wherever dead people's souls go? And why could I see her?

Seeing souls was not a power of mine, I have never been able to see them. Suppose I could now, what did it mean?

So now I was trying to find out that answer. But no matter how much I searched through books and puzzled over it I had no answer but one: the soul wasn't at rest. It wanted something.

But what?

Who else to ask except my best friend the Sorceress?

I got up early on Wednesday morning and sneaked into her room.

"Fab!" I hissed, shaking her. She was tossing around in her bed, murmuring.

"No, I don't understand," she whispered. "Come back!" she yelled, sitting up with a jolt.

Then she saw me. "Oh God!" she said scrambling in her bed, pulling her covers up.

"Fab, it's me!" I said, holding the lantern higher so she could see.

"Ann!" she cried. "What on earth –?" She sat up, rubbing her eyes. "What is it?"

"You were mumbling in your sleep," I said.

"Really?" she said her eyes widening. "What did I say?"

"It was kind of incoherent…." I admitted.

"Oh," she mumbled. "Is that why you woke me?"

"Uh… well I needed to talk to you. Can you come down?"

I climbed out the window, and jumped down the roof. She came the same way after about fifteen minutes, dressed for the day.

"I miss doing that, you know," she said.

"What's stopping you?" I asked.

She raised her eyebrows "It's alright for you, but if I do it as well…."

"Alright for me," I laughed. If only.

"Why did you wake me?" she asked. "Are you alright?"

"I wanted to tell you something," I said slowly.

She waited. "Uh remember that girl who died? The one Lyra saw a vision of?"

"Yeah," Fab answered, nodding.

"Well…" I hesitated before I blurted, "I saw her!"

"Saw who?" she asked, looking confused.

I took a deep breath. "I saw the dead girl… Rose."

Fab frowned before saying, "That's not funny, Ann."

"I'm not joking, Fab," I said, my nervousness turning to indignation.

"Don't be silly Ann. You probably saw someone else whose name is Rose."

I hadn't been looking at her while I had said this, now I looked at her and without even blinking, I said: "I saw the dead girl Rose."

"You think you saw a dead person?" she asked.

"Noooo," I said slowly, "I know I saw a dead person."

"It isn't funny, Ann!" She looked cross.

"When did I say it is? I'm dead serious Fab. Do I look like I'm joking?" I asked, angry now. How could she not believe me? Okay I did play pranks on people a lot, but even I wouldn't joke about such things!

"Why do you think I woke you up at four in the morning?" I asked. "Just to play a stupid prank? I saw a dead person! And I can't tell anyone else, that's why I told you! But if you think that I'm lying, then fine! I'll just figure it out by myself," I said, turning towards the woods, ready to storm off, when she caught me by the shoulder.

"Okay, okay. Calm down," she said hurriedly. "I'm sorry. Of course you're serious. Just calm down."

I took deep breaths, and shut my eyes tight, trying to regain composure.

"Ann…" she said slowly. "I know you're not playing a joke okay? But even if I wanted to believe you," she shook her head "it's not possible. You can't see ghosts!"

"But you can! I mean I can, at least!" I insisted. "How can I prove to you that I'm telling the truth?"

I felt the desperate need to make her believe me.

She frowned "Maybe if I could see for myself…"

"See Rose?" I asked dubiously.

"No, of course not," she said. "I meant your mind."

"No," I said flatly.

She was taken aback. I couldn't show her my mind! It wasn't like before! What if she saw… about my Soulfire? I was always thinking about it, she would definitely see it. I couldn't let her see that I was… destined to die soon? Possibly. How could I tell her something I hadn't yet come to terms with?

"Why not?" she asked, confused.

"Because…" I searched around for an excuse, "I just can't okay? You can believe me or not."

She had been in my mind a few times, though of course she hadn't seen everything. When I entered her mind I made sure that I didn't broach too much and that both our memories didn't mix. But this was different. This she *would* see.

"But…" she frowned, "Ann, what's wrong? What aren't you telling me?"

"Nothing," I said a bit too quickly.

"Ann…" her blue eyes burned into me. "Tell me."

"I will, okay?" I said, trying to buy time, "but not now, I will later. Just not now. Please."

She sighed. "Fine, I believe you. Now what?"

"Now," I said a smile spreading on my face, "I show you the dead girl, Rose."

"Rose?" I called when we reached the tree. "Rose? Are you – oh hi."

I smiled at Fab. "Fab this is Rose, Rose this is Fab."

Fab shook her head and said in a soft voice, "Ann, there's no one here."

"Of course there is!" I said panic rising in me. "She's right in front of you."

Rose was looking at me, her head cocked to one side. How could Fab not see her?

"No, there isn't." Fab said.

"How can you not see her, she's right there—?" I looked at the spot where Rose had been standing a moment before but wasn't there now. I took a turn around the whole tree. She wasn't there.

I sucked in my breath, my hand on my forehead. "She was here... just a minute before."

Fab looked uneasy.

"I'm going mad," I said softly, "oh Thor, I'm going mad."

"You're not mad," she murmured.

"No," I agreed, then continued dejectedly, "I only see people who are dead, when nobody else can. I'm not mad. I'm a lunatic, a crazy lunatic! I should be on medication. Oh hell, I should be put in some asylum. I'd probably be kicked out of there too," I continued, before Fab took me by the shoulders and shook me.

"If you're mad, I am too!" she said. "Because I've been dreaming about weird stuff too. Like someone hunting me. And trying to kill me and stuff."

I grimaced. "That doesn't make you mad."

"Well... define mad," she said with a smile.

"How about seeing people others can't see?" I said.

The bell rang, "DONG DONG DONG."

"Well, we'll figure this out... afterwards."

I nodded and followed her. I turned back and looked at the tree, and for a minute I thought I saw a flash of blonde hair. Probably just me hallucinating.

Sundays were my favourite days, because we didn't have lessons that day. I got into my favourite green tunic and brown trousers. My boots were a bit muddy; I would have to clean them today.

I was planning to skip breakfast and go roaming in the forests, when someone knocked on my door.

I opened it, it was Lyra and Kristen.

"We're going to town soon, you coming?"

I hesitated. If I did go with them, then I wouldn't get the day to myself, but I had been spending an awful lot of time by myself lately. I would only think too much and put myself into depression, especially with the whole seeing ghosts thing going on.

"Sure, let me just braid my hair and I'll be down."

They nodded. I shut the door and quickly combed my hair. It had grown longer, which was saying something; it was already till my waist. I braided it quickly, then bounded out of my room using the door this time, after what seemed liked weeks.

On the way, I entered Fab's room, without knocking, which is why she screamed.

"Ann!" she said pulling her dress down. She was wearing a light green gown. "Hey, we match!" I said, as I jumped onto her bed.

She groaned. "Well-mannered people knock before entering."

"Yeah," I said with a grin. "But I'm not well-mannered, I thought we all agreed on that?"

She rolled her eyes, then suddenly grinned. "I wanted to show you something. But... it might scare you a bit."

"Puh-leese." I guffawed. "I saw you in your underclothes, what could be worse?"

She didn't answer me; instead, she floated five inches above the ground.

I yelped and stumbled away from her, tripped on the leg of her bed, and fell.

"Whoa!" I said rubbing my head, sitting up and staring at her. "Hell, when did you start floating?"

"Ilatagite taught me," she said, looking proud. "I can fly!" and she zoomed about the room albeit in a cramped manner since the room was small.

I watched, with my mouth wide open.

"Now, I'm jealous," I said, meaning it. Why couldn't I have some awesome magic like that? Why did I have to be the one being haunted?

She grinned and lighted onto the floor, gracefully.

"How'd you do that?" I asked, on our way down.

She shrugged. "Guess there are some good things about being a Sorcerer."

"Damn, I should've been one!" I said, shaking my fist at the air.

"Ann!" said Lyra, running towards us as we went down the stairs, "you won't believe what just happened!"

"What?" I asked, taken aback.

"Irena slapped James!"

"What?" both Fab and I said in unison.

"Why?" I asked, eagerly. Ah, the foul little gorgon had got it!

"Apparently," she said with a giggle, "he err tried some inappropriate behaviour with her!"

"You're kidding!" Fab said as I danced around in joy, singing "Yes, yes, ye-aah!"

"Nope," she said grinning wildly. "She said he had it coming."

"Ann…" said a voice stopping my dance mid-way. "What are you doing?"

"Aero!" I laughed, "I was just uh you know celebrating."

"Celebrating what?" he asked with curiosity.

Feeling a bit devious I said, "Your love, dear cousin! Congrats!"

Fab and Lyra gaped, Aero flushed.

"What do you mean?" he stammered.

"Noooothing," I sang, sliding down the banister. "Come on girls, let's go!"

I skipped all the way to the town, joyously. If someone asked me if it was because of what happened to James, I'd say no. I wasn't such a sadist. But if you asked me why I was so happy then, I didn't know. I just was. Only the girls were there on the trip, we were finally away from the boys. I guess that contributed too. Dawn was getting on my nerves. He looked at me as if I was some new specimen or something. And around the boys I had to behave, pshaw!

I congratulated Irena; in fact I spent the whole walk to the town congratulating the girls.

"Congratulations, Kal!" I said. "Since you've been such a kind friend you are rewarded with one day with… wait for it… the bloodhound Fergus!" Fergus was one of Ilatagite's bloodhounds which he had moved away because Kal was terrifed of dogs.

Kal rolled her eyes. "You've lost it!

I skipped about her, throwing flowers on her. I jumped and snatched some leaves and tore them apart and then skipped over to Kristen. She glowered at me. "Don't even think about it."

I pouted, sighed, and turned away from her. From the corner of my eyes I saw her relax and I chose that moment to chuck the whole thing in her face and then, with a hoot of laughter, I ran.

She chased me.

We ended up falling into the stream instead of crossing the bridge.

"Oh god, Ann!" she cried, "you've lost your marbles!"

"Never had them," I said as I climbed out of the stream, dripping wet.

"We can't go to town like this!" she said.

The others had joined us by then, after crossing the bridge like sensible people. I was feeling a bit tired now, my energy drained.

"Maybe you should go back?" suggested Vandra. "You both aren't really *presentable.*"

"Says who?" I demanded, but even I had to admit I didn't want to go to town with wet clothes that clung to my body. Had I gained weight?

"Let's just sit here," said Kristen. "The rest of you carry on, and when you come back we both will be here. We'll probably be dry by then."

"Or…" I suggested "let's ditch going to the town and…" I winked at Fab. Reading my mind she grinned and as casually as she could, she sidled towards Kal and bumped her on the waist with strength, pushing her into the water.

"Oops," Fab said, chortling as Kal splashed about in the water, yelling. "My mistake."

"Aaaghh!" she cried launching onto Fab and grabbing her leg, pulling her into the water.

Fab screamed. Kristen and I started attacking the others, splashing water on them and cajoling them into the stream. Finally it was only Lyra who was on the banks. I strode towards her with a grin, my clothes dripping wet and heavy.

"C'mon Lyraaaa, you know you want to get wet…" I sang.

"No!" Lyra said shaking her curls. "I don't! Don't you come near me Andalucia! Don't you dare!"

My grin widened. "Aw, don't be like that." I made a grab for her and caught her arm.

She shrieked "AAAAANN!"

I pushed her towards the stream, which was easy as she was so tiny. And then everyone grabbed her and pulled her into the stream.

"I feel so satisfied," I announced, standing on the banks, with my hands on my hips. They all exchanged looks, before Kal suddenly screamed: "Get her!"

That I had not expected at all.

A frenzy of hands grabbed me, and dragged me into the water. I gasped as water went into my nose, mouth and eyes. They were all squirting water on me, I ducked but someone was holding onto my leg. I kicked about, resurfacing.

"Ha!" said Kristen dripping wet. "Got you!"

I stuck my tongue out. "No. You didn't!"

"We did too!" said Lyra.

"Fine, you did," I admitted, snorting water out my nose.

Then we all started splashing water at each other like crazy. "Let's play a game!" suggested Josie amidst the chaos.

"What game?" Fab asked. I was digging the stream's bed with my right toe, the water level was only up to our chests, so it was okay. Otherwise I would be in trouble; I didn't know how to swim.

"How about one of us tries to catch everyone else in the river?"

"Sure!" said Kal.

"Okay everyone. Kal," I said with a grin, "is going to catch us! Scram!"

Kal looked indignant but everyone was already swimming or toddling away from her. I waddled away.

That's when I saw those eyes again, the first time since that night. I screamed, as something grabbed my leg from under water and pulled me down.

It was only Kal. I surfaced, gasping for air.

"Got you!" Kal said, swimming towards the others who were screaming about, paddling in the water.

I turned and looked at the spot where I had seen those eyes, but they weren't there anymore. Had I imagined them?

Blue eyes. Blue like…

Okay, Ann, you are losing your mind. First you see people who no one else can see, and now you feel creepy eyes are watching you.

It couldn't possibly have been your dead brother. What's wrong with you Ann? And yet those eyes…

Maybe I *am* going mad.

17: Fanged Deceiver

In the darkness he waited for her.

She would come soon and he would wring the truth out of her. He had already told his master about the girl's prophecies and visions but it was only the last prophecy about the Sorceress that had enraged his master.

He would have to find out what else she had seen. She said she would come; he had compelled her enough to.

Soon everything would fall.

And it would be him, not the blue-eyed bastard who would deliver Her to his master. Surely, he would be rewarded and if not, the feeling of having beaten Adrian would be enough.

He saw her come and quickly gathered his thoughts. This would have to be quick. He had no time to mess around as much as he wanted to.

Lyra walked dazedly into the forests. He stepped out of the shadows.

"Did anyone see you?" he asked.

She shook her head.

"Did you have any more visions?"

She hesitated. He took her roughly by the shoulders and asked again, making sure to keep eye contact.

"It's coming," she whispered.

"What is?"

"The end."

If it was, he was on the winning side. And his master would protect him. Perhaps once he delivered the girl he would hold a position of more power.

"Yes," he smiled, revealing his fangs, "your end has come."

18: Death of a Seer

Fabiana

I felt so tired, yet equally euphoric, after playing in the river. It felt so good to loosen up after such a long time, I didn't know the other girls could be so much fun. But Larissa hadn't been too pleased when we came in, dripping water all over the floor.

When we sat for dinner I finally got time to ask Ann about Rose.

I hesitated. "So... um, what about Rose?"

"Rose?' Kal asked. She was sitting right opposite me. Lyra's head shot up as Kal said, "The dead girl Rose?"

Ann immediately covered. "No, of course not! Fab's favourite flower is rose, she was just telling me."

"Mine too!" Josie said suddenly.

Roses weren't my favourite, violets were. But Josie prattled on in her tiny voice.

"What's yours, Ann?" Vandra asked.

Ann looked amused as she answered, "Wild lilies."

Wild lilies were rare; they were a pure white colour with streaks of blue and purple erupting from the centre and fading when they reached the petal tips.

"Of course," Vandra said with a smug look. "Aren't their vines supposed to contain a poison which they inject on innocent people who go too near them?"

"Well..." Ann said, chewing thoughtfully, "then you probably shouldn't get too close to them."

I didn't think Ann was talking about the lilies. Vandra didn't think so either because her expression changed.

"Do you know," she said loudly, so loud that even the boys stopped their chatter to listen to her, "I hate the type of people who think they are superior to others, don't you Fabiana?"

I flinched, why was she asking me? "Uh..."

"I do," Josie said cheerfully.

"Oh yes, Fab. Don't you just hate those people?" Ann huffed, shaking her head and clicking her tongue in displeasure. I stepped on her foot. She looked at me and shrugged.

"Do you, Ann?" Vandra asked. "Hate those people, I mean?"

"Most definitely," Ann said, nodding. "They're an abomination to the world." It was clear to everyone that Ann was mocking her.

Vandra's eyes flashed angrily.

"My Ma said Arni's sycamore tree has grown so huge it even shades your house," said Kal from opposite me. I think maybe she sensed the danger and wanted to avoid it. She couldn't have picked a worse topic according to me.

Ann seemed to think so too because she smiled tightly.

"You know my brother Trevor, right Irena?" said Vandra. "He has been invited to the castle *Dracone Helle*`."

Oh god, really? What was with her? Even Irena looked annoyed. "He's to become the king's personal bodyguard," she announced.

Marcus and Cassius exchanged looks. Dawn just stared at her. James looked unruffled, as always. Quinn and Elvin continued to eat as though nothing had happened. I tried to follow suit.

"Obviously, some people might not like this. They might think that my brother is vulgar or whatever. That he only got this post because my father was the king's steward once..."

"Nobody thinks that," Josie said quickly. "I'm sure he deserves it," she said, nodding.

I knew Josie could sense the tension because of her powers, and now she was trying to avoid a fight by using her powers even though she didn't have a clue what was going on.

Ann was playing with the rice on her plate, stone-faced.

It didn't seem to me like Josie's powers were making it easier.

"It's alright Josie," Vandra said. "I know some people's opinion of my brother."

"To have an opinion about something," Ann muttered quietly but loud enough for Vandra to catch it, "you have to think about it. I doubt many people sit and think about your brother you know. No offence but we have other things to do."

I sighed. Sometimes Ann just wouldn't shut up and let go.

Vandra flared up. "You don't know a thing about him—"

"And I don't want to either," Ann said. Ann was sitting poised. Something was wrong. And then it clicked. Ann was reading Vandra's mind. Which was horrible because we all knew Vandra hated Ann to the core, though for what I just couldn't imagine. Except, maybe because Ann did punch her brother and break his nose.

"You're just jealous because I have a brother!" she said.

Ann's fists clenched. "Vandra…" she said in a deadly soft voice.

Aero looked nervous, exactly how I felt.

"Ann, remember last time," I whispered to her quickly. "We can avoid this."

Just breathe, I'm here, we'll get through this; an echo of the past. I frowned. Not now Fab.

"I have no reason to be jealous," Ann continued coolly, not heeding me. "You don't have the first clue about what a good brother is."

"And I suppose you do?" she asked shrilly. "You, whose brother was a fraud, a cheat?"

"Vandra! Her brother's only five!" Kal said in indignation.

"Not him," Vandra hissed. "I'm talking about her elder brother."

Ann's jaw was twitching. Kal looked at Ann with confusion. Not many people knew about Ryan.

"Vandra, please," I beseeched.

"Your brother is the reason Selene is like this! He *ruined* her life!"

Who the hell was Selene?

"Your uncles did that," Ann said coldly. "Your uncles ruined her life. Not my brother."

"He killed my grandfather! He killed him!"

I looked at Ann, shocked. Ann was shaking, her face red.

She shot up. "Vandra if you had any self-respect you'd shut up," she said through gritted teeth.

"You think you're so superior, wearing his clothes and walking around. YOU'RE NOT!" she yelled, "I'M GLAD HE'S DEAD! I'M GLAD SHE WAS SAVED FROM A MONSTER! HE DESERVED IT"

Ann was shaking with anger.

Larissa came running into the room. "What's going on here?"

"Nothing," I said quickly. "Just… a misunderstanding."

Ann stood up, knocked her chair to the floor with her hand, and then stomped off.

I got up but Aero was already headed to the door. I hesitated before sitting down. Ryan had killed someone? Vandra's grandfather? What? What was going on?

Vandra stormed off as well. Lyra wasn't there either. But the other girls looked at me, and I sighed, shaking my head in shock.

Everyone was silent. James had disappeared in between the fight, or had he even come for dinner? Nick and Aero had gone behind Ann. Quinn had also left. Elvin looked uneasy. Dawn looked appalled. He looked at me, and I knew that he knew what was going on.

He must've seen everything during the fight, from Vandra, and probably from Ann too. She must've let her guard down, like she did whenever she was agitated.

That night I didn't get much sleep. I hadn't gotten a chance to talk to Ann and I thought maybe she needed some time to herself.

I went to sleep with a disturbed mind.

I felt like I had just fallen asleep when someone shook me awake. "Fabiana, wake up."

"Kristen?" I said groggily. "What are you doing? How did you even get in?"

"You hadn't locked your door," she said. "I have the keys as well, Larissa gave them to me."

"Why? What's wrong?"

"Didn't you hear her scream?" Kristen said, her face crumpling.

"Who?" I asked, my heart pounding, immediately thinking of Ann.

"Lyra," Kristen whispered, her eyes brimming. "She's dead."

We were all assembled in the lounge, all of us still in our nightclothes. No one had thought to change, who would too?

Everyone was shocked. Ilatagite had left hours back for the castle, and we didn't know when he would come back. Larissa said she'd informed him. She was the one who told us. Lyra hadn't been seen since dinner, she said. Larissa was frantic, she alerted the townspeople about Lyra. They found her. It was too late then.

Lyra was dead.

I glanced at Irena. She was sitting still as a statue, tears just flowing down her face. It was Ann who was sitting beside her and patting her back, murmuring softly. Josie was sitting close to me, her hands curled together. She was shaking.

I wiped away my tears. Larissa was serving us all tea, but her hands kept shaking.

"Here, let me," Kal said, taking the tray from her. I took a cup from Kal, and we offered each other a consoling smile.

It is in such times of need that you find yourself looking at others for support and courage. I could see in everyone's face the sympathy for Irena, even in the boys'. It was, after all, her sister... Us girls sat around Irena murmuring in consolation, but who could make her feel better? She had just lost her sister. Nothing could compensate for the loss. Irena had always pretended never to like Lyra, but I had noticed in many situations she was always there for Lyra. When Lyra had the fever, Irena was by her bed. When Lyra had her fits, Irena was there looking after her. Family was family.

Poor Irena.

"I've sent word to Ilatagite," Larissa said, trembling. "He'll be here soon. The villagers recovered her body. Irena, love, if you want to see her you can but I wouldn't recommend it." But Irena was already on her feet. Larissa sniffed and walked out the room, Irena behind her.

I felt her grief, her anguish.

"I feel so sorry for her—" said Vandra.

"I can't believe this," Kristen said.

"Why would—" but Kal was interrupted by a heart-stopping scream. A cry of anguish and pain.

Ann held her head in her hands, rocking back and forth. I felt renewed tears flow down my cheeks as suddenly I was gripped by an image of a mauled body. The neck hung from the body, held by a sinew of skin, there was blood all over her front. I couldn't see her face but even then, I recognised Lyra by her red hair.

I felt the anguish, the disbelief of Irena, I felt the sympathy and anger of Ann. I felt the shock of everyone else too, their disbelief. *ANN!* I cried in pain, unable to take the rush of emotions that weren't mine. *What are you doing?* But she didn't hear me. She was so overcome by the feelings of Irena; I could sense it. Could the others feel it too? Or was it just me?

Ann! Get a grip! Please!

She heard me, and she answered *she was murdered! How could this happen? Again! First Rose, now Lyra… what's going on? Oh Thor, oh God, what's happening? What's happening Fab?*

Ann, please. Please, calm down. I can't take it all. Your emotions… are flooding me Ann! Yours and Irena's and everyone else's too!

I'm sorry, I don't know how that happened, she said as I felt the emotions withdraw slowly. But I was still distressed by them. Is this how she felt all the time?

Larissa re-entered the room. "It is your right to know," she said unsteadily, "that Lyra was murdered."

No one was surprised. "I am supposed to tell you all to pack. Ilatagite will come soon to take you to the castle," she said.

There was an outburst.

"What?" said Kristen.

"You can't do that!" I said as Elvin argued, "We haven't even finished our training."

"It is the Sorcerer's wish," Larissa said quietly.

"The training time is not up yet," Quinn said quietly.

"He told my parents when you took me that I could see them before we went to the castle," said Vandra. "I want to see them. I'm not going anywhere without —"

"Please go pack your belongings. He will be here soon," she said quietly, turning to go.

"That's not fair!"

"We're not going! We're leaving."

"Where can we go?"

"The kingdom needs you," Larissa said. "As magicians you have a right to protect us normal folk. It is your duty. Or else we will all die."

Irena had re-entered the room. "Everyone will die otherwise also," she said, her head held high despite her red puffy eyes. "My sister was a seer. And that is why I believe she was murdered. She knew that we would lose the war, because even amongst us there are spies."

"Irena, child, I think you need some sleep."

"I will rest," Irena said, "after I finish saying what I have to say, Larissa." The mood in the room had changed.

"Ilatagite has scared my sister and Dawn, he blackmailed them, brainwashed them into thinking they had to serve the land. That their own life was worth nothing except to serve the kingdom!"

"Child, enough," Larissa said, and she didn't look so scared anymore. In fact, she looked scary.

"Ask Dawn! He will tell you the truth!" Irena continued. Everyone looked at each other, Dawn wasn't in the room.

"He wasn't with us…" said Cassius slowly.

"I don't think I've seen him for a while now…" Marcus added.

"He's run away," Ann said, shocking the room into silence.

"He told you?" Marcus asked her with wide eyes.

"No," she said pulling a letter out of her tunic pocket. "He left a letter. I was reading it when…" her voice trailed away. "The gist of it is that he had talked with Lyra and both of them knew that this war was pointless, we would lose. Unless, something about the Four again—if they stepped in maybe we would be safe. But Lyra had told him that she would die soon. So he ran away." She folded the letter and tucked it into her pocket.

"You will all please pack your belongings and assemble here," said Larissa.

As soon as she left, everyone was in an uproar. The boys were livid.

"He can't just —"

"What does he think?"

"Just because he's the royal Sorcerer!"

"What about our families?"

"What about our choice?"

"We never had a choice," said sensible Quinn.

"We can always run away," someone suggested, "like Dawn. I'm sure we can hide..."

"For how long?"

"From the kingdom? Are you crazy?"

"Everyone, please," Kal tried saying. She looked at us for help. I didn't know what to say, Irena was swaying on her feet. The poor thing, it was her sister that was dead. I didn't think she had the energy to be sitting here any longer. I walked towards her from behind the settee.

Kristen stepped in. "There's no point yelling and shouting. We have time now; I say we bolt."

"Irena," I whispered, "I think you should rest."

She nodded, letting me help her up. She leaned on me, and we walked towards the door.

"I can't believe... she's dead," Irena sobbed, once we were outside. I patted her, not knowing what to say. "I should've looked out for her, I should've. But I was too jealous of her."

"Irena, it's okay," I said, but she continued.

"No, it's not. I should've looked out for her. But I... my stupid ego, damn it. Our mother always liked her more than me, she had more friends than me, and she was a seer! She had everything I wanted."

"Shh..." I said, feeling miserable. Suddenly there was a movement. I turned, but no one was there.

"We should—" I started to tell Irena, then screamed.

Irena lay sprawled on the floor, her neck broken, and blood flowed onto the floor.

Shock, that's what I felt as someone's hand came over my mouth, firmly. The person turned me around so I could see their face, it was James. My eyes widened, and I tried to scream again. He lifted me quickly, and then he ran out the front entrance with me kicking and screaming wildly.

I couldn't even see where we were going; he was running at an unbelievable speed. My mind was reeling; I didn't understand what was happening. The image of Irena lying dead was still fresh in my mind.

Then suddenly I was thrown on the floor. I was in the woods. I scrambled, trying to get to my feet. But I had somehow twisted my ankle. I yelped in pain.

Then I saw him, and I forgot everything else.
Blood dripped from his hands, from his mouth.

My breath caught, as something clicked in my mind. "You—you're the one who's been committing the murders."

He smirked. "Yes, I have a very huge... appetite."
He licked the blood on his hands. I shuddered.

"Blo—blood is your food?" I murmured in disbelief.

"Of course," he said, "I am, after all a... what do you call it? Jinn, is it?"

"No," I said shaking my head, feeling faint. "No, you can't be! Ilatagite would've known! Someone would've known!"

"Ilatagite would never know," he said with vehemence, his chain with a huge crystal dangled before my eyes, glinting maliciously. "He's a weak Sorcerer. He doesn't even deserve to be one! My master on the other hand, he is the greatest Sorcerer alive!"

I frowned, unable to comprehend what he was saying. "But—Ilatagite's the last Sorcerer."

You will be a Sorcerer like no other, stronger than me, stronger than Him.

But I knew that wasn't true, and so did he.

"Is he?" James asked his brow cocked. "What about you, then?"

He was slowly coming closer to me. I couldn't move. My broken ankle wouldn't let me.
I started to sob.

"DON'T CRY!" he snapped, and I flinched, frightened by his tone. "I can't stand snivelling girls."

"What do you want?" I sobbed. "What the hell do you want?"

"You see, Fabiana," he said, in a soft voice, "I am a jinn, a blood drinker, vampire, whatever you choose to call it. And I am immortal."

I bit my tongue, how could he be immortal? No one was immortal. It didn't make any sense.

"As long as I consume blood I will always be. I have super strength, super speed! And I will never age."

"That's not possible," I whispered, horrified. What kind of monster was this?

"But it is," he said. "I'm living proof, sorry, dead proof," he continued, seeing my confusion. "Of course there is a price for this."

"Your humanity?" I choked out.

"No," his smile widened, "my soul."

My insides turned to water. He didn't have a soul, how can a person not have a soul? How can a person be alive without a soul? Hysteria bubbled in me, he wanted to kill me, consume my blood. But then why hadn't he killed me before?

"What do you want with me?" I asked, my voice surprisingly strong. I tried to summon my magic, anything to use against him. But it didn't come, it wouldn't come. Despair clung to me. I would die. He would kill me.

"Oh I don't want anything with you," he said kneeling next to me. His fingers lingered on my throat and my heart stopped. "As tempting as your blood is, I can't drink it," he said withdrawing his hand; I relaxed. "My master wants you alive."

"Why?" I whispered.

He shrugged "I came here for that purpose. Because my master knew that there was a Sorcerer amongst that old fool's students. But when I came here—" he stopped with a cruel smile, "I was for a long time confused between you and that friend of yours," he spat. "But soon I realised she wasn't a Sorcerer, just a freak who could see ghosts. When she met that weakling, Rose's spirit, I was sure she would find out it was me. But Rose couldn't remember who had murdered her, she couldn't remember anything. But I still feared that your freak friend would find out. I told my master. He trapped the spirit of that stupid girl. He told me to keep an eye on both of you. I brought you here and your friend will follow to save you, then I'll have you both. And I will hand you both to my master."

Behind my back, my hands were searching for something, anything that I could use against him.

"I followed her into the woods, without her knowledge. Often, I was so frustrated I thought I'd rip her little white neck and feast on her blood. But I wasn't sure if she was the Sorcerer or you, so I held back. I watched you too, until one day I saw you going into Ilatagite's room. From that day I saw you go to his room every night, and I thought maybe you were... entertaining him." His eyes glittered with malice.

I shrieked, "Bastard!" and hurled the rock I had found at him. It hit him in his eye and he yelped.

With a burst of speed he slapped me. I fell against the tree, my cheek smarting, tears streaming down my face.

"Silly girl, you think you can hurt me with a rock?" he snarled.

"You have no idea what I can do! I could kill you, I could!" I started crying loudly.

"Stop that! Stop it I said!" he shook my shoulder, I didn't look at him but I held back my tears. "If it wasn't for my orders..." he hit the tree on which I was leaning, with force, and it broke into two. I felt my heartbeat flail.

From out of nowhere, a huge wolf leaped and jumped onto James, pulling him down. I scrambled against the tree, screaming on top of my voice as James wrestled with the wolf. I couldn't move. I couldn't do anything.

I was helpless.

"Fab!" someone cried. It was Ann. I had never been so relieved to see her in my life as I was now.

"Ann," I sobbed, "he's a monster, he killed Irena and Lyra and all those other girls!"

"Shh..." she said, "we have to get you out of here!" A leopard had joined the fight. Marcus. And an eagle was clawing at James.

"I can't walk," I wept. "I can't, my ankle—it's broken."

"I know," she whispered. "Here, lean on me." She helped me to my feet. I let out a gasp of pain.

"Ann! It was him, he did something to Rose, he trapped her spirit—"

"It's alright Fab," she murmured. "Let's just get out of here, fast!" she said. "Aero!"

"Take my hand!" We both did. We were suddenly thrown into a whirlwind and next, we landed with a crash in the Academy.

"Elvin! Kal!" Ann cried. "Help us out!"

I was still crying, more with pain than shock.
"Where's Ilatagite?" I asked, stifling my moan.

"He's still not here," Kristen said, holding a roll of bandage in her hand and giving it to Kal. Kal started winding it around my ankle, as Elvin placed his hand on my cheek, cursing under his breath.

"What happened?"

"After you left the room," Ann explained "Larissa came in again and asked for you. When we said you went out with Irena... she lost her mind. She... snarled and ran out the room. Then we heard you scream, but by the time we came out you were gone, and Irena... was dead. We thought at first that Larissa had done it."

Ann suddenly got up. "Josie, come with me!" They both quickly went up the stairs. I couldn't move.

Kristen picked up the story. "Larissa came out with a knife." I gasped. "And she attacked us. So Quinn hit her on the head and knocked her out." She gestured at the place under the stairs where I saw a pair of legs.

"But since you were gone and Larissa was unconscious we figured someone else was involved."

"And we noticed that James was missing—" Elvin said. "I always had a bad feeling about him."

"One man, one of *them*, tried to enter but he couldn't. I think Ilatagite put some protection charms on the Academy. They can't enter. But James can and he may be able to bring them in." She looked fearful.

That's when I noticed Vandra slumped against the stair railings. And the scratch marks on Kristen's face that were bleeding. Aero had a cut on his arm. Elvin was hurt too. Kal looked shaken.

"I don't understand..." I mumbled.

"Quinn, Marcus and Cassius changed and attacked the two monsters."

"Those creatures must have done something, broken the enchantments," Kristin shrugged.

"That's the worst," said Aero. "These creatures are really strong. Almost... invincible."

"They're immortal," I said.

"Immortal?" Kristen gasped.

"No, they're not," said Elvin. "Quinn attacked that man. I think... werewolf bites are fatal to them. And so is wood."

"Wood?" Aero asked.

"That's what Quinn did after he knocked that man out. He stabbed him with a wooden shard."

"How does he know so much?" Aero asked.

"He lived in the wastelands didn't he?" said Josie. "He told me that in the wastelands, to survive, you needed to be tough."

Everyone looked shocked.

"He told you this?" Aero asked in shock.

Josie nodded.

"Then what happened?" I pressed.

"Well," Kristen said recovering, "Ann knew that it was James who took you. He was the only one missing. Besides... he's so obviously evil." She shuddered. "So she, Aero, Marcus, Quinn and Cassius left."

"I had to leap," said Aero. "I've never done it with so many people but..." he looked proud of himself, "Ann had an idea where you might be. So I tried to get as close as possible to where you were. It still took us about five minutes to find you, then Quinn and the twins changed and attacked James... the rest, you know."

Gratitude overwhelmed me. "Thank you all so much."

"It's okay," said Aero as Kristen interrupted, "Leave all that, what will we do now?"

There was silence.

"We know you're a Sorceress," said Josie softly, "and it's okay that you didn't tell us. But... is there anything you can do?"

I shook my head. "I'm not that powerful, Ilatagite was just teaching me..." it felt so good to be able to tell them all this, they knew now. I didn't have to hide it anymore. "I don't know how to kill the creature and I can't really do much."

Kristen sighed with frustration as Aero asked, "What do we do now?"

Suddenly Ann came down the stairs, Kal and Shandre behind her. "We run," she said very calmly.

19: Escaping

Andalucia

"Run?" asked Kristen. "Where to?"

"We have to go," said Elvin. "Those monsters might come after us. They wanted to kill us all."

"What?" Fab spluttered.

He looked at her pityingly. "Fabiana, they don't want to lose the war. If the king has more magicians, he has a better chance. And we are the only known magicians left that they could reach."

Suddenly the door was thrown open, and I thought with horror that James had escaped and come back to kill us all. But it was only Quinn and the twins. Josie ran up and hugged Quinn, shocking us all. He returned the hug, lifting her off her feet.

"Whoa..." said Marcus watching them with surprise. "Today is really... full of surprises."

Something in me ached, I wanted to be held and comforted too.
What's wrong with you! You have to get Fab out of here, remember?

Cassius closed the door behind him as Quinn put Josie on the ground and said "The blood-drinker is dead. I knew something was wrong about him from the start, never thought... whoever he works for must be very strong." His jaw clenched. "More will come. He said so, before he died, that more are coming. For you." He jerked his head at Fab. She shuddered.
"What do we do?" Josie asked nervously.

Quinn continued in his deep voice, "They will try to kill us wherever we go. That is why I say we go to the one place where we will have at least a little bit of safety. I think we should go to Dracone helle`."

"What?" said Marcus "But – but then we'll never be able to leave!"

"Perhaps, but it is the lesser of the two evils," Quinn said.

"I want to go home," Vandra sobbed. "I can't fight. I can't. Let me go home!"

I felt pity and anger. I didn't even have that choice open. But that didn't mean the others shouldn't. "For those who want to go home, Aero can leap you. You just have to show me where your house is, I have some amount of telepathic abilities," I said. No one looked too surprised. Quinn was smiling, I think he suspected. "But it doesn't matter anymore if we're on the warfront or not. Unless we win this war, everyone's going to die."

"I don't care. I want to go home, please," Vandra said.

"What about us?" Marcus asked.

"If we go home Mother could be attacked," Cassius told his brother.

This made everyone uneasy. Now the tables had turned, no one wanted to go home. Elvin said he was going to the castle. Most of the others nodded too, hesitatingly, uneasily. There was no other choice.

"I can take you," Aero said, "to the Capital. But what about you, Ann?"

I looked at Fab and felt everyone waiting for my answer. I didn't know what to say.

"We won't be coming with you," I said slowly. "We're not going home, it's too dangerous. But…"

I couldn't continue because a blast of heat hit us. Someone screamed.

"Everyone hold hands!" Aero yelled, as the Academy was set on fire.

"But our things—"
"What—"

"Quickly!" Aero cried. I grabbed Fab's hand, helping her stand, and then Aero's. Everyone else linked hands and we were thrown into a whirlwind. The breeze was cool and the smell of smoke was gone.

We were in the town.

"We can't stay here," I said quickly. "The people here could be endangered. If we go home we endanger our families. You have to go to the castle before those men come after us."

"What about you and—"

"Josie, give me the bag." She handed it over, looking confused. "Fab and I have to go somewhere else. It's for the best, trust me."

"But she's a Sorceress," Marcus said.

"She's more valuable than any of us," Elvin mumbled frowning. "How can she stay back?"

"We're not staying back! We have to figure it out—"

I could see the smoke rising from the Academy.

"Please, trust me," I said. "There are spies like James everywhere. We can't come to the castle, it could be infiltrated."

"Then why should we go there?"

"Fab is a Sorceress, it would be like walking into their arms."

"Which is what you want us to do?"

Some of the townspeople, what was left of them, came out bleary eyed and saw the smoke.

"Fab, come on, we have to go," I told her.

"Ann where..."

"Trust me." I mentally called him again. He was nearby.

"But where are you..."

"I am going to the castle," Quinn said loudly.

"Me too," Josie said, linking hands with him.

"Aero, I have to go. We have to," I told my cousin. "Take care."

"Ann where are you going?" Kristin asked.

"They're after Fab, we have to hide," I told her. "We're running away until we figure out whom to trust."

"What about us?" Kal asked.

"It's up to you. But don't go home, it could endanger your family," I said as he came. Thank Thor!

"Whoa!" Elvin said as Shadow galloped towards us. He was saddled; I didn't have the time to question him.

I climbed on. "Fab, come on!" I urged. She hesitated before taking my hand and sitting side-saddle.

"Take care," Aero muttered, distressed.

"We'll be fine," I assured him.

I looked at Kristin and Kal, and felt a pang. "I'm sorry. But you'll understand later, I hope. Take care," I told them.

And then Shadow took to the night.

Though it felt like we were safe, I knew better. I knew those monsters were after us to get to Fab. And yet we couldn't ride forever. Fab was holding me tightly. I felt her near my barriers and I lowered them to let her in.

Ann, where are we going?

Ilatagite was afraid this would happen. He told me. He's given me instructions.

When? She asked shocked.

That day when my potion went wrong.

We're not going home are we?

Not now Fab, maybe sometime in the... future. We rode silently for a while.

What about Irena?

She's dead Fab. I felt Fab's grip tighten on me and I cringed.

He was a jinn Ann, a jinn. How come no one realised? How come Ilatagite didn't realise?

Didn't he mention a strong master? A Sorcerer?

Yeah but apart from Ilatagite, I'm the only Sorcerer.

Maybe not, I said gravely, there's a lot we don't know. Ilatagite didn't tell us a lot.

Shadow stopped and Fab jumped down. He had brought us to a cave on a hill but we were still in Rivendell.

I had no idea what to do, where to go, whom to trust.

I took a deep breath. I had to follow Ilatagite's instructions. I walked into the cave, it was dark.

"Uh, Fab, a little light please?" A flame roared in Fab's hand and I took the pouch and the bowl Ilatagite had given me from the bag. Then I took the vial and poured a silvery liquid into the bowl

"Ann, what are you doing?" Fab asked, staring at me like I'd lost my mind.

I emptied the contents of the pouch into the water. It shimmered. "What did you put in that?" Fab asked with wide eyes.

"Something Ilatagite gave me."

"What's happening, Ann?" she asked sobbing. "One minute everything was okay and now…"

Sparks flew out of the bowl. I leaped back. Fab stifled a shriek as a silvery orb rose from the bowl and wavered in the air.

"Ilatagite?" said a woman's voice.

Fab and I stared at each other in paralysed shock.

"Ilatagite?" the woman repeated in an urgent tone.

"Uh," I coughed "Um, no. I'm a student of his. He gave this to me."

"Who are you? What is your name? Where is Ilatagite?"

"The Academy was attacked," I said moving closer to the bowl. Fab eyed it with nervousness. "Ilatagite instructed me to er…"

"Are you the Sorceress?"

I gaped at Fab whose eyes were wide. *Go on, tell her,* I mouthed.
Fab looked worried, *but who is she?*
We have to trust Ilatagite.

"No, I am." Fab said looking uneasy.

"I see. And where are you now?"

"In a cave on a hill," I said.

"A hill?" The lady's tone was sharp. "Where is this hill?"

"In Rivendell, near the town."

"Help will come now. Don't leave the cave. Pour the liquid onto the soil."
And then with a splash the silvery orb fell into the bowl.

"What was that?"

"I have no idea," I muttered nervously as I took it and slowly poured it on the ground. It formed a star and then sank into the earth.

"Can we trust her?" Fab asked me fearfully, "whoever she is?"

I shrugged. "We'll just have to trust Ilatagite."

Fab slumped against the cave's wall. I picked up the bowl, it was empty, no trace of the contents remained. I dearly hoped that we hadn't made a huge mistake in trusting this strange woman.

"What about the others, Ann?" she asked. "We should've gone to the Capital."

I shook my head. "I was warned not to." She frowned. "I was dreaming just before well... Lyra..." I gulped.

"I was dreaming too..." Fab said. "Someone's after me Ann."

"I know. The Spirit in my dream told me."

"But why?"

"I'm not sure," I sighed, "but I was warned against going to the Capital."

"But can we trust the Spirits?" Fab asked me. "If we're just a game..."

I bit my lip. "Fab, take rest, you look terrible."

"I don't think I'll get sleep," she said blinking her tears away.

"Try," I said.
She sighed and lay down on the floor, but before she fell asleep she said, "I'm going to ask you all this later Ann, when I'm less tired."
I smiled grimly.

Once she slept, I got up, and stood outside the cave, then took out Dawn's letter.
I hadn't read out everything he had written, because some things I... couldn't read out.

Ann,

I'm sorry I couldn't say goodbye to you. I really am. But this was a sudden decision, and... I couldn't face saying goodbye to you. After that girl died, Lyra became extremely paranoid. She used to come and tell me, because Ilatagite wanted us to go to the kingdom before the training was over, she knew I could relate to her. She told me that she was scared, that she felt she was going to die soon. She told me this war was pointless, that we would all die anyway. That there was some dark magician, a Sorcerer who... who started the war. And do you know what she said his name was? The Night Prowler. Yes. Remember the time you wondered how he accomplished his 'feat'? It was because he was a Sorcerer. It's him we're fighting against, we don't stand a chance. He's very powerful.

Lyra also... felt people were coming for us, for all of us. Including... your friend, Fab. I know you've been keeping secrets from me Ann. I know that's why you don't want me to see your past. Lyra told me about Fab, she had a feeling Fab was a Sorcerer.

She is, isn't she?

But I never knew the weight of your secrets until tonight, during that outburst with Vandra.

I'm sorry, I hadn't meant to pry. But the images flooded me, and I know now that you will understand what I mean by that.

I only saw flashes, I don't know everything... but I know you went through a lot Ann. And I wish... it hadn't happened to you.

But I wanted to tell you that... Ann, there's a part of your past which is locked. Even from you. I don't know who locked it, but someone did, someone who had the same magic as me I think. You won't be able to access those memories. But you need those memories; I think there's going to be a time when those memories play a crucial role in your life. Specially the memories of your... brother's death. And I think it's about time you told someone... about the murders you witnessed; I think the king would really like to know Ann. It's not your secret to keep.

I could unlock them for you, but I have to go now, before it's too late.

I'm sorry again for not saying goodbye. Also for not saying this before—I love you. I could never tell you this before but I can't leave without saying this.

Forgive me for not being able to tell you this personally. I hope I see you again, and that you don't hate me when you do.

Love, Dawn.

I wiped my eyes, tucking the letter into my pocket. I thought about Ryan. I tried to recall what had happened that night, but I couldn't. I could only remember flashes, blood so much blood. I lied when I told Fab that my brother was killed because he was involved with the minister's daughter. That was true but not the real reason he was killed.

My brother was killed because he assassinated the queen.

I thought about the figure kneeling before Nellie's grave. I thought about the feeling…

I stared into the darkness, wondering what fate awaited us as I closed my eyes.

Can the dead walk?

The story of Ann and Fab continues in the second book of the Game of Lives series – Flight. Trapped in the Game of Lives, played by spirits unseen, they find themselves as mere chess pieces in the hands of the Spirits. As the darkness looms over in the name of war and an ancient evil power, they find that they can only place their trust in each other as their closest friends and family are taken by death. Fabiana who is the first ever female Sorcerer struggles to get a hold on her magic and Andalucia tries to come to terms with her unusual powers as her past continues to haunt her. Now out in the open, exposed to the bitter truth, the girls have to accept their roles and fight for their world or die trying.

Acknowledgements

There are way too many people to thank, who have inspired/helped me directly or indirectly, so here goes:

To Bunn, who inspired the character of Fab, thank you for listening to all the various mad plots I had in mind, for giving me ideas, for the laughs and the memories! I hope I've captured a part of our friendship at the very least.

To my parents, thank you for putting up with me staying up way into the night 'cause "night is when I'm awake and my brain juices really flow!" For encouraging me, for trying to act interested when I rambled on (it's not your fault! it's called YA for a reason!), for bearing my excitement when I figured something out and frustration when I couldn't, for believing that a writer's block could be cured by coffee and cake, for the books I keep asking you to buy, a special thanks to my mom who is the reason I am such a bookworm and love literature... thank you!

To my little brother who asked me if he was the inspiration for Ann's younger brother (Yes, you are. Now you know!), and wanted the five-year-old to be a hero, slay dragons and whatnot.

To all my friends, you may not know it but you've inspired a lot of the student magicians in the academy. Thanks for going through bits of my story, encouraging me, goading me on!

To all my English teachers, who inspired me to take Literature, improved my language and ideas, truly.

To Devika, my editor, who went through the manuscript, edited it and was patient enough to give me her feedback!

To Subhra uncle who was my last hope at having a decent book cover! Thank you!

To my dear computer who has gone through a great amount of turmoil because of me, sorry for ramming away on you. To all the books in the world, to all the gifted authors who create magical worlds for us. To God, for all these people in my life, for the memories, the ideas, everything!

About the Author

Gowri Rekha is a young Millenial who started writing at the age of 15. She was born in Kochi, grew up in Dubai, Indonesia and Chennai, and is currently doing her BA in English Literature when she isn't writing, teaching, reading or day dreaming. The final version of the first book in Gowri's four-book series, Game of Lives evolved along with its creator, over a period of six years! Gowri lives in a World of Books, with a Big Mug of Coffee for company. She loves sarcasm and hates compliments, so if you read the book, just send her some snarky notes and she will love you for that!

www.sorcerersandspirits.com
www.gameoflives.net

Happy Reading!